Blissful Beginnings

By Sue Vout

Contents

Acknowledgements

I thank all of the wonderful people who believed in me and that I was capable of telling stories to the world.

Especially to the editors/writers at Creative Book writers, you all rock.

Dedications

"I love you as certain dark things are to be loved,

in secret, between the shadow and the soul."

— Pablo Neruda, 100 Love Sonnets

To my husband, without whom, my achievements would never have been possible.

I love you for being so patient with me when I am lost in my imaginary world, consumed by the words.

Prologue

Life was very simple while I was growing up. I just had to study and eat and be with my mummy and daddy. There were no worries apart from when the sun goes down, where does it really go or why daddy had to go on long business trips. Every year before my birthday, my parents would take me on holiday. They had taken me to see Disney land, and it was the most unforgettable moment of my life.

I was a shy girl when I joined high school. I was good with studies but did not have many friends or even a boyfriend. I was pretty, but my quiet and reserved nature had made it difficult for the guys to approach me. I was happy staying in my own bubble. I liked my life the way it was.

Just before my 15th birthday, daddy had to go on a business trip, and my mother accompanied him to it. It was supposed to be short and quick. I remember my daddy kissing the top of my head before leaving and assuring me that they would be back by the next evening. Mummy had said, "We will be back in no time at all, sweetheart." She had hugged me, and they had left. They had really left me that night, as their car met with a terrible accident on the highway that night.

I got to know that night what they mean by turning one's world upside down. Mine did. The days that came after went in a blur. The funeral was held a week later after the accident, and that was when the neighbors had asked me if I had some relatives, which I did not, so the only option was that I was sent to the care home. I thought the death of my parents was terrible, but the real terrible began after I ended up at home. I was raped in the initial month of my reaching the care home, and then it had become an addiction. I couldn't live without sex.

I wasn't the worst. The girls I knew were into trafficking, drugs, and whatnot, but I had a goal in mind. I had to become someone, not losing myself in the darkness. I had tried to find love; that was what I craved the most, but after getting my heart broken several times, I gave up on it. I only wanted sex; no strings attached. Not until I met the man I fell in love with, and then my world turned upside down; again.

Chapter One

I had just come out of a relationship with Shaun, well if you called it that having constant hard sex as soon as we were home. I sometimes laughed that we fucked like wild rabbits. It was all going well until I had caught him necking a blonde in the night club who was showing off her large assets in front of him. His excuse he that was drunk, but it didn't look like that to me watching them from the balcony of the night club. The club was heaving, Shaun said he was going out with his mates, but I couldn't see any of them with him. The lying bastard, I wondered how long this had been going on; he didn't seem any different at home sharing the flat between us. Luckily it was only rented as having a mortgage would have caused a large headache having to sell it later.

I was having a night out with Tina; she was a friend from college. We met on the course and continued to meet up at least once a month for a night out.

"Tina, do you know who is that blonde woman Shaun's necking near the end of the bar?" I asked, sounding casual.

"Fuck Caz, what's Shaun doing with her?" said Tina in a surprised voice.

"I don't know, but I'll find out when he gets home." I shrugged casually playing it cool.

"She's the biggest slag around," said Tina even more surprised on how cool I was seeing Shaun with her. We quietly watched his intensions with the 'slag'; he was all over her like a rash.

"Aren't you going over and smack him one?" asked Tina unable to control her concern for me anymore.

"No, I'll wait until he gets home and then I'll kick his head in. I don't want to be shown. I can't keep a man and cause a scene." I said, staying calm, and Tina stared at me in disbelief. I laughed at her expression.

It was midnight when I got back to the flat after saying goodbye to Tina and promising her that I would keep her updated on Shaun. Luckily it was a Friday night which gave me time to go through his things bagging them up ready to throw them out together with him. He wasn't going to mess me about, despite him being good in the sack; I wasn't prepared to share him. We had only been together two months, so my feelings for him weren't heart wrenching it was easy to let him go, not only that I had been leaving my heart cold. Time and circumstances had changed me a lot. I didn't cling into people or things anymore, what had to go, had to go.

It didn't take long gathering his stuff together having only half a dozen black bags to fill; if there were anything I had missed I'd either send them to the charity shop or chuck it out. I wanted to erase him from my life for good.

It was 3 am, and he still hadn't come home. I turned over to look at his side of the bed. He was going to pay for this, the bastard. No one fucks me about; I have been fucked about all my life but not anymore. It was about 4 am when I heard the key in the lock. I could hear him trying to creep in thinking I wouldn't hear him. He must have seen the black bags in the hallway, but he pretended to be oblivious to them following his way into the bedroom. I could hear him undressing before he slipped into our bed, his hand sliding over to my breast snuggling up to my back.

I removed his hand off my breast as I laid flat on my back, and I was about to say something, but I heard him starting to snore, jerk. I could have punched him there and then, but I needed him sober to listen to what lies he was going to tell me, so I turned over and waited until we were up to have this conversation.

I only had a few hours' sleep that too with so much disturbance, with Shaun snoring most of the early hours. As I woke up and looked up the clock, it said 8.15 am so I decided to get up to make a coffee. Slipping on my short robe, I made my way to the kitchen to make my coffee. As I was pouring the water into the mug, I heard Shaun raising in the bedroom. I was ready for him with my guns ready. Shaun padded through the kitchen, acting all normal.

"You just made coffee? He yawned as he came out of the bedroom.

"Yeah get it yourself," I said drily, walking off back into the bedroom to get dressed.

"Oh, what's up with you now?' asked Shaun. His voice laced with sarcasm.

Shaun made himself a coffee and followed me back to the bedroom. I could see him looking at my body as I dressed up, my tattoo showing on my back from waist down to the top of my buttocks. I could feel his presence next to me as his hand touched my tattoo gently. I flinched by his touch.

"Caz, I've got something to tell you." began Shaun waiting for me to turn around, but I didn't and carried on dressing myself until I had finished.

Once I had finished, I turned around to face him; blue eyes looked at me, waiting for me to say something. I looked at him up and down, his fit body and sexy hair before I started.

"Yeah and I've got something to tell you, too," I said, sounding annoyed.

"Yeah?" said Shaun looking all innocent. "What's wrong, babe?" he asked, sounding concerned.

"I suggest you tell me first," I said abruptly. Shaun put his coffee down on the chest of drawers next to him before approaching me with his arms held open to hug me.

"Don't touch me, Shaun, just tell me," I said harshly wanting him to spit it all out already.

"Well I don't know how to say this," he went on. "but I'm leaving you Caz. I just can't do this anymore." He stopped, waiting for me to explode.

"Well, you won't have to take long in packing as I have already done it for you," I said calmly, walking out of the bedroom into the kitchen.

"But how did you know I was leaving?" asked Shaun sounding shocked to see me so calm. It was obvious that he had expected a show.

"I saw you last night at the night club all over that blond slag," I said, still sounding calm.

"Er no, I'm moving in with Jo from work," replied Shaun looking a little sheepish.

"Well, obviously she doesn't know you well enough does she, Shaun?" I threw it his way, saying it with sarcasm. He didn't know what to say now he had been caught out by his actions from last night. "Oh and Shaun I'm going out now, so by the time I get back I want you gone and put the keys through the letterbox on your way out," I shouted, stepping out and banging the door shut.

I held it together as I got into my van to head off to a job that could have waited until Monday, but I needed to go somewhere out of Shaun's why else it would upset me. Some more pushing and I would have probably punched him in the face for being let down like this. I was in a man's world doing a man's job I had to be tough

18

having plenty of rude comments on the way; my journey had never been easy. I was a builder; busy setting myself up since I left school having no one to help me through the process. I was determined to reach my goal, knowing where I wanted to be in life. I had saved up money to enrol myself on numerous courses to learn the different lines in the trade of the building industry. Despite being tall and slim, I could lift as much weight as a normal guy giving the men a run for their money. I worked out at the gym three evenings a week, and with being street smart at an early age, I took on courses in all types of self-defence, so I was prepared for anything physical, but not always mentally.

I was fifteen when my parents had died, leaving me no choice but to go into a care home. My Uncle lived abroad and was always working away, so he never contacted me, clearly because I would be a burden to him and who likes a burden on them? I didn't really know him anyway, so it was no big deal. While growing up, bullying was a big issue with having no one there to help you. Hence growing up the last few years had been a tough job. I knew I had to follow my path in life.

The school was a rest bit having not to deal with girls nicking your things or the lads coming into the bathroom while you showered. You had no space of your own I was glad when the day came for me to leave home being let out into the big wide world. I was glad it was over.

While I drove through the traffic, I thought that I must find someone to share the flat with. Luckily it had a second bedroom, so that was a bonus, whether it was a guy or a girl I wasn't bothered as long they paid their half of the rent. My job was on the other side of the city; the traffic was nose to tail being a Saturday morning. Everyone would be out shopping seeing that the weather was warm with temperature due to rise higher next week. Music was playing on the radio; I usually selected rock playing it loud when I was working singing with the music and dancing when I had the chance. I suppose I looked a bit of a rocker too with my dark shoulder-length curly unruly hair and a little black eyeliner I loved to wear to match the tone of the music. I think that was what turned Shaun on when I first met him on a building site as he was the projects manager for the site. It all started with him seeing the tattoo on my back. He was watching me with the site foreman as I was lifting and carrying pipework into the houses, ready for fitting and connecting. My vest was riding up, exposing my tattoo every time I bent down to pick up a bundle of pipework. I was least bothered about the fact that it might be driving someone crazy.

Shaun came over to see how I was doing with the plumbing. I saw his eyes glued to my vest top, revealing my cleavage as beads of sweat ran down my face dropping into my cleavage. His blue eyes focused on my cleavage before he spoke.

"Hi Caz, how are you getting on with the plumbing?" he asked, looking deeper into my cleavage. I stood up as I continued saying it was going well and should be finished by the end of the week.

"Oh, good." He smiled as we walked outside to bring another bundle of pipework inside. He walked with me as I bent down, picking the bundle up, revealing the tattoo again. He hovered over me while I picked it up and followed me into the house like a puppy.

"Caz would you like to have a drink with me sometime?" I suddenly heard Shaun. After putting the bundle down, I get up to face him, his blue eyes looking at me for an answer.

"Yeah, ok, then," I said, putting him on the spot.

"Cool, tonight if you like?" said Shaun pleased I hadn't turned him down. I had my reasons; I needed a fix of sex, knowing he would be obliging being a Friday.

"Is 7 pm, ok?" he asked as I continued with my work, looking excited.

"Yeah, that's fine," I said as I walked away from him.

Shaun picked me up at 7 pm; he was wearing jeans with a black tee-shirt, making a change not being in a suit for once. It had been a warm day that continued into the evening. Every evening, I showered and washed my hair being into a physical and dirty job. After a long refreshing shower and washing my hair I had decided to wear a short red dress for a change, as I always wore jeans or sometimes trousers at work depending on the weather. The doorbell rang, Shaun was on time. I opened the door after grabbing my bag, and there he was, standing there his blue eyes staring at me as though I wasn't there.

"Babe, you look gorgeous," said Shaun kissing me on the cheek. I was taken aback by his kiss and comment.

"Yeah ok, cut the flannel," I said, shrugging it off.

I slid into the front seat of his BMW, waiting for him to start the engine.

"So where would you like to go?" he asked with a huge smile.

"Not bothered I'll leave that to you," I said, giving him a quick smile.

"Well, do you have any wine in your flat? We could have a drink there first," he asked, pushing his luck.

"I'll tell you what, how about you come with me and we'll go straight into my bedroom, where 1 can fuck the living daylights out of you?" Shaun couldn't believe what he was hearing; I was offering it to him on a plate.

"Yeah, sure." he jumped out of the car, opening the door in case I changed my mind.

I opened the door to the flat with Shaun close behind like a puppy. He wrapped his arms around my waist as he shut the door with his foot. I turned to kiss him; his hands roamed up my dress, desperate to get into my undies.

"Shaun, would you like to fuck me now?" I asked, standing there waiting for him to decide.

"Of course Caz you have been turning me on since you came on the site," said Shaun groping my breasts. I grabbed hold of his hand towing him to my bedroom as I whipped off my dress, revealing my lacy underwear and the full sight of my tattoo. I could see his length bursting to come out. I turned to face him as I started to undress him, he helped me with the undressing, down to his boxers.

"Shaun, I am going to give you the best blow job you have ever had in your life." I grinned as I went down on my knees, pulling his boxers down to reveal his waiting length. I teased him kissing his length as I massaged his balls, he started to moan.

"Fuck Caz what are you doing to me? I am going to go crazy." I started licking his length, making my way to his tip as a small tear escaped from his tip. I licked it tasting the salty drop, flicking my tongue on the sensitive tip of his length. I felt powerful, in charge as I looked at him going berserk.

"Oh Caz, I'm going to come." he moaned louder this time. My pleasuring him was pushing him to the limit. I finally took his full length in, sucking him hard and making him come in seconds, his moans were pure pleasure. I swallowed his hot salty liquid and licked him dry before I stood up. He was panting with his eyes still closed from the pleasure I had just given him.

I kissed him on the lips as he opened his eyes.

"Babe, I have never had a blow job like that," said Shaun kissing me as he forced his tongue in my mouth. He unhooked my bra, releasing my breasts. His eyes widened as Shaun saw them for the first time unleashed.

He pushed me onto the bed, slipping my undies off. He grinned as he slid down, pushing my legs apart sucking on my wetness as he fingered me. I moaned as I wriggled my hips with his tongue playing on me.

"Shaun fist me," I whispered. Within seconds, he was fisting me as he pressed my clit. My pleasure was intense as I came. "Keep going." I moan loud as the pleasure intensifies, coming again. I started panting with the sensation as beads of sweat started to roll down my neck. Shaun came up to face me, kissing me hard on my lips his hand hard on my breasts massaging them until his lip reached my nipples.

"Oh Caz I need to fuck you, now," he whispered, as he had soon recovered from his last climax.

"fuck me then," I said, bringing his head up to kiss him hard on the lips as our tongues collide. He is soon ready to be inside me. He slid in, desperately to get his release.

"fuck me hard Shaun," I whisper with my eyes shut, enjoying this moment with him. He pumped me hard, making my breast wobble, sending him into a frenzy before he came flopping on my body with the force he had applied. Our hearts beat fast with the fast pace of sex we just had. I had missed it not having a fix for over six months. It was good that it was Saturday the following morning. I made sure Shaun was at it all night. I blew him and rode him as he fisted me and massaged my breasts and nipples, making me come over and over again. I made sure he was totally fucked.

Over a period of time despite finishing to job on-site, Shaun still came around to the flat as we fucked each other hard until Shaun couldn't take it anymore. He moved in with me at last, not able to control it anymore. As soon as we were home together, it was straight to the bedroom for hard sex.

The traffic started moving as the traffic lights changed to green. I was only a mile away from the job, and then it dawned on me why he was moving out. I had a high sex drive, and he wasn't able to keep up. Was I too much for him? Had I driven him away?

Fifteen minutes later, I pulled up outside the gates of a large mansion. I pressed the buzzer on the intercom waiting for someone to answer.

"Hello,?"

"Oh Hi, you rang about some plumbing you need to be done?" I said speaking into the intercom.

"Yes, come in, I'll open the gates." said a male voice from the intercom. I waited for the gates to open driving in and making my way up to the front of the house. The driveway snaked around a wood setting, thick with green foliage and a variety of coloured flowers following up to the tarmac driveway to the front of the house. The house stood well off from the main road making the position a quiet spot with the trees stopping the drone of traffic from the main road. The house was totally surrounded by woodland having a large lawn area at the side of the house, but I should say it would be all the way around the house, being of some age having tall windows and a huge solid oak front door.

I drove into a parking slot marked out at the front of the house. Parking up, I walked over to the front door and pressed the button on the side of the door, and within a few seconds, the door opened as a tall, dark haired man probably forty appeared.

"Hi, Caz come on in." He smiled as I stepped inside into a large hallway with a large staircase rolling up and around heading to both sides of the house. The oak wooden polished floor sparkled as the sun shone through the large windows.

"Call me Lloyd; I do have a few jobs that need to be done, this being an old house," said Lloyd walking towards a side door of the hallway.

"Would you like a coffee first?" asked Lloyd entering the huge stainless kitchen looking rather clinical.

"Um, yes, please," I answered, looking around the huge kitchen. Lloyd set the coffee machine going, switched it on as it made bubbling and rattling noises going through its cycle.

"So Caz how long have you been doing this sort of work?" asked Lloyd eyeing me up. I shifted slightly in my seat, not sure what he was thinking.

"Nearly six years," I replied. "Why do ask?" I asked him, being blunt.

"No, I was just interested," said Lloyd as he eyed my cleavage.

I thought is this guy was thinking that I was not up to the job or had he had something else in mind. The coffee machine stopped making noises as the water started to pour out. Lloyd rushed to get the coffee and, in a minute, he was ready with two mugs of steamy hot coffee. Lloyd handed me a mug while he went to the fridge and picked up the milk.

"Sorry," he said, looking embarrassed. "I forgot if you take milk."

"No black is good, thanks," I said as I sipped the hot liquid from my mug. Lloyd poured a drop in his mug, placing the milk back into the fridge.

"What's the job you need doing?" I asked needed to get on, with having to find someone to share the flat with me plus I needed to get some grocery and do my laundry. We walked out of the kitchen back into the large hallway to another door which led to a swimming pool.

"Fuck this guy must be loaded." I thought walking alongside the pool to the other end, where there was a changing room. Lloyd pointed to the shower cubicle saying that the tray was leaking and if I could reseal the tray; "fuck is that all?" I thought thinking it was going to be something like moving pipes or adding a toilet or something but resealing? Crap.

"Why don't you have a walk-in shower instead of a tray? you wouldn't have to bother then about sealing, as it would be tiled and sealed." I suggested making out I knew what I was talking about.

"Mm I never thought of that," said Lloyd rubbing the stubble on his chin. "Yes, ok, when could you do it?" he asked.

"Hmm, I probably could start the week after next," I said, not expecting him to give me an answer straight away.

"Yes, that's ok. Just ring me the day before to let me know when you're coming," said Lloyd smiling as we made our way back through the house. Lloyd showed me to the door and watched me walk to my van. I could feel his eyes burning into my butt. Mm, he probably needs a good blow job I thought with a smirk jumping into the van.

Chapter Two

It was after 11.30 am by the time I got back from my job; the traffic was still heavy, but at least Shaun had gone pushing the flat keys through the letterbox. It felt quiet now that I was on my own, but as they say, when one door closes, another one opens. I threw my van keys on the table and walked through to the kitchen to make a coffee. Shaun had left a note on the side table.

'Hmm, I wonder what he had to say in his defense now.' I switched the kettle on and picked up the note to read. It said;

Caz, I am so sorry it had to finish like this, I didn't want to leave, but you were killing me having such a high sex drive. I loved your blow jobs, but I needed some breathing space and to be back with the lads. I know you had seen me with the blonde girl, but there was nothing between us apart from sex. I loved the time we had together and hope at some stage we could meet up for a chat sometime. Love Shaun x

I knew I was right; he couldn't stand the pace. That sorted the men from the boys. I screwed the note up, throwing it into the bin as the water boiled as I poured the steaming water into my waiting coffee granules. Once I was done with it, I went through to the bedroom, stripping the bedsheets to get rid of the smell of Shaun. I needed to start fresh now I had no one to share my bed with.

It was nearly 2 pm by the time I had sorted the laundry and cleaned the flat throughout, giving it a sweet fresh smell. As I was about to go out to buy groceries for the week, I heard a knock on the door. I opened the door to find a tall guy, fit and muscular with shoulder-length blond messy hair leaning against the sidewall of the door.

'Yes?' I said abruptly, staring into his ice-blue eyes.

'Oh, hi, I'm Russ.' He smiled, standing straight, and now he had my attention. 'I hear you're looking for someone to share the flat?' He continued with the same smile that reached his blue eyes. He had caught me off guard. I nodded, taking a more in-depth look at his body, his bare arms revealing tattoos down both his arms with a piercing in his left brow and an ear lobe.

He looked great. I smiled too, thinking I could pull him in and fuck him hard there and then. 'Where did you hear about that?' I asked, sounding casual as I crossed my arms and looked at him.

'I saw Shaun in the bar. He mentioned you might be looking for someone to flatshare, seeing that he had to move on due to moving jobs,' explained Russ, hoping I would say yes.

'Oh, did he? You better come in then,' I said, opening the door wider for him to enter.

Russ stepped in, waiting for me to go through the living room. 'So, what's the story?' I asked, not beating about the bush.

'Well, I've just been sofa surfing for the last couple of days with a mate while I've been looking for a flat, but they are so hard to come by,' said Russ sounding disappointed in the search. 'I work with my mate on that large development. Their building is over the south side of the city. It is supposed to be about five years' work.' Russ gave me the details with a puppy dog expression, trying to convince me to take him on.

'Okay. Do you have any habits? Spill.' I raised my eyebrow.

'I don't know what that means, but no, I hope not. I do like a tidy place, though.' His face was serious, and it looked like he was honest. I told him what I wanted to go towards the rent with extras for the utilities. He was happy with the deal and asked when he could move in. I decided he might as well move in now, having someone in the flat was better than none.

Russ had borrowed the work's van, so I gave him a key to the flat. I then showed him the spare bedroom, which was smaller than mine, but it was a room, and he needed a bed, so I let him start to bring his gear over while I went out to do the grocery shopping. I just hoped I wasn't making a mistake again.

'Still, this is life, and you have to make the most of what you have, life is too short anyway,' I told myself. 'Would I finish up fucking him?' The question popped up in my head. Yes, probably. I smiled and closed the door behind me as I stepped out to go for groceries.

The traffic was still heavy as I made my way through to the supermarket, and I had to queue at the checkout too, which was pretty annoying. By the time I got back, it was almost 5. Russ was already in the flat and had almost sorted his stuff out.

'Let me give you a hand with those groceries.' Russ rushed towards me as he saw me and took serval bags from me.

'Gee, thanks,' I said, handing him the bags and sighing in relief. I dumped the remaining bags on the side with having to bring a couple more from the van.

'Caz, what line of work are you in?' asked Russ helping me with unpacking and stacking the groceries. Shaun hadn't spoken to him about me.

'Well, I'm a builder,' I said, waiting for the comments to come back.

'What do you mean a builder?' asked Russ thinking I worked in an office of some sort.

'A builder as in plumbing, electrics, woodwork, plastering, brickwork. Do you want me to carry on?' my voice was laced with sarcasm.

'Wow, you're too beautiful and fit for that,' said Russ looking at me in the eye.

Ignoring his comment, I went on, 'Well, what do builders usually look like?' with my hands on my hips.

'You must come and work on the site where I'm working; it would make the days more interesting to see you there,' said Russ raising a brow at me.

'You can cut the flannel out,' I said, finishing off putting the groceries away and putting the kettle on for coffee. I made two mugs of coffees and took them into the living room.

'So, what are the plans? Are you going out tonight?' I asked, trying to initiate a conversation with him.

'Nah, I was out last night; I need to catch up on my sleep.' Russ shrugged sipping his coffee.

'Ahaan, I am making beans on toast if you would like to join me,' I asked, looking into his ice-blue eyes, and then my eyes wandered to his messy hair.

'I thought you'd never ask.' He grinned at me as he jested. I rolled my eyes, smiling at him as I sipped my coffee. We watched some TV together until it was 10 pm. Russ decided to call it a night as I noticed while watching TV he was napping; He must have had a big night last night.

Sunday was a day to rest. If Shaun were still here, it would be more sex until midday, but having the luxury of sprawling out over my 6ft bed, it was comfortable drifting off to sleep after waking up at 6 am. I could hear

Russ banging about in the kitchen, probably trying to find his way around where things were kept. I turned over in the bed and glanced at the clock; It was 10 am.

Fifteen minutes later there was a knock on my bedroom door. 'Caz, are you awake? I've made you some toast and coffee,' said Russ sounding not sure whether it was a good idea or not.

'Yeah, come in,' I shouted as I turned overlaying for a few seconds before sitting up. I pulled the duvet up to my breasts as I was sleeping without anything underneath the duvet. Russ had a towel wrapped around his fit tanned body showing the tattoos that stretched over parts of his body. His muscles flexed as he brought in the tray, laying it on the bed.

'Hmm, and what is this for?' I asked, looking into his eyes and grinning.

'It is for letting me share your flat,' replied Russ, not knowing where to look, seeing that I had been sleeping naked.

'Oh, where's yours?' I asked as I picked a piece of toast and bit into it.

'In the kitchen,' said Russ turning to go.

'I'll tell you what? Why don't you bring your breakfast and slip into my bed with me?' I said, waiting for his response.

'Oh, I'll just go and put my boxers on first,' said Russ, a little shocked with what I had asked him.

'Nah, don't bother, just bring your breakfast,' I said, taking another bite of toast.

Russ was soon back with his toast and a mug of coffee; he slipped them on the side before sliding into my bed.

'You can take the towel off. I'm not going to bite,' I said, teasing him and smirking.

He was so fit and those sexy tattoos. I wondered if he would let me fuck him. Russ pulled out the towel, knowing we were both naked in my bed now.

'So, what are your plans for today, Russ?' I asked, making normal conversation as we ate our toasts.

'Nothing really,'
said Russ looking slightly uncomfortable.

'Mm, so how would you feel if I gave you the best blow job you will ever have?' I said, picking up the tray and putting on the side cabinet next to the bed.

'What?' His expression was filled with shock. 'Did I hear you right?' asked Russ again, not taking it in what I had just said.

'Yeah, but I just need to use the bathroom first.'
I moved the bed cover over to get out of bed. I then
tottered over to the bathroom naked. I knew Russ would be
watching my naked body with my tattoos in its full glory.

As I came back from the bathroom, Russ had
finished his breakfast and was lying there in my bed,
waiting for me to give him the time of his life. I pulled
back the cover to expose his fit body and climbed on top of
him as he wrapped his muscular arms around me. He felt
different from Shaun, probably because I shocked him,
and he was not prepared for what he was about to have.

I kissed his lips softly, making my way slowly
down his neck as he started to moan with my touch. I
could feel his length beginning to rise. I moved my hand
down to hold his length as he moaned some more. His
hands gripped the bed in ecstasy as I was bringing him to his
limit. I cupped his balls, shoving them into my mouth and
sucking them gently. His length was ready to burst into my

mouth as a tear leaked from his tip. I slid my tongue up his length, flicking the tip, and he moaned, 'Caz, I can't hold on any longer,' as pleasure overwhelmed him. I took his full length to the back of my throat, sucking him hard to release his desire making him come within seconds. His hot salty liquid hit straight down my throat as I licked him clean. His eyes were closed, and I still could hear his moans of pleasure and heavy breathing. I smiled proudly to myself.

I started to kiss his body again, making my way up to his lips. He grabbed hold of me, rolling me over onto my back as he started kissing my neck and taking hold of my breasts, kissing them all over. My nipples hardened with his touch while my arousal was on fire. He sucked hard on my nipples. My fingers were gripping his hair, waiting for him to go down as I needed my entrance stimulated.

His hands slid down my body pushing my legs apart and lifting me to access my entrance with his tongue. My wetness was ready, waiting to be sucked in. My moans were loud enough to bring the flat down. I called his name as his tongue played with me as it entered me.

'I'm on the verge of coming,' I whispered to Russ to fist me. His fingers started to move in until he was fisting me, taking me to the next level and, at last, making me explode with pleasure. I had beads of sweat rolling down my neck. I panted with pleasure, and Russ kissed his way up to my lips.

'You were right about the blow job; I've never had that mind-blowing experience,' whispered Russ kissing me on my breasts; my arousal was still on fire.

'Russ, there are three things I need to ask you,' I spoke amidst my pants.

'Mm, what's that beautiful?' said Russ kissing my body.

'Firstly, if you want, we could stay in bed all day and have sex. Secondly, I don't like my sexual exploits talked about outside these four walls, and thirdly, you can go and get the coffee,' I said, grinning at him.

'Yes, to the first question, no, I wouldn't go to the second and yes to the third.' He laughed as he slowly slipped out of bed, kissing me harder on the lips before walking out of the bedroom. He did not bother to cover his modesty. His shyness had soon disappeared. I waited for him to come back with the coffee to offer him my fully naked body to consume.

By the time he had made the coffee and came back into the bedroom, his erection was pleased to see me. I also needed his length hard inside me.

'I see you're waiting for me.' I teased him as he handed me a mug of coffee.

'Well, what do you expect? I have been lying next to a beautiful bird,' said Russ smirking.

'Cut the flannel,' I said, opening my legs for him to enter me. He soon glided in, pushing his length inside me. He started kissing my neck as I began to moan in pleasure.

He held it as long as he could, but within minutes, he pumped me hard, releasing his pleasure inside me.

Now the fun began. I rolled him over, kissing his body all over until I went down to his length. I spread his legs apart to access his balls. My hand lifted his balls to expose his entrance as I flicked my tongue around it, making him flinch as though he wasn't expecting me to go that far down.

His entrance was moist with my tongue as I licked every part of his balls, relaxing him as he started to moan. I then started to massage his length with my other hand, lickings and sucking his balls. I slowly pushed my finger in his entrance, making him flinch and then relax as I pumped his length, sucking his balls harder.

He was very responsive while taking my finger as I slid it in and out slowly. I was sure that after a short while, he would release his pleasure in my mouth again.

'Oh, Caz, you are so good,' Russ gasped as I slid two fingers inside him. My mouth slid up to the tip of his length as tears started forming, waiting to explode in my mouth.

I picked up the pace with my fingers inside him; he moaned as he was on the verge of finding his release. I took his hard length to the back of my throat, sucking him hard to release his pleasure within a couple of seconds.

'Oh, Caz, I have never had so much pleasure as I am having with you. I don't know why you haven't had a partner; you would keep a man so happy,' said Russ rolling me over kissing my lips softly, moving his hands to my breast to massage them.

'Mmm, you can keep doing that.' I start to moan with the sensation; he was sucking my nipples in the process.

'I could suck you all day,' said Russ looking up and raising a brow.

'I'm all up for that,' I smirked back at him.

'Well, let's try it then,' said Russ going down and parting my legs to drink in my wetness. I arched my back as my hips followed his tongue.

'Russ, fist me,' I whispered, and my demand was granted. I exploded my wetness for him to drink. We laid back on the bed, exhausted with all the work out we had just done.

We laid in silence for a while, but then I started to get up. 'Seeing that your coffee has gone cold, I'll go and make some fresh.' I made a move to get up from the bed, but I was pulled back by Russ, who had wrapped his muscular arm around my waist, pulling me back onto the bed. He went down on me again, making me explode in pleasure quickly.

'Oh, Russ, you know how to keep a girl happy.' I appreciated him panting from the pleasure. 'We need coffee.' I finally said. 'Come on; you can give me a hand.'.

I grabbed the mugs full of cold coffee from the side of the bed and took them into the kitchen. I did not bother covering myself. It was just the two of us exploring each other's bodies. Russ walked through in the kitchen, naked, and stood close behind me. It was good to feel his hot muscular body next to mine. My sex drive was on over-ride, and I needed him to fuck me in the kitchen.

His length was ready to take me as I jumped up, enveloping my legs around his waist, taking his hard length inside me. He balanced my weight in his strong arms, holding my buttocks as he thrust hard. I rode him, and my tongue entered his mouth, making every thrush harder. Our tongues played with each other as we tried to eat each other. It was intense, as we both found our pleasure in sync. I was so happy that I had found someone with a sex drive as crazy as mine.

We managed to make the coffee and drink it before heading off to the bathroom for a shower together. Despite the flat being rented, I wanted a double shower, so the landlord agreed at my expense to change the bathroom around. I was happy with that knowing I wouldn't be alone in there. We showered together, washing the sweat and sex off our bodies, but before we finished, I asked Russ to take me again. He was already hard waiting to enter me. I stood with my legs apart, showing my butt, and he bent down to kiss it. He pulled the cheeks and licked the back entrance as he inserted his finger inside. I moaned loudly.

'Russ, enter me,' I begged as the water ran over us. I felt his length entering me, sliding in slowly as his fingers inserted me in the front.

My intense pleasure kicked in, 'Russ fuck my arse harder,' I whispered, my voice shaking with pleasure. He pumped me harder and faster.

'Oh, Caz, your arse is so tight. I'm going to come.'

'Russ fist me, we can come together.' I pleaded. I hung onto the rail as my intense pleasure exploded at the same time Russ came inside me.

After our intense pleasure in the shower, we were back in the bedroom and sank in the bed. I was exhausted, with every cell of my being begging me to rest, but with Russ around, my sex drive had grown more significant than ever, and there was no way we were going to stop any sooner.

'It was incredible.' I smiled big.

'I bet it was,' Russ replied and bent over to kiss my lips. We had all day, all night to continue it.

Chapter Three

'Would you like to eat out tonight?' I asked Russ placing my hand on his taut body.

'I was thinking of eating in,' smiled Russ turning over and pressing his body over mine while his hand dived on my breasts for a massage. I started to moan, closing my eyes because it felt so good.

'We'll get the food delivered in,' I whispered with my eyes still closed, enjoying the sensation.

'Good idea,' said Russ as he straddled me; his desire was definitely on overdrive. As he went down sucking on my wetness, his hands were still massaging my breasts. My pleasure kicked in, making me come instantly, and he drank my wetness.

'Russ, fist me hard,' I whispered as the things started to get wilder once again. He pumped his fist inside me, and my wetness was proof of my pleasure as I exploded within seconds. 'Russ, fuck me, please.' I pleaded, still shaking with pleasure. He entered so slick and pumped me hard, with my legs opened wide to feel his full erected length and his balls. 'Russ, I'm coming,' I screamed as we came together. We stayed locked together lying on the bed exhausted by the explosive sex we just had, and eventually, we both drifted off to sleep.

I woke up after having a well-deserved sleep with it being a very energetic day for a Sunday. Russ was still partially lying on me with his hand cupping my breast and his leg over my body. I stirred to see what time it was feeling hungry having only eaten some toast that morning which Russ had made for me; how thoughtful of him.

Mmm, do I want him to get into a relationship with him or use him as my fuck buddy? I thought as I turned to look at his fit body, his messy blond hair, tattoos and tanned skin from working on the building sites. I'll have to think about that.

I started to get up trying not to wake Russ while slipping out of bed; groggily, he rolled over, spreading himself further over my bed. God, he looks so hot and sexy even when he is asleep. I admired him for a few seconds, staring at his naked body while he slept.

I slipped on my short robe and wandered into the kitchen in need of a coffee. Flicking the kettle on, I nipped to the bathroom for a wee while the kettle boiled. It was nearly 6 pm, and I was starving. I decided to have Chinese food delivered if Russ agreed with that. The kettle had boiled as I padded back to the kitchen to make the coffee, but Russ had beaten me to it. He was pouring water into the mugs. I put my arms around his waist, hugging him and pressing my breasts against his hot body radiating heat.

'Hey, I'm getting hard already,' said Russ playfully while pouring the water. My hand glided down to his length, testing his hardness.

'I think you need a good blowing.' I smirked, kneeling down to take his length deep into the back of my throat, sucking him hard. He moaned as he leaned back and closed his eyes. After a while, he sighed and released his full pleasure in my mouth.

'Oh, Caz I've never had so many blow jobs as you have given me today,' murmured Russ pulling me up and kissing me hard on the lips as our tongues entwined. My robe started to slip off my shoulders as Russ pushed it off, exposing my naked body.

He effortlessly picked me up and then placed me down to the kitchen floor to drink my wetness. He winked at me before spreading my legs wide for access. I started to moan and lifted myself up, moving with his mouth. I didn't have to ask him to fist me. We had started to know each other's needs to trigger our pleasure spots. After having another explosive orgasm in the kitchen and catching our breath, food was very much needed. The workout we had had all day had made us hungry. Russ said he would pay for the food, for letting him share the flat and for also being a sex goddess. I give him a light punch on the arm for his jest and being so thoughtful.

After our meal, I cleared away the trays and bags and made coffee to settle down for the night.

'What time do you have to be at work tomorrow?' I asked, hoping it was not the same time as me.

'I'll be up at 6 am. Need to be on-site at 7.30 am. Jamie's picking me up at 6.30 on the High Street.' said Russ wondering why I was asking.

'That's okay then at least we won't clash in the bathroom in the mornings, as I am not normally a morning person,' I said, sounding relieved.

'Caz, where do we go from here?' asked Russ suddenly, squeezing my hand.

'Umm… I don't know, we can just play it by ear if you want,' I replied, sounding as though I was not sure about what I wanted.

'I'm always here for you Caz if you need me,' smiled Russ as he put his muscular arm around me. I curled up to him to watch TV. It was around 10.30 pm, I was ready for bed. Russ was already asleep as I moved to get up, waking him in the process.

'Russ, I'm going to bed, and you need to be up early in the morning, too.' I grabbed his hand to pull him up from the sofa.

'Yeah, you are right,' said Russ rubbing his eyes, looking half asleep. He kissed me on the cheek and said goodnight as he headed off back to his bedroom. This was going to be my second time in a while sleeping on my own, but I needed to start some time.

It was Monday morning, and I could hear Russ moving around in the kitchen. The sun was shining through the thin curtains that hung up in my bedroom, and I stretched out in my bed now that I had it to myself. Whether it was because I was on my own or the full day of sex yesterday had given me a good work out, but either way, I was feeling refreshed. I heard a knock on my bedroom door before the door opened. Russ had made me coffee.

I sat up not caring to cover my breasts as he handed me the mug.

'Russ, you are so thoughtful.' I caressed his cheek with my hand. He bent down to kiss me gently on my lips, he was starting to arouse me.

'Russ, fuck me before you go,' I commanded. He pulled the cover back to expose my naked body and took the coffee from my hand. He put it on the bedside cabinet. I tugged on his work trousers to get to his length as I turned around to open my legs, ready to receive him inside me. Russ was soon thrashing his hardness inside me. I moaned loudly making the most of his length as I moved my body with his for fulfilment. He was pumping me as hard as he could. Our mouths were eating each other, my fingers wrapped tightly in his hair as we came together. He collapsed on me with the instant release I had given him. He started to massage my breasts for a couple of minutes, and I closed my eyes to receive the pleasure.

'Russ you have wonderful hands,' I said shaking with the gentleness of his hands on my breasts.

'Caz, I need to get to work,' said Russ wishing he could stay to have a re-run of yesterday.

By 7 am, I was up to have a shower before I left to finish the job I had started last Monday. Most of my work was with the local council. I planned other work around the jobs I had taken on and was now starting to get enquiries from the upper-class clients living in the most expensive part of the city. They paid well, never asked for a quote or quibbled over the invoice and seemed happy with the work I was doing. My bank balance was nicely growing with the new clients. The council had been refurbishing a row of council houses and had asked me if I would stripe out the pipework and replace the boiler with new. They had a year to complete all the houses and were working on a budget. Mine was fixed, only charging for labour having no upfront costs to purchase.

I just had the boiler to plumb up and flush through the pipe, making sure there were no leaks, it would take me most of the day to finish off. We had to finish by 4 pm for the reason that some of the guys that worked for the council only worked until 4 pm and were responsible for locking up. By 3 pm I had finished, the day had been hot and even hotter when I had to test the heating and the pipes making sure they were working and leak-free.

I was home by 4 and went straight into the shower to wash away the day's sweat from the heat of the day. I was soon back and went down to the gym to work out. I wasn't sure what time Russ would be back but continued my single life without Shaun.

It was 6 pm by the time I got home. I had another shower and a change of clothes that I had taken with me to the gym.

'Hi, my goddess,' Russ sounded upbeat now he had somewhere to stay.

'Hi, my sex on legs,' I called back smirking at him.

'I was going to cook, but I didn't know where you were or how long you would be,' said Russ getting up from the sofa where he was watching the TV.

'Oh, that's a change! A man cooking for me?' I laughed out loud. 'But no, it's okay, it will only be something simple like salad,' I said, taking my gym gear from my bag and slipping it into the washing machine for a quick wash.

'I can do that,' offered Russ following me into the kitchen.

'Russ, I don't expect you to be my slave.' I smirked and then reply in a serious tone.

'I'd love to be your slave anytime my goddess,' answered Russ grinning as he made his way to the fridge.

'Yeah, you would soon get fed up with me and start seeing sense,' I said, pulling the plates from the cupboard.

'No ways. I'd never get fed up with you goddess,' said Russ extended his arms to reach me so he could hold me, making me laugh.

'Yeah we'll see,' I said taking the bag of salad from him.

We had our meal with Russ insisting that he would wash the dishes and make a drink while I put my feet up and watch TV. I didn't argue with that. He was so refreshing. Shaun expected me to do everything for him. I was glad he was out of my life. Russ brought through hot drinks as he settled down on the sofa with me. I curled up in the curve of his arm, the heat from his body radiated off him, and I could hear his heart beating. He smelt divine as if he had had a shower before I got home, it was all too good to be true. We chatted about our days' work. Russ was bricklaying on site but had other skills when one job finishes another would start. I told him that I usually go to the gym three days a week and depending on the clients I worked for, sometimes worked until 6 pm. Russ wanted to cook so it was agreed that we would text each other the times we would be home. As the evening moved on, I started to doze off while we watched tv. It was nearly eleven when Russ woke me up saying I should go to bed.

'Hmm, yeah I must have dozed off.' I yawned and got up to go to the bathroom. I came out of the bathroom as Russ waited outside the door, waiting for his turn. 'Russ the door will always be open for you,' I said, reaching up and kissing him goodnight on his lips as I padded off to my bedroom.

The following morning was going to be a hot day; my bedroom was rather warm already by 6 am as I woke up feeling the heat. I could hear Russ in the kitchen, and within 10 minutes, he had brought me coffee. He looked so sexy having his skin all tanned up from yesterday's heat, and his messy unruly blond hair and ice-blue eyes. He was wearing a vest top exposing his tattoos and rippling muscles; yeah sex on legs.

'Morning, my sex god.' I greeted him with a smile. The sight was brightening my day.

'Morning, my goddess,' he said as he bent down, kissing me gently on my lips. I raised my brow giving him the 'come on' signal pulling the covers back from my bed. I whispered to him, 'fuck me hard before you go to work Russ.'

'Caz are you sure? Because I'm not bringing coffee to get into your undies,' said Russ grinning.

'Oh shut up and fuck me,' I ordered, laying back with my legs open waiting for him to release his beast inside me. We kissed hard as though we couldn't get enough of each other. His beast released his hot, salty liquid inside me, mixing together with my wetness. We stayed locked together a few minutes before he released me after giving my breasts a two-minute relaxing massage. God how I loved this. My feelings were starting to change despite only been with him a couple of days.

I was starting with a new client who needed an outside building to be renovated as office space. Alex's wife wanted him to have his own space separate from the house, being rather noisy. They also had a couple of kids running riots around the house while he was trying to work, so his wife Jess insisted he had his own space.

The morning was heating up, and I knew that I would be sweating heavily while preparing the area for plastering. Luckily, I always carried plenty of water with me. The traffic was heavy; Jess didn't want me to start before 9 am due to her taking the kids to school. It was 8.50 am when I pulled into the driveway leaning down a long stone track off the main road to the house.

The large six-bedroom house of the Victorian era had outbuildings standing in a large plot surrounded by trees and lay to lawn. Jess didn't seem the gardening type. She was blonde and petite with long well-manicured nails and soft-looking hands as though she had never done a day's work in her life.

She was the so-called housewife, while Alex worked his butt off to sustain her lifestyle and look after the kids. I wasn't sure what line of work he was in but whatever it was must be highly paid knowing houses in this area were worth a couple of million-plus. Jess drove up the driveway, knowing I would be waiting to let me into the building. Her 4x4 pulled up next to my van as she quickly got out tottering across in her coloured heels wearing a flora printed flowing dress, looking as though she had plans of going out somewhere.

'Sorry you had to wait; the traffic was horrendous. I came back as quickly as I could,' she said in a fluster.

'Oh no problem I haven't been waiting long,' I said, shading my eyes with my hand as I spoke to her.

'Caz, if you can drive your van around to the building while I get the key, I'll meet you around there,' said Jess trotting off to the house as her mobile phone started to ring.

I drove the van around to the back of the house parking up outside the building and waiting for Jess to come over with the key to let me in. The surrounding grounds were covered with trees dotted around a large plot of lawn area having flower borders with a variety of various colours and textures. It was like walking into a state home with grand manicured gardens. Jess would definitely have a gardener to keep this looking so well. I must have been waiting for nearly ten minutes before she came out to let me into the outbuilding. Jess was still on the phone as she came out but quickly ended the call as she approached me.

'Sorry Caz that was a friend of mine, they wouldn't let me get off the phone.' She said, sounding slightly sheepish. Mm…was she having an affair? I wondered seeing how fresh she looked and smelt while passing me the key to unlock the outbuilding.

'I have a slight change of plan, it probably will take you a lot longer than you anticipated,' said Jess looking at me with a sheepish grin.

'Oh, what are you thinking?' I asked.

'Well, I know we said it was just the plastering, but I was thinking of fitting in large bi-folding doors to let through more light into the building. What do you think, Caz?' asked Jess smiling at me.

'Err, yes, I can do that, but it will cost a lot more,' I said after hearing her out.

'Don't worry about the cost. I'll leave it with you to design this outbuilding for my husband with no expense spared,' said Jess now in a hurry to go.

'Mm… okay, leave it to me, but just one thing. You don't mind me being here starting early and sometimes leaving later in the evening?' I said, needing to maximize my hours of the day.

'No, not at all,' she shook her head and handed me the key. 'I hadn't had the time to throw the rubbish out. You can keep the key,' said Jess walking off as she looked at her watch. The woman was becoming a pain adding to my workload, but she was going to damn well pay for it.

I needed to hire a skip and some machinery to lift the RSJ to support the top for the bi-folding doors. Luckily the bi-folding doors would be fitted by the manufactures, so I had no worries on that part. It took me an hour to plan the outbuilding to bring in the maximum light but still have the personal space without people looking in, but the doors and glass would be expensive. Once the skip arrived, I could start to clear out the building, which led me to believe it would be empty, taking more of my time on the project. While I waited for the skip to arrive, I made a few phone calls on the bi-folding doors and glass asking for an estimate and lead time. I coughed at the prices and would have to speak with Jess on the price before committing to order them.

It was lunchtime by the time the skip had arrived; I had already tidied up some of the stuff inside. It took me most of the day to clear it all out of the building. Some of the stuff I thought was too good to chuck so I put them to one side to take home to sell at a later date. By 5 pm it was now clear and ready to start knocking the bricks out for the RJS to slide in, I had ordered it, and was due to arrive the next day together with the lift to manoeuvre it in its place.

By 6 pm, I was home feeling sweaty and dirty and a little miffed with Jess changing her plans on the outbuilding. I had totally forgotten to text Russ the time I would be home. It hit me while I was unlocking the door to the flat, but I was surprised to find has wasn't in. No wonder I hadn't heard from him. There had been no signs of him coming in and leaving again. He must be working late or out with his mates. I was a little disappointed as I was starting to get fond of him with his thoughtful ways. Seeing that he wasn't in, and I have had a crappy start with my new client with her changing her mind. I headed off to the gym to release some tension. I texted Russ that I was at the gym and wouldn't be back until after 8.30 pm and not to cook anything for me as I would get something while I was out.

I checked my phone to see if Russ had texted me back. He texted to say he had something to ask me when I got back but wouldn't say what. I was intrigued by what it was. After a stress releasing workout, I showered and changed into fresh clothes before setting back to the flat. It was nearly 9 pm by the time I got back from the gym still wondering about what Russ was going to ask me. Russ was in the kitchen, making a drink when I arrived.

'Hello, my sex goddess. I'm making a drink, would you like one?' said Russ filling the kettle with water.

'Yes, please sex god,' I grinned as I pulled my gym gear from my bag and pushed it into the washing machine.

Russ made the drinks and brought them through into the living room. I had switched the TV on putting my feet up on the sofa while waiting for my drink. Russ sat down next to me, handing me my drink as we curled up together to watch the TV. I waited for him to ask the question he had texted me about as I didn't what to push it.

We chatted about the day's work. I told him how my new client changed her mind from being a quick, simple job of plastering to a total refurb extending my workload needing to work the Saturday and Sunday to reduce the time scale on the build. I was due to start at Lloyds on the following Monday morning.

Russ hadn't mentioned his text yet which I wanted to hear about.

'So what did you want to ask me when you texted?' I asked him finally.

'Well, I was going to ask you if you would like to come to a rock concert at the weekend with a group of us? We are also camping out, but if you're working, it puts the kibosh on that,' said Russ sounding disappointed.

'Ah, my sex god is so thoughtful for thinking about me. I wish I could, but Mrs Moneybags changed her mind, extending the job, so you know.' I shrugged sounding a bit miffed knowing I would have enjoyed the concert and camping out. I kissed him on the cheek, thanking him for asking me. Russ gave me a hug as I snuggled into him, feeling the heat and smell of his body. He was lush. I would miss him over the weekend while having an empty flat.

Chapter Four

To my utter disappointment, Friday morning had soon come around. Russ was going to the concert that evening, and I would miss him since I had to work late. Russ brought my usual coffee in at 6 am. I knew that I was going to miss him despite it only being for a couple of days.

'Russ, I'll miss you,' I said, looking into his deep blue eyes.

'Aw, I'll soon be back, my sex goddess,' Russ assured me, kissing me on the lips. I snaked my arms around his neck, pulling him down onto my bed and kissed him. As I snogged his face, our tongues started playing with each other. Our moans of passion began to fill the room as Russ turned over, pulling the bed cover back before going down to taste my wetness.

'Oh Russ, I'll miss you, babe,' I moaned, arching my back as I felt his tongue on me. He pulled his trousers down to enter me.

'Russ, fuck me hard,' I ordered, moaning with the pleasure he was giving me. His hardness slid in, pumping me like a piston until he released himself inside me.

'My God, Caz, I can't get enough of you,' said Russ panting with his recent release of pleasure. His hand took hold of my breast for a massage, and I moaned, enjoying these last moments before he left. I wouldn't see him until late Sunday evening.

After Russ had pleasured me before leaving for work, I decided to get up and start my job earlier than usual. I turned up just after 7 am with the traffic not too heavy. The sun was beating down despite the early morning, and was it was due to get hotter. Jess had agreed to pay for the bi-folding doors, which were expected to come in three weeks. It had left the side of the outbuilding exposed, but the weather wasn't due to change for the foreseeable future, so it didn't matter about a temporary fix to cover the opening. The RJS had been placed to support the roof and the sides of the building with the bi-folding doors giving light inside when they finally arrived. I was pleased I didn't have to work around these costly doors being the last thing to be put in.

My mind wandered to Russ and him asking me out to the rock concert. I wished now that I had said yes instead of coming here, but the money was excellent, and the job needed to be finished as soon as possible to start the job for Lloyd. I flicked through my playlist for the rock songs and set play turning the volume up as I started to work. Within half an hour, Jess had turned up.

'Caz, can you turn your music down?' shouted Jess as she approached me. I turned it down, wondering what she wanted. 'We can hear your music in the house, my husband came back late last night and is still asleep.' continued Jess sounding slightly annoyed.

'Oops, sorry, I thought you would be out.' I shrugged. She had never been home all week.

'No, I'm in all day, so could you please keep the music down?' said Jess turning around to leave as she tottered back to the house.

Fucking bitch, I thought as I continued my work.

There was already running water in the outbuilding, making it easier to connect to the toilet and washbasin. I just had to find the main sewage drain to connect to the toilet. Luckily enough, I found that running along the side of the outbuilding. Everything seemed to be running smoothly, and I was relieved.

I was outside knelt in the trench, which I had dug while fixing the pipes when a shadow came over me. I continued working completely, ignoring the presence shadowing me.

'You have a nice tattoo,' I heard a male voice. I stopped what I was doing as I looked up with my hand protecting my eyes from the sun.

'Gee, thanks,' I replied as I began to stand up.

'My name is Alex, Jess's husband. I wasn't expecting to find a fit chick like you working on this.' He introduced himself, sounding surprised, with his eyes glued onto my cleavage.

'Well, you'll be surprised to see what I can do,' I mumbled as I continued with the pipework.

'Hmm, I wouldn't mind finding that out,' Alex whispered under his breath. 'So, is Jess keeping you on your toes with this work? I know she is one for changing her mind.'

'Yeah, just a bit,' I said without looking up at him. He stood there watching me for a while, with my cleavage in good view. I ignored him and twisted the pipes together until I could hear Jess calling him from the house. I could sense him undressing me with his eyes in the trench and being turned on by my tattoo as my vest top was riding up my back.

It was 6 pm by the time I left to go home. I had only seen Alex and Jess that day. The skip was due to be replaced with an empty one ready for me to start the boarding and the skimming the next day being Saturday. It had a little bit of electrics to sort out first, though. I was home before 7; the flat felt different without Russ not around. I was missing him already. 'Fuck, what is wrong with me for feeling like this? I asked myself. Russ seemed different from other guys I had been with or was he?

He seemed to be more caring and thoughtful, which I liked in him apart from his incredible sex drive matching mine. I needed to go to the gym, spending an hour de-stressing over the day's work.

I was back on the job the next day by 7 am. There was no one in sight, so I kept my music down as I started working on the wiring before the plasterboard was put up. It took me an hour to finish when Alex came over with a tray of coffee and biscuits.

'I thought you would like some coffee,' said Alex putting the tray on the bench at the back of the wall. I hadn't taken much notice of him yesterday being in the trench with the sun shining and blinding my vision and him hovering over me. Alex was about 6ft tall and had dark, short, curly hair and grey eyes. He was wearing jeans and a blue tee-shirt which was hugging his fit body.

Yeah, I could fuck him, I thought as I picked up a biscuit and started to nibble it.

'So how are you getting on?' asked Alex looking around the building.

'Not too bad, the plumbing and the electrics are now finished, so I'm just about to start boarding up.' I took another biscuit, ignoring Alex again.

'You're doing a good job,' Alex nodded with approval. 'Would you like me to give to a hand with the boarding?' asked Alex picking up his mug of coffee and taking a sip.

'Well, I thought you would be out with Jess and the kids.' I was surprised by the offer of assistance by someone paying handsomely for my services.

'No, she's taking the kids to her mother's. She lives on the coast, so with the weather so hot and the kids not at school, she thought she could take them for the weekend.'

'Ahaan, you're looking after yourself, then?' I was still surprised by Alex, not going with them.

'I have spent a lot of time on my own for the last couple of months,' said Alex sounding a little miffed. I didn't ask why, as I did not like getting involved with personal problems.

'Yes, thanks, that would be great if you helped.' I was grateful thinking this would move the job more quickly.

After coffee and biscuits, we started to plan out the boarding. The ceiling had to be done first, so Alex held the boards while I nailed them into place. I noticed his muscles as his tee-shirt rode, upholding the boards up for me; they were taut. I also noticed he was watching my body as my vest top rode high in the middle of nailing the boards into place. We were both watching each other's moves.

'I need a drink,' I muttered, hammering the last nail into the board; it was getting hotter despite working inside. I could feel beads of sweat trickling down my neck.

'I'll nip over to the house and make a drink,' offered Alex relieved that we had stopped.

'Sure, thanks,' I nodded, sitting my butt on the floor to reach for my water and gulped it down in one go.

Alex came back with a tray of sandwiches and two mugs of coffee and placed them on the floor where I was sitting.

'I've made some sandwiches as well,' said Alex pushing the plate toward me.

'Wow, you're domesticated,' I said with a little sarcasm.

'Yes, I should be, living on my own four nights a week,' told Alex as he picked up a sandwich and took a bite.

'You only come home on the weekends, then?' I asked, biting into my sandwich.

'Yes, that's what comes with running a business and being on top of your game,' said Alex sipping his coffee now.

'What made you go into building work?' he asked, changing the subject over to me.

'Er, I suppose I have always thought about doing this ever since I was young,' I replied shortly, not giving him any of my life story.

'You're so beautiful and fit to be doing this. I would have expected you to be in modeling or design of some kind,' said Alex sounding sincere.

'No, I like the physical and outdoor life,' I said, getting up to go to the bathroom, which was in the main house near the back door.

After a half-hour break, we started to complete the remaining boarding of the ceiling. It was getting late in the afternoon with the heat of the sun beginning to die down to a more comfortable temperature. We were on the last piece of boarding when I lost my balance while hammering the final nail and fell off the step ladders. Alex was soon there by my side to scoop me up as I fell, but we both landed on the floor with Alex falling on top of me. I banged my head slightly on the floor. Alex stayed laid on me, staring into my eyes and then suddenly kissed me on the lips softly.

I laid there thinking, do I reject him? But then he had rolled up his sleeves to help me out when most of these posh clients looked down on you.

'Caz, can I make love to you?' asked Alex kissing me gently on the lips. I was gobsmacked.

'What? Why me?' I asked, sounding surprised.

'I have been watching you since I came home. You are so beautiful, and your body is so perfect. I want your body next to mine,' he whispered in my ear.

'What about your wife?' I frowned.

'She's too busy spending my money and going out with her friends. She hardly has time for me,' said Alex making excuses for her.

He started kissing my neck and slowly worked his way down to my cleavage. Despite my sweat, he licked my body, sweat, and dust from doing all the work did not faze him. My arousal had woken up as his hands started to touch my body. He cupped my breasts, making me gasp with his soft touch, my arousal roared.

'Oh, Caz, I need to be inside you,' he whispered again, sliding my bra over my breast to take my nipple in his mouth. I moaned as I arched slightly, needing this so much. I could feel his hardness on my body, waiting to enter me. Alex lifted me slightly to unhook my bra and releasing my breasts as he cupped them gently, squeezing licking and sucking both nipples. My arousal was now on fire.

'Alex, I need you inside me,' I mumbled, his touch was so soft and gentle it was making my wetness explode.

He started to unbutton my trousers before slipping them off. After that, he unbuttoned his jeans to expose his hard length waiting to enter me. He slid his mouth down my body to my wetness, his tongue playing with my wet core. I moaned in pure pleasure.

He massaged my breasts, flicking my nipples and sending a sensation down my body.

'Oh, Alex,' I whispered, 'you are making me come over and over again.' He kept filling me with pleasure as he drank in my wetness. 'Alex, would you like me to suck you?' I asked him. He came up and kissed me on the lips with the taste of my wetness and whispered.

'Later, I need to be inside you.' He slid his length inside, holding it for a few seconds and then began to pump me hard. Within seconds he shot his hot, salty liquid inside me.

'Caz, that was so good,' He kissed me on the neck while lying on top of me with his length still inside me. We laid there a few minutes before he got up to dress. I still laid there with my half-exposed body while he dressed. 'Will you stay with me tonight?' he asked me, looking at my body hungrily. I started to get up to hook my bra and pull my trousers up.

'Mm, I don't know. I need fresh clothes and a shower.' I said, but then it occurred to me that I would be home alone. 'What about your wife?' I asked.

'She won't be home until tomorrow evening, and you can do your laundry while you are with me. We can also have a shower together,' suggested Alex helping me up off the floor and grinning.

'Well, I have nothing to go home for, so yeah, ok, I'll stay.' I shrugged. Alex grabbed hold of me and bent me back, smothering me with kisses. I was going to make him happy for one night. He needed a break from his boring wife.

It was after 5 pm by the time we had tidied up outside before walking over to the main house. We ventured into the kitchen as Alex switched on the coffee machine and asked me if the salad was ok for our evening meal?

'Yeah, that's great,' I said. The kitchen was huge, with white fitted units and built-in appliances. There was an island in the middle of the kitchen being used as the kitchen sink. 'Where's your washing machine?' I asked Alex looking around the kitchen.

'Oh, we have a laundry room for that,' said Alex pointing to the door on the left. It was near the door we had come through from outside.

'Umm, have you anything I could wear while my clothes are being washed?' I questioned looking lost as I was in a house, I shouldn't be in.

'Yeah, I'll get you one of my long tee shirts,' said Alex nipping upstairs to fetch me one. I walked around the kitchen, opening the cupboards and touching the surfaces and basically being nosey. Everything seemed to be in its place and clean as though the kitchen didn't get used much or that Jess had a cleaner as I couldn't imagine Jess cleaning like the gardens outside.

Alex soon came down with the long tee shirt and handed it over to me as I went off to the laundry room. It was large with plenty of spare room for storage if need be. After finding the washing liquid, I turned the machine on for a quick wash. Alex's tee-shirt covered me with the hem touching the bottom of my butt. By the time I had changed and switched the machine on, Alex had the salad prepared. It had various cuts of cooked meats. He placed the plates onto the kitchen table for us to sit and eat.

'You look sexy in that,' smirked Alex, as he came over kissing me on the lips and squeezing my butt.

'I'm ready for a shower,' I said, sitting at the table.

'Hmm, so am I, and I can't wait,' said Alex raising a brow. I grinned as I started to tease him. I was eating my meal in a way that I was giving him a blow job.

'Caz stop it, or I'll have to come over this table and fuck you,' he said, and his grey eyes sparkled.

'You just wait. I'm gonna make you have it tonight,' I said, licking my lips as I teased.

We finished our meal, resisting each other but teasing as I helped him with the washing and drying of our pots before heading off for a shower. The washing machine had finished its cycle, including the drying, so I pulled them from the machine, which didn't look too bad as I would have thrown an iron over them. The kitchen led out into a vast hallway to expose a broad stairway dividing the rooms into two wings. The hallway had oak wooden flooring with neutral colour walls and coloured textures in a modern twist. A huge chandelier hung from the ceiling, with wall lights dotted around the hallway. It must have cost a fortune, the weight of it, and the cleaning. Alex took hold of my butt as we climbed the stairs turning left on the top. It looked as though both sides were mirror images as the corridor ran through the top floor to the bedrooms.

We headed down to the last door at the end of the corridor as Alex opened the door, squeezing my butt again.

'I'll go and switch the shower on,' said Alex as he gave my butt a further squeeze before heading for the shower. The bedroom was impressive, having a four-poster bed with matching furniture in an old but new kind of way. The decoration was a more relaxing soft shade of pale green with darker shades of textures and matching bedding.

'Come on, my sexy builder,' called out Alex from the bathroom. I placed my freshly laundered cloth on the chair near the door as I padded over to find a large bathroom, which was making my bathroom and bedroom in my flat look small. It was tiled throughout with plain white and pale green tiles split with a board of coloured pattern of darker green and red. The shower was huge with no tray, walking straight in with a large shower head. Alex was already in, exposing his fully naked body. His body wasn't as muscular as Russ's, but he was in good shape.

I peeled off Alex's tee-shirt, exposing my nakedness to Alex as I entered the shower. Alex enveloped me into his arms, pressing his body next to mine. I felt his length in need of attention.

'Oh, Caz, I've been looking forward to this moment.' He placed a kiss on my neck as the water poured over our dusty and sweaty bodies from the day's work. I started to moan, leaning my head back as he ran his lips over my body. His hands cupped my breasts, gently massaging them, making me groan with lust and arousal.

'Oh, Alex, you're making me cum just with your touch,' I moaned as he went down, spreading my legs apart and pressing his mouth on my wetness. The sensation was intense as I exploded with pleasure, and my wetness increased. His finger entered me; he pumped his fingers one at a time until he started to fist me. The desire was overwhelming as I exploded.

'Alex, you're pressing all my right buttons,' I panted.

'I need to be inside you,' Alex turned me around and entered me doggy fashion, holding my breast while pumping me slowly. I was going insane; my arousal was burning red hot. I was breathing heavily with so many orgasms. After a few minutes, Alex finally exploded inside me. He pressed his body against my back as I was pressed against the shower wall. His hands were still massaging my breasts.

'I need you Caz, I missed this so much,' he whispered. I was lost for words and felt sorry for the guy missing out on his pleasures.

'Alex, you have my body all night enjoy it,' I said as I turned to kiss him passionately on his lips. He squeezed me tight, so happy that I was with him for the night.

After washing off the day's work and making out, we finally headed into the bedroom.

'Alex, what is your sexual fantasy?' I asked, looking into his come to bed eyes.

'Well, I think I'm having it now,' he said, taking me into his arms and planting a soft kiss on my lips.

'Alex, I want to fuck you all night and please you; you deserve it,' I said, kissing him harder.

'Hmm, show me Caz; it would make me a very happy man,' whispered Alex.

I was sure that by the time I walked out of his bedroom, he would have lived all his sexual fantasies with me.

Chapter Five

"Well, let's start then," I said, eyeing him and then sliding down his body kissing and licking slowly. He moaned loudly in pleasure, closing his eyes as my lips skimmed down his body. His length began to rise; I pushed his legs apart to access his balls, cupping them with my hand and squeezing gently.

"Oh, Caz this feels so good." His voice sounded hoarse, not more than a whisper. I started to rub down his length while I kissed and sucked his balls. His length soon became full, so I stopped rubbing it. I licked and brushed my lips around his length to the tip teasing it with my flicking tongue. "Caz, I'm going to come." he cried, waiting for me to release him. His tool exploded and started spilling slightly; I licked the taste of his hot salty liquid.

"Caz you are killing me." he tightened his grip on my head, wanting me to finish him off. I took his length down to the back of my throat, sucking hard, giving him his release of pleasure. The hot salty liquid flowed to the back of my throat, and I swallowed it in one. I licked him dry and then kissed him on the mouth to give him a taste of his juices.

He pulled me over, pinning me to the bed. "Caz I've never had such a good blow job as I have had tonight with you. My wife won't do it; she does not do anything for me. You are one in a million and making love to you has made me so happy." He told me, kissing me on the lips.

"Well, we will have to make the most of the night and suck you all night, then?" I teased, sticking my tongue out at him.

"Hmm, and I want to rub my hands over your body and taste your wetness on my lips." He teased back as he started making his way down to my wetness. My legs opened reflexively to gain maximum pleasure as his tongue played me. I cried with pleasure as he started to insert his fingers one by one inside me until he was fisting me, twisting his fist inside me. I screamed as I exploded and he drank on my wetness.

"God Alex, you know how to please a woman." I panted.

"Oh, I wish we could stay here forever," said Alex licking my body up to my neck as he took hold of my breasts to massage them.

"Mm, I love this," I said. He made me come all over again just by massaging my breasts.

"Caz, ride me?" asked Alex now his length was ready to be mounted. I obliged his demand slipping onto his length, straddling to get his full length inside me. He shut his eyes in pleasure as I started to ride him slowly.

His hands were on my breasts, massaging them, and I soon came again. I quickened my pace, and his moans became more demanding as I started to ride him hard until he came releasing his pleasure inside me. His hands were roaming over my body.

"Oh, Caz, I am so lucky you came into my life," said Alex breathing heavy with the release of pleasure I had just given him.

We laid on the bed for a breather, with Alex's body pressing half on mine with his hand running all over my body, guess he couldn't get enough of me. His sex drive was good so far, but it was still early with a long night ahead. I wanted to fuck him hard until he couldn't take any more, that should make up for the time he had missed being married to his wife. I started to run my hand down his body, reaching his length, rolling him on his back. I started to kiss his body and licked him.

"Caz straddle me if you're going down so I can squeeze your butt and taste your wetness." I obliged him straddling over as I took his length in my mouth, sucking him hard, bringing his erection back to life. He soon came, and I swallowed his hot salty liquid. He in returns started to fist me while I was straddled over his head, enjoying the pleasure as his other hand squeezed my butt. I was in heaven, so I soon came, and he pulled me down to his mouth to lick my wetness. I moaned as he teased my core with his tongue, forcing me to come again.

"Oh, Alex, you keep making me come over and over again," I whispered all exhausted.

"Alex, I need to try something," I said, kissing him softly on the lips.

"Yes, what's that?" asked Alex wondering what I was going to do.

"Wait and see." I moved down his body, slowly pressing my breasts on him on the way down to his erection. "Alex, open your legs wide," I ordered. He obliged without question. I cupped his balls gently squeezing as he started to moan in pleasure, I squeezed them harder. Another moan of pleasure escaped his lips. I licked and sucked his balls as I squeezed harder, licking his balls further down to his entrance to make it moist as I started to insert my finger. He flinched but relaxed as I started to rub his length. I pushed a little more as I felt him relax more, after a minute I inserted another finger coming up to take his length and sucking hard to simulate him, relaxing him further as I pushed further.

My fingers were soon sliding easily as I pumped his length with my mouth, making him release his love juices in my mouth. His pleasures were released as he brought me up, sucking my mouth to taste his self on my tongue.

We were both panting hard, sweating with our work out. "Alex, can we go into the shower? I need you to do something for me." I commanded him.

"I'd do anything for you, my angel," said Alex cupping my face. After 15 minutes, we were in the shower. "So what would you like me to do?" asked Alex as water flowed over his body.

"I want you to take me up my back passage," I say.

"Wow, Caz this has been a fantasy of mine, you will make a man very happy," said Alex enveloping me in his arms under the flow of the shower. Firstly, he massaged my breasts after which he fisted me, making me wet and aroused.

"Alright, Alex, take me now." I turned around facing the wall; his length was hard and ready to take its journey inside my rear. I bent over, pulling my cheeks apart, waiting for him to insert his length into my passage. I felt the tip as he started to push, his hands cupping my breasts. I moaned with the sensation as he pushed further.

"You're so tight," exclaimed Alex.

"Alex fist me," I whisper, he inserted his fingers in my front as he pushed further inside me. He started to pump my rear and fisted me, making the sensation kick in.

"Alex pump me more." He obliged pumping harder as the sensation grew bigger and further until I exploded. My moans of pleasure were so loud they could bring the walls down. I kept shouting his name. He exploded at the same time as we locked together for a few seconds before releasing each other.

Alex spin me around, pressing his body on to mine, squeezing my breasts hard. He then kissed me, and my body all over. He was deprived of his sexual pleasures for so long. I let him use my body until he spoke.

"Oh, Caz, you have made me a very happy man," said Alex as he started to wash my body.

"I'm glad I could be of some service." I sounded like a hooker. After we dried ourselves, we were back in bed.

Alex was on fire with his hands all over my body yet again; I laid there, taking the pleasure of his hands massaging my body. He pushed my legs apart sliding his tongue into my wetness, making me explode again for more wetness for him to consume. He fisted me bringing another explosion of wetness; he drank me making his way up to my breasts for another massage and kissed me heavily on the lips tasting my wetness as he entered me holding his length inside me, waiting as he couldn't take it any longer.

We laid on the bed, exhausted from our continuous sex.

"You have a good sex drive," I said to Alex considering his wife was not great in the bedroom department.

"Mm, I must confess I have had a helping hand a friend of mine gave me a while back so I thought I'd try it tonight." He confessed.

"Oh, how long will it last?" I asked, sounding inquisitive.

"I don't know they say it all depends on the person taking it," said Alex turning over kissing my nipple. "I must say you have a high sex drive for a woman." He ran his hand down my body.

"Yeah, I just love having sex." I nodded rolling over and taking hold of his length to massage. He started to moan as I took his length in my mouth and sucked him hard bringing up to release.

"Caz, you're going to kill me tonight at this rate," said Alex moaning as he shot his lot in my mouth.

"Yeah, but what a way to die?" I said jest.

"Hmm yeah," whispered Alex in the moment of release.

It was getting on for 4 am. I had eventually fucked him until he laid there exhausted despite him having taken something to help him in that department. I wasn't going to let any guy beat me in the bedroom department, at least I didn't need a helping hand like Alex, but he would have a night to remember. He slept like a baby entwined in my body as though he didn't want to let me go. We managed to get three hours of sleep as the sun started to poke through the gap in the thick curtains. It was going to be another hot day.

I needed to crack on with the rest of the boarding in the outbuilding, hoping to complete that task the same day. I started to stir untwining Alex from my body. He groaned as he rolled over, giving me a chance to escape to the bathroom for a quick shower. I stood under the shower as the water massaged my body, cleaning the sexual pleasures of the night.

It was when I felt a presence behind me as a pair of hands cupped my breasts to massage them. Alex pressed his hard length tight to my body. I started to moan with his lips kissing down my neck as I leaned back to expose more of my neck.

"Caz, can I take you from the back?" whispered Alex sliding his hand down to my wetness. I obliged seeing that this would be the last time I would see him after today. I bent down, and his hands massaged my butt parting my cheeks to insert his hard length. He started to push as I moaned. His hands cupped my breasts, squeezing them hard as he pushed further into my passage. The sensation was intense as he pumped harder.

"Your arse is so tight." moaned Alex as he pumped me faster until he released himself inside me slowing down as he still pumped. I Hadn't come with Alex, who was in a hurry to fuck my arse. He spun me around pushing against the shower wall his body pressing on mine showering me with kisses as he fisted me. I screamed in ecstasy as my arousal kicked in. His hands cupped my breast as he nipped my nipple, I quince with the sharp pain he was giving me.

"Alex, you're starting to get a bit rough with me," I said, sounding concerned.

"I'm so sorry I can't get enough of you; I need your body next to mine," Alex whispered while kissing down my neck.

"Alex I need to get back to work." I went on, trying to end his night of sexual pleasure.

"Caz will you stay awhile longer I want to play with your body? I'll pay you," said Alex sounding desperate for my body.

"Alex I'm not a whore, you know," I said, sounding miffed by his question. I pulled away from him and stepped out of the shower.

What a fucking insult it was, the thought of him paying me to play with my body. If he paid me, would he treat my body any different? I wondered.

The bi-folding doors were coming early due to a cancellation on Wednesday so I should be finished by the end of the week. I needed to get this job finished and out of the way before this gets out of hand.

"Caz I am sorry please will you stay? I have to leave by midday to go back down to London for the week, and my wife will be here next weekend." Alex followed me and grabbed my arm to stop me. "I have another fantasy; I would like to tie you to the bed and play with your body." He sounded desperate.

"Well, I'm not sure," I said as I started to walk to the bedroom.

"Please Caz I won't hurt you," begged Alex desperate for me to stay.

"Alex, I need to get on with the job." I made an excuse to turn him down gently.

"Look, Caz, I will pay for time, but please don't see it as paying for a hooker," said Alex as he kissed my neck.

I was soon tied to the four-poster bed, spread-eagled and naked. Alex was naked as he started to play with my body, fucking me hard in a frenzy as though he had never had sex for a long time. His mood changed with the next hour kissing and licking my body all over, paying special attention to my breasts and wetness making me come over and over again. He had managed to fuck me four times before releasing me of my bondage. It had been quite a pleasant experience.

Alex made some toast and coffee before he had to pack to go back to London. Then he dropped me a bombshell by asking to see me again.

"Alex, I can't! you're married, and this was just a one-off." I said dismissing the question.

"Caz you make me happy I need you in my life," said Alex touching my hand across the table.

"Alex, you only need my body you can use someone else's body," I said, moving my hand away.

"No, Caz I need yours, I don't want anyone else." retorted Alex a little uptight. Alex could have a right temper on him if he didn't get his way it seemed. I needed paying for the job I was doing; would he hold it against me and not pay if I didn't agree?

I would have to play with this one. "I'll think about it," I said, getting up to start work. Alex took hold of me, cupping my face and kissing me hard on the lips as he pressed me against the kitchen wall, squeezing my breasts.

"Caz I need to fuck you in the kitchen before I go." He pulled me down on the kitchen mat slipping of my trousers and panties fucking me hard to release his pleasure before he left that morning.

I needed to get this job completed so I could be paid before Alex took control of the situation. Luckily, he was away in the week only coming home at the weekend, so at least I would only see him once. I had to phone Lloyd to let him know that I couldn't start that week and had to complete a job that took longer than I thought. Lloyd was happy for me to start when I could fit it in and just to let him know the day before I was ready.

With Alex helping me with boarding the ceiling, the rest was easy as I nearly finished the area apart from one wall. I was tired of having Alex playing with me all night and most of the morning. I tidied up before leaving for the day being gone by 4 pm. It had been another hot day with the temperature to drop slightly next week. I was pleased as the plastering could go off too quickly and crack apart from being able to spread it over the boards. The traffic wasn't too bad going home being a Sunday with the shops closing at 4 pm.

By the time I stopped at the supermarket for some essentials, it was just after 5 pm. Russ wasn't at home when I got in, after putting away my few groceries I dived into the much-needed shower. I had sent my playlist going listening to the likes of Bon Jovi and kiss, I wished in one way I had gone with Russ to enjoy the concert to unwind and enjoy the atmosphere with Russ for company. With the music fairly loud I didn't hear Russ come in, only his naked presence as he stepped behind me in the shower.

His embrace felt different somehow; I thought there might be something there between us. Russ cupped my breasts as his body pressed against mine, his hard length waiting to enter me. I moaned as he kissed my exposed neck.

"I've missed you," I mumbled turning around, wrapping my arms around his neck, kissing him gently on the lips.

"Hmm, I've missed you too," replied Russ as he moaned while we kissed.

"Tell me about the concert?" I asked, smiling at his beautiful face and eyes.

"I'll tell you after I've fucked you," said Russ pushing me against the shower wall as he lifted me onto his hard length. I shimmy down to feel his full length inside me; he was ready to explode inside me.

"Russ release yourself, and I'll bring you back up again with my mouth," I ordered as I could felt the tension of his release. Within seconds he had released inside me his pleasure now empty, for me to replenish it. "Russ fist me first," I whisper, he obliged as he slowly started to fist me while sucking on my wetness as I came.

I knelt as the water sprayed over us. I cupped his balls while rubbing his length; he moaned with the sensation I gave him. His hand was resting on my head as he leaned back slightly with his legs apart. Within a couple of minutes, he was hard as I took his length in my mouth, sucking him hard. We washed each other's bodies. He

119

hadn't had a wash since Friday, and I needed a shower from the few hours' work I had done that afternoon.

It was after 6 pm when we both had sex in the shower before getting dry to think about making something to eat.

"I'm making spag ball tonight is that ok with you Russ?" I shouted through from the kitchen.

"Sounds good to me my sex goddess." Russ padded through in his short robe enveloping me with a hug kissing me on top of my head. I turned around, releasing the tie on his robe; it opened to expose part of his naked body.

He did the same with mine. "Take me, Russ," I whispered, kissing his taut chest.

"Come on, my goddess." He lifted me onto his length, holding my butt with his muscular arms; I shimmy on his length, feeling the fullness as I rode him. Our tongues danced around each other as we both come together.

"Oh, Russ I had missed you," I repeated kissing him gently on his lips before I dismounted him.

"Me too," said Russ bending over kissing me passionately on the lips.

Monday had soon come around, and with no break, I was feeling a little tired; also I was due to start my period, which luckily only lasted three days. Russ brought me coffee as usual before going to work.

"How's my sex goddess this morning?" He smiled, putting the mug of coffee on the bedside cabinet. I laid there, feeling tired and needing some painkillers.

"Bit crappy, would you mind and get me some painkillers please?" I asked, not sounding my normal self.

"Oh, my goddess, what's a wrong sweetheart?" He asked with concern, kissing me softly on the lips.

"I am due my monthly it makes me tired, and I get cramps," I told him as I touched his cheek to reassure him

I was ok but having to put up with my monthly's. Russ went off to find some painkillers for me before heading off to work.

"Here you are, sweetheart." He kissed my forehead, handing a couple of tablets for me to take.

"Thanks, Russ," I smiled as I took them swallowing them with a gulp of coffee he had brought in for me.

"Are you sure you're going to be ok sweetheart? I can stay with you if you want," said Russ concerned.

"No I'll be ok once the painkillers kick in and thanks, Russ you're a sweetie." I kissed his cheek. Russ hugged me before leaving.

Once Russ had gone, I laid there waiting for the painkillers to work. I was thinking of Russ how thoughtful and concerned he was about me. No one had done that before but only used my body, but there again, I used them to suit my needs. But Russ was someone different from the rest, could I stay with one man, I had tried it with Shaun, but now I could see it was only sex. Was Russ going to be any different? Time would tell I suppose.

With that, I closed my eyes and drifted off.

Chapter Six

It was nearly 9 am by the time I was back to finish the outbuilding for Alex and Jess. Jess wasn't around when I got there to my relief; she was becoming a pain in the arse, either telling me to turn the music down or change her mind on something on the outbuilding every day. What she needed was a good fucking, preferably up the arse.

I had a few more boards to complete with only to finish off once the bi-folding doors were fitted. It took me most of the day to skim the ceiling being the hardest bit to do with having to stretch and work more or less upside down. It didn't help much with my period to start today. I persevered with the task to finish it that day. It was after 6 pm by the time I was happy with the ceiling and went to wash out my tools ready for the next day.

I texted Russ to tell I would be home before 7 pm and he quickly texted back to say that he was home and would make something to eat. I reached home around 7 pm, Russ had a meal ready, despite it being salad I wasn't all that hungry. He kissed me as I walked in, dumping my work bag in the hallway.

'How do you feel sweetie?' asked Russ giving me a quick hug.

'Mm, could be better,' I mumbled walking into the living room and flopping onto the sofa. Russ brought me my meal on a tray. 'Oh Russ, you are a darling,' I said gratefully taking the tray from him.

'You would do the same for me,' said Russ going back into the kitchen.

Hmm, I suppose I would. I thought. We sat on the sofa eating our meal while we watched the TV after which Russ cleared the dishes and washed them. I laid down on the sofa; my cramps had returned, and I desperately needed some painkillers. Russ came through with a couple of mugs of hot drinks, placing them on the coffee table.

'Would you like me to get you some painkillers?' asked Russ reading me like a book.

'Please,' I whispered, starting to get tired. Russ was soon back with a couple of painkillers as I took them with the drink, he had brought in. I laid between his legs as we both relaxed on the sofa, his arms hugging me for comfort. We watched the TV for an hour, but I was slowly dozing off.

'Russ, I'm going to bed.' I yawned, getting up to head for the bathroom first before settling down for bed.

'Yeah, I think I'll go as well,' he said as I switched the TV off.

The following morning Russ brought me a coffee with a couple of painkillers.

'Hi, sweetie. How're the cramps?'

'Not too bad,' I say, smiling. 'Thanks, Russ, you're a diamond,' I say, pulling him down for a kiss.

'I'd do anything for you, sweetie,' says Russ kissing me back.

'Aw thanks, you're so thoughtful my sex god.' Russ disappeared off to work as I laid there feeling slightly under the weather. Russ seemed to appreciate women's monthlies.

I managed to get to work after 7.30 am. Mrs Moneybags was in; I could tell seeing the 4x4 in the driveway, she would be taking the kids to school shortly. I started to mix the skim plaster kicking up the powder dust as the mixer started. I couldn't mix too much due to the weather being as hot as it would dry too quickly. I started on the opposite side of where the sun was shining, as it would give me enough time before the sun came around.

It was just after 9 when I heard Jess's heels coming over from the house.

Oh, fuck! What's she after now? I thought.

'Morning, Caz. It's looking good, isn't it?' she said, looking around at the skimming I had done.

'Yeah, not too bad, considering it's so hot,' I said as I continued to mix some more plaster.

'Are you going to tile around the hand basin and the floor?' she asked.

'Well no, I hadn't planned on it yet,' I said, thinking fuck, here we go again!

'Well, I was hoping you could finish it all together, you know the painting and wooden flooring,' said Jess standing with her hand on her hips waiting for me to answer her.

'Umm, I got another job to start, and I've put them off once already,' I replied, hoping she would find someone else.

'But I was hoping you would do it; Alex is so pleased with what you have done so far,' she said, waiting for me to say yes to it.

I bet he does; she doesn't know half of what he's been up to. I thought, but I needed the pay so kept my thoughts to myself. 'Yeah, okay, but it will cost more,' I bargained.

'Oh, Alex is paying, money is no problem,' said Jess as she turned to totter off back to the house.

'Fuck!' I thought I shouldn't have stayed the night with him; now he'd have a hold over me.

By Thursday, I was back in form, dragging Russ in bed with me that morning, I needed him inside me to which he obliged giving me my massage. As soon as he had gone to work, I got up, going in early myself since I had extra work to do. The 4x4 wasn't in the driveway when I arrived.

I wondered where Jess was at this time of the morning. The kids would still need taking to school. The bi-folding doors were in, looking smart with the glass reflecting as a mirror so you couldn't see in giving some privacy. There was just a little remedial work to finish off the skimming around the doors. I now just had the painting and the tiling, together with the flooring to finish to complete the job and was hoping Jess wouldn't think of anything else for me to do.

I heard a vehicle pull in the driveway, and 10 minutes later, I heard heels walking across from the house. God, it was Jess again.

'Hi, Caz. How are things going?' asked Jess, sounding upbeat.

'Yeah, ok,' I said.

'So, do you think you'll work this weekend?' she asked.

'No, I have to start another job tomorrow.' I shook my head, finding an excuse to keep out of Alex's way.

'Oh, that's a pity. Alex is home all weekend, and I am going down the coast with the kids again, I thought he might give you a hand. It will also give him something to do,' said Jess sounding disappointed I wouldn't be here.

'Well, I'm sure he'll find something to do,' I said as I continued my work sounding casual.

I gave Lloyd a call to let him know I would be starting tomorrow if that would be ok with him. He was delighted by the sound of my voice. At least I wouldn't be seeing Alex. I texted Russ to let him know I would be home by 5 pm and asking him what time he would be home? But he was already home and was about to text me saying he would cook. I was starting to care for him and loving him in a different sort of way. I was on time as Russ had cooked spag ball and was just plating it up.

'Umm, hmm, you're becoming a nice little housewife,' I jested hugging around his waist.

'Well, don't be telling everyone,' said Russ kissing me on the cheek. We took our meal into the living room, switching the TV on while we ate.

'I'll wash up,' I said, collecting the empty plates.

'No, you stay there, I'll do them,' said Russ being assertive. I didn't argue as I laid out on the sofa. Russ brought through hot drinks and placed them on the coffee table.

I laid between his legs as he put his arms around me, kissing the top of my head. I was starting to feel slightly guilty now for having sexual pleasures with Alex the previous weekend while Russ was at the concert. Russ seemed to be growing on me, being so thoughtful and caring. I had never met anyone like him. I must try and avoid seeing Alex if I was going to finish the job off and get paid without him wanting more from me.

By 10 pm I was feeling tired, stirring to get up from the comfort of Russ's arms.

'I'm going to bed,' I told him as I took the empty mugs into the kitchen to wash. Russ padded through into the kitchen and enveloped me into his arms asking me if I was feeling ok?

'Yeah just a bit tired,' I assured him turning to give him a peck on his cheek. Russ cupped my face giving a long passionate kiss on the lips.

'Aw, Russ you're a nice guy.' I hugged him. 'Come and sleep with me tonight?' I whispered to him while still hugging him.

'Are you sure that's what you want Caz?' asked Russ being it a workday.

'Yes, please.'

Within 10 minutes, we were in my bed together. I was curled in his arms as the heat radiating off our bodies mingled together. The comfort of his arms was making me feel safe and secure.

'Russ, make love to me.' I requested, needing his love.

'Oh, Caz I was hoping to make love to you,' he went on, turning me over to kiss me so passionately on my lips I felt it was love radiating through. My arms enveloped him, kissing him passionately. His lips slid down my neck, skimming over my body as I started to moan with his touch, his hand on my side, sliding down to my buttock as his body pressed further into the mine.

'Caz, with the short period of time I have known you, I'm starting to fall in love with you,' whispered Russ kissing my body. I moaned with his pleasuring as I whispered that the feelings were mutual.

'Russ, take me, I need you inside me,' my voice was hoarse; his embrace around me was so comforting. Russ entered me slowly staying inside me, kissing me more passionately as he went.

'Ah, Russ, why hadn't I met you sooner? You are breaking my shell,' I whispered, starting to love this man who was in my bed. His lovemaking was so surreal I had never experienced so much love as I was having with him.

I slept well in his arms, soaking his heat. Russ stirred around, and I saw the time, it was 5.30 am. He would be going to work soon and bringing me coffee as usual.

'Hello, my love,' I said in a sleepy voice as I turned to kiss him on the lips.

'Hello, gorgeous.' He returned my kiss with the same passion. I melted as his hand roamed over my naked body.

'Russ, make love to me before you leave for work.' My words were lost in his lips and skin. His love was so intense he made me explode on the inside; I loved this man more every minute.

As soon as I drank the coffee Russ had brought, I decided to get up and start the new job at Lloyd's. I was there at 7.30 am. Lloyd was waiting since the crack of dawn; he seemed to be a morning person. I drove up to the intercom pressing the button, waiting for Lloyd to answer, but the gate started to open straight away. I drove in with the gate closing behind; he seemed very security conscious. I snaked up the colourful driveway to the house where Lloyd was waiting at the large grand oak door.

'Hello, Caz, the coffee is on,' said Lloyd opening the door wider for me to enter. It was the first time I took notice of him. He looked to be around forty with flecks of grey hair showing at the temple, with his matching flecks of grey in his designer stubble, making him look sexy. He had pale blue, intelligent eyes. He seemed to be fit underneath his jeans and loose-fitting blue shirt. I wondered if he had a wife like Alex to spend his money.

After we had drunk our coffee, we chatted a little about nothing special. Lloyd gave me a tour of his house, having only seen the kitchen and the enormous hallway with the staircase dividing the house into two leading up to the bedrooms either side of the house. The house seemed similar to Alex and Jess's. They must have had the same designer with having four-poster beds with old and modern mixed with the soft furnishings. I walked around the bedroom, touching the fabrics, so soft, thick showing quality and how expensive they must be.

'So,' I said, turning around. Lloyd stood close slightly taller than I looked into my cleavage. 'Where's your wife?' I asked side-stepping away from him, avoiding eye contact.

'I'm not married,' said Lloyd following me as I walked towards the door.

'Oh,' I said, surprised seeing the house so plush with a woman's touch.

'Does that bother you?' he asked with concern.

'No,' I said, thinking why he was asking if I was concerned if he was married or not. I ignored the question, his single status, and comment as I continued to head for the staircase to look at the job in hand.

'Would you like another coffee?' offered Lloyd entering the pool area.

'Yes, please,' I said, giving him an excuse to stop following me like a puppy. The pool looked inviting, so smooth, waiting for someone to dive in gliding through the water. I walked to the shower room near the side to assess the job in hand to estimate. It would take me just over a week, depending if I worked the weekend. Lloyd came in with two mugs of coffee handing one over to me.

'So, how long do you think it will take?' he asked.

'I think probably just over a week,' I said slightly unsure, depending on if I worked the weekend.

'Oh, that's ok, just take your time,' shrugged Lloyd looking down into my cleavage. I should have my eyes in my tits at this rate as most men I speak to stared right there. I wondered if he wanted a good fuck and a blow job, but thinking of Alex, I didn't want him to have that hold over me, owing me money. Not only that, but I was thinking about Russ, too. Our lovemaking was intense; I didn't want to hurt him.

Lloyd went off, while I started stripping the shower cubicle out. It seemed straight forward; I noticed while taking the shower tray out, it had been leaking badly, causing a large damp patch with tiles starting to come off the wall. The drainage didn't seem to flow, washing away some of the dust I had made. I didn't order a skip seeing that the van would be large enough to take the old shower and tile debris away, with having the expense of making it to landfill site across the city.

I would have to make two trips, which was a pain having to go through heavy traffic, costing me my time. I shouted out to let Lloyd know that I was going to the landfill site to take the rubbish from the shower room. Within a couple of minutes, Lloyd was there.

'Could I come with you?' he asked, sounding like he needed some company.

'Yeah, if you like,' I replied, sounding ok with having a passenger with me.

'Caz, I would like to give you a remote for the electric gates and a key for the house,' said Lloyd, handing over the key fob.

'No, thanks. I don't want to be responsible for the fob and security,' I said, refusing to take it.

'Please, Caz, take it. There may be the odd day I could be out,' Lloyd tried to persuade me to take it.

'Well, just let me know when you're not going to be in, and I'll work around you,' I said, determined not to take the key. Lloyd took my hand, slapping the key/fob into my hand; I took hold of his slapping it back. We continued this game until we started laughing together with Lloyd, winning the game.

Lloyd climbed into the passenger side of my van as I shut the back doors, now ready to go. Lloyd showed me how the fob worked on operating the gates as we approached them to go out. We pulled out into the traffic heading for the landfill site going around the ring road of the city. It was going to take at least a couple of wasted hours. Lloyd seemed quite happy seated with my stuff and the dust in the van. I wasn't the cleanest of people for keeping the clean vehicle inside. As far as I was concerned, it was a working vehicle.

We started chatting in general, where I found out that his wife had died five years ago in a burglary that went wrong, killing her in the robbery and Lloyd injured. I felt sad for his loss, having everything but nothing in his life apart from the memories of his late wife. He had moved to this area to get away from the bad memories and the house where it had happened.

'I am so sorry to hear what happened to you both. Did they find the people who did it?' I asked, putting my hand on his hand, squeezing it.

'No, the police had arrested two guys, but the court threw the case out due to lack of evidence.' I was gutted for Lloyd not getting justice for the loss of his wife. I squeezed his hand for comfort, and then focused on the traffic, waiting for the lights to change.

'It's been five years, and I need to move on with my life,' said Lloyd trying to stay positive.

'I know what you mean. I lost my parents when I was fifteen and had to go into a care house until I was old enough to be let out into the wide world. My uncle lived abroad and was always working. I would have been a burden on him. Not only that, but I also didn't know him, so it was just as well I went into care.'

'We seem to have similar loses in our lives, don't we, Caz?' He squeezed my hand in return. The lights changed green as the traffic started to move edging the van forward until half a mile gathering speed.

We finally arrived at the landfill site and had to weigh the vehicle first to work out the charges of the rubbish. We were then told where to go to empty the van. I reversed up to the heap opening the back doors to clear out the debris. Lloyd stepped out of the van, giving me a hand with clearing the rubbish.

'Lloyd, stay in the van. It's what you're paying me for,' I barked, shooing him away.

'No, Caz, I need to help you,' said Lloyd giving me a grin and a shove. We jested and played teasing each other making comments to each other as we laughed together.

By the time we got back, it was nearly 4.30 pm. I turned into the driveway pressing the fob key for the electric gates to open; a sensor activated the gates to close the length of a vehicle away from the entrance.

'I think I'll call it a day, Lloyd.' I turned the vehicle around parking outside the front door of his house.

'Please come in for a coffee before you go?' asked Lloyd, hoping I would.

'Well, I was going to go to the gym, but make it a quick one,' I said, getting out of the vehicle. Lloyd seemed pleased being in my company; we had got on so well, laughing and cracking jokes.

'Why don't you have a work out in the pool instead?' asked Lloyd, trying to persuade me to stay longer.

'Er, I haven't got anything clean to change into,' I said, making an excuse.

'I still have a few bits left that my wife never wore, you look to be of similar size, and you can use the bathroom downstairs near the kitchen.' He suggested.

'But they are your wife's,' I hesitated.

'Look, Caz, I need to move on, so please take them,' said Lloyd sounding persistent. I had always fancied swimming in the buff, not that I was bothered covering my modesty.

'Ok, you win,' I said, giving him a playful punch on the arm.

His smile made him more handsome with his designer stubble. After his sad loss and the drama of what had happened five years ago, had he been without the comfort of a warm body enveloping him? I wanted to help him get back on track, not forcing the issue.

145

Lloyd brought me a couple of large fluff bath towels, black leggings, and a long v neck top to wear after my swim. I had a quick shower, washing the dust and the dirt off before heading off to the pool with a towel wrapped around me. I sat on the side of the pool, testing the temperature of the water. I was surprised that it was warm. I took off my towel as I slid into the pool. The water wrapped itself around me, soothing my naked body as I started to swim. It was exhilarating, free of clothing, and no distractions of people bumping into you.

I had half an hour of swimming nonstop when I noticed Lloyd coming in with mugs of coffee. I swam to the side where he placed a mug of coffee.

'Thanks, I needed this.' I smiled, taking a sip of the hot liquid. 'Why don't you join me?' I asked, sending a spray of water over him.

'No, you can have the pool to yourself,' said Lloyd looking slightly embarrassed with me being naked in the pool.

'You can swim, can't you?' I asked jokingly.

'Yeah, I swim every day,' said Lloyd. With that, I grabbed hold of him, pulling him towards me. He lost his balance and fell into the pool, fully clothed. He came up gasping for air as I made a quick getaway swimming fast to the other end of the pool, but despite being fully clothed and coming up to find the bearings, he had soon caught up with me.

I started to splash him, and soon, we were splashing each other, laughing and joking, pulling each other under. After half an hour of horseplay, we swam back to the shallow end. Lloyd got out first as water ran from his clothes. I got out behind him despite being naked - I wasn't bothered. I picked up the large bath towel as Lloyd's eye met mine, seeing me naked.

147

'Oh, sorry, Caz,' he said as he looked the other way.

'Lloyd, it doesn't matter,' I said, walking up to him for a hug. He was lost, not knowing whether to hug me back. 'Lloyd, I want to help you,' I whispered. We stood for a few seconds in silence before he spoke.

'I don't know what to do,' said Lloyd sounding lost from five years ago.

'I will help you if you let me.' I hugged him around his waist. He slowly wrapped his arms around me, as he could feel my bare skin.

'Oh, Caz, I need someone to hold, to be by my side, I've been lost for five years,' whispered Lloyd hugging me tightly. We stood for a few moments before releasing each other.

'You better get out of those wet clothes,' I said, wrapping the towel around my body.

'Yeah, I suppose I should.' nodded Lloyd looking as though he needed help in undressing.

'Would you like me to come with you to undress?' I asked, pushing it a bit.

'Yes, please,' said Lloyd as with both collected our things and padded out of the pool area.

Chapter Seven

We ended up in his bathroom; I helped him in stripping off his wet clothes. Underneath his wet clothes was a fit body; he must have spent hours in the pool. I tried to cover his modesty while he took off his underwear, but he wasn't that bothered. Suddenly, he lost his balance and grabbed hold of me in an attempt to steady himself; as a result, our towels dropped to the floor. We stood naked in front of each other.

I couldn't help but notice he had a rather large package down there. "Wow!" I thought.

"I'm so sorry, Lloyd," I stammered picking up the towels from the floor.

"No, I should be the one saying sorry," said Lloyd taking a towel from me.

"Lloyd, please, if you want to let go of the past, I want to help you." I went for a hug pressing my breasts on his taut chest. His arms enveloped me as we stood, hugging each other. "Would you like me to stay with you tonight?" I whispered.

There was a silence for a few seconds before he said "Yes, please. I would like the company."

"We need to dry our hair," I commented, pulling away from his body.

"Caz, you are a good person." Lloyd pulled me into his chest, enveloping me once more.

"We both have losses in our lives, and I know what it's like, the struggle to let go." I hugged him back.

We both towel-dried our hair and put clean, dry clothes on before going to the kitchen to sort out something to eat. The clothes Lloyd had loaned me were a good fit only with the top being slightly smaller, that pressed my nipples through the fabric.

"You look good," smiled Lloyd as his eyes scanned me up and down. Was he thinking of his late wife? My heart went out to him. It took me a few years myself to overcome my sadness and depression, but I had to think forward to take my mind off my loss as everything fades but is never really lost and we have to move on.

I texted Russ, informing him that I wouldn't be home tonight, not explaining why. I didn't want him to know my past despite telling Lloyd as he was the only person I had ever opened up to. It was after 7 pm when I had texted, but there wasn't a return text yet. I wondered where he was? I was growing fond of him seeing how he had been since moving in and the ways we made love, but did he really have feelings for me or was it a front?

Lloyd cooked something simple and made coffee afterwards. We took our coffees into the living room, which was so big with a choice of seating on three sofas. The room had high ceilings with fancy coving, dividing the white painted ceiling with a soft shade of pale brown blending into the solid oak flooring. The soft furnishings also had shades blending in making it homely with a large inglenook fireplace for the winter evenings. There were two large chandeliers with wall lightings dotted around the large room. The room wasn't overwhelmed with too much furniture though, with old and new working well together.

Lloyd had the oversized plasma TV making my 50" look rather small. We sat together on one of the sofas as Lloyd put his arm on the back of the sofa. I moulded myself next to him as his arm softly wrapped around; we watched a little TV in between chatting until 10 pm. I was getting tired of having done a lot of physical work and the lengths in the pool.

"Lloyd, I need to go to bed. I'm tired." I yawned getting up to move off the sofa.

"I'll come with you if you don't mind, but I need to lock up first," said Lloyd.

"Mm, okay." I nodded, waiting for him to come back.

I eyed the four-poster bed as we entered the bedroom, I had never slept in one, and it was looking inviting for a good night's sleep. Lloyd also had a spare toothbrush for me to use.

"I have a long tee shirt if you would like to wear that in bed," Lloyd offered, pulling a drawer out.

"No, I don't wear anything if that's okay with you," I said hesitantly.

"Oh, okay, I don't either," said Lloyd, unsure of the situation.

"Lloyd just lay with me. If something happens, it happens." I shrugged, trying to reassure him.

"Hmm, right." He chewed his lip.

I got into the bed first while Lloyd spent a good ten minutes in the bathroom before slipping into bed. I could feel the heat radiating from his body as he touched mine.

"Hey, would you like me to hug you?" I asked as he laid there, staring up at the ceiling. He didn't say anything, but I moved so that I was hugging him into my body with his head resting on my breasts. His arm wrapped around mine as though he needed to be loved. We silently laid there for an hour, and I was starting to doze off, but Lloyd started to stir, his hand running down my body.

"Oh, Emma, I miss you so much," he whispered as his hand touched my breast. His soft touch sent a tingle inside me like no other before, not even like Russ.

This man, deprived of his late wife's love, was living in the past and needed to get out of this depressed state. Suddenly, he realized I wasn't Emma and pulled away from me.

"Lloyd, it's ok," I said, reaching over to him and snaked my arm over his body, pressing it next to mine.

"I miss her so much." He sobbed.

"Lloyd, you need to focus on the future, or you will never get away from your depression. I know it because that's what I had to do," I said, hugging him tight and planted a kiss on his shoulder.

I stayed close to him all night trying to give him comfort where possible. It was nearly 6 am when I woke up; the sun was peeking through the space in the curtain. I must have turned over in the night with now Lloyd's body pressed next to mine with his hand over my breast and a leg over my body. I could hear his breathing as he slept like a baby. I didn't want to wake him, but I needed to go for a pee. I slowly tried to unravel him from my body without waking him, but as I got back into the bed, he stirred.

"Hey. What time is it?" he whispered.

"It is nearly 6 am," I replied, slipping back into bed before turning to face Lloyd. "Good morning. Did you sleep well?" I asked, touching his cheek with the back of my fingers.

"I did," He smiled. "It's been so long I haven't had a good night's sleep." Lloyd leaned his face on my hand to feel the touch deeply.

"Lloyd, would you like me to stay as long as you need me?" I asked him after a brief pause.

"Don't you have anyone waiting for you?" Lloyd said.

"No, not really. Only a flatmate." I said not saying anything about Russ.

"I would love that; you're very thoughtful." Lloyd kissed me on the cheek.

"It goes deep," I said as a tear rolled down from the corner of my eye. Lloyd hugged me wiping the tear away as we laid in silence.

I was in my work clothes from yesterday with no clean clothes to work in as I was staying with Lloyd. I decided not to wear my underwear and only slipped on my trousers, bra and top. I needed to go to the flat to sort out some clean clothes to bring back with me. Lloyd made some breakfast, poached eggs on toast. It was a change, as I normally missed breakfast and only had coffee.

Lloyd went to work in his study despite it being a Saturday while I continued clearing the last of the rubbish away from the shower room. I was going to call into the flat after having to be at the landfill site before midday. It was Saturday, and I only had to work half a day.

It was another two hours' drive through the heavy traffic despite it being a ring road around the city. I pulled up outside the flat feeling rather grubby, needing a change of clothes. I unlocked the flat door, and as I stepped in, I could smell perfume. Had Russ had someone here last night while I was away? As I walked further into the flat, I noticed a pair of heels in the living room. These were definitely not mine. At this point, I could hear moaning coming from Russ's bedroom. He had a woman with him. All those words he had said to me, bringing me coffee and pretending to be caring was a load of bullshit. My judgement had been wrong; why had I let him in?

I packed a few things in hold all and slipped out before Russ noticed I was there. Just as well I wasn't broke, but he certainly had some explaining to do. I drove back to Lloyd's house, thinking about letting Russ into my heart. I thought I was hard coming from a care home, losing my parents at fifteen years old, making it hard with no one to turn to and having to live on my wits.

I walked into the house, heading for the kitchen as I badly needed a coffee. I made one for Lloyd and took it into the study. Lloyd was on the phone but waved me in; he seemed to sound better in himself as the telephone conversation was business. I didn't know what line of work he was in whether he worked for himself or a company?

Lloyd wound the conversation down as I brought a smile to his face.

"Hi, how's your day going?" asked Lloyd sounding better.

"Yeah not too bad, I called at the flat to pick a few things up," I said, avoiding my discovery with Russ and the woman he was entertaining. I sat on the end of a two-seater sofa sipping my coffee, while Lloyd finished off typing whatever he was doing before closing his laptop.

"So, how do you fancy having a swim with me in the pool?" said Lloyd sitting back in his chair sipping his coffee.

"Hmm, that sounds good, but I will need a shower first." I was covered in dust and dirt from the rubbish I had taken to the landfill. Lloyd took our empty mugs through to the kitchen while I went upstairs for a quick shower to rinse off my morning's labour.

Lloyd was already in the pool swimming his lengths as I came in with a towel wrapped around my body. He saw me on the edge of the pool and swam over.

"Come on, I'll race you," said Lloyd splashing me.

"I know you will beat me," I scoffed, defeated already before I had started.

"Come on, you don't know that," said Lloyd splashing more water onto me. I dropped my towel and jumped in making a big splash; the wave of water rose and engulfed him. As I came up, Lloyd took hold of me as we started to play fight for half an hour with laughter and jovial banter. We finally had a race with Lloyd beating me hands down, which I knew I wouldn't have a chance at with his practice every day.

I was at the side of the pool panting with the energy I had been releasing swimming as fast as I could when Lloyd swam up to me and hugged me so I couldn't move.

"Caz, you're such a tonic being here," said Lloyd looking into my eyes and touching my cheek with his finger. But before I could reply Lloyd took hold of me and dunked me under while swimming off to the other end of the pool. I gasped for my breath, taking off after him where he was waiting.

I dived in, pulling his legs down and he came down with me. We struggled, grabbing hold of each other before we surfaced. He held me to the side and gently kissed me on my cheek.

"Thanks, Caz." He swam off to the other end of the pool and jumped out, showing his full firm naked body before wrapping a towel around his waist. I wanted to make him happy sexually, but he was still grieving. Well, time would tell. I swam over and jumped out after him; Lloyd was waiting with my towel in hand. I wrapped the towel over my breasts, tucking the end inside. We hugged each other, but I could feel no sexual need from his body below.

We both dried ourselves before changing into fresh clothes and headed for the kitchen to make coffee.

"Lloyd, how do you fancy going out tonight for a pizza, and call in at that new wine bar that has just opened?" I asked casually.

"Well, I don't know, pizza sounds ok, but I'm not too sure about the wine bar," said Lloyd a little uneasy.

"Okay, just the pizza then?" I took hold of his hand to reassure him.

"I'll order a taxi for 6 pm and after we can walk back seeing that it's a nice evening," I told him about the plan.

"Well, I can drive." He offered.

"No, we will get a taxi," I said, being assertive.

"On one condition that I pay for the taxi and the pizza," said Lloyd being assertive back.

"No. It's my suggestion, my treat." I said firmly.

The taxi was on time and took us to the city, which was about five miles away. Lloyd was dressed casually in black jeans and a white shirt looking rather handsome with his designer stubble and blue eyes. I wore my skinny jeans with a loose fitted red and white v neck top. Lloyd seemed lost being away from his home, so I took his hand as we walked into the pizza hut, taking a seat near the back of the dining area.

"Are you ok, Lloyd?" I asked, sounding concerned.

"Hmm, yeah, it just feels strange that's all," said Lloyd looking around the place.

"We can go if you want." I did not want to push him.

"No, I'm ok, let's eat." Lloyd picked the choice of pizzas on the menu. We chatted in general as Lloyd started to relax, having ordered our pizza with drinks. We spent nearly two hours in the pizza hut ordering another round of drinks after which I paid. We set off back towards Lloyd's home for a pleasant stroll in the evening air. We walked hand in hand with finally wrapping our arm around each other.

As Lloyd opened the gate to walk up the driveway, I asked him if he had a gardener.

"No, I do it myself," said Lloyd, not saying much about it.

"Oh, I thought you had a gardener, it's so stately home looking, you're so good with the choice of colours." I complimented.

"Yes, my wife used to do the gardening. She had an eye for it being a landscape gardener," said Lloyd as the gates closed behind us.

"So, you have continued her work?" I asked, sounding interested.

"I've only copied what she used to do at our old place down south," said Lloyd sounding a little sad. I squeezed his hand as we walked.

Lloyd started to machine the coffee while I went into the living room to switch the TV on. Despite the late evening and the long walk back from the pizza place, I was wide awake. I slipped off my pumps, placing my legs up onto the sofa until Lloyd came in with the coffee.

He came over to sit with me, slipping his shoes off and placing his legs up on the sofa, too, just like me.

"Come lay with me." I moved over for him to squeeze between my legs, shoehorning him in as we got comfortable with his head on my chest and my arm around him resting on his chest.

"Caz, I have enjoyed tonight," said Lloyd squeezing my hand.

"Yeah me too." I kissed the top of his head. Lloyd started to open up about his wife. How they met, how she looked, how long they had been married, the things she liked, the holidays they went on, her work and with a slight laugh her bad habits.

I would have loved to have met her; she sounded as though she lived life to the fullest, my kind of person. I remembered a friend who was on one of the courses I was on a few years ago.

"I had a friend similar to your wife she was fun to be with until she moved abroad and we lost touch," I told him thinking what would she be doing with her life now.

I spoke about losing my parents in the accident when I was fifteen, becoming moody, tearful and keeping myself to myself, not wanting to be with people until I had to go into the care home. Where I had to share with other girls in the dormitories and some of the boys were right dick head.

When you used the bathroom, the boys used to come in some would nick your towel and left you no choice but to go back to the dorm naked while the other watched laughing and giggling making rude jesters until one of the cares came to sort them out. I had to grow up fast from the day I lost my virginity in the bathroom by a boy when there wasn't anyone around.

"Hmm you've had it tough," said Lloyd stroking my arm.

"Yeah well, I decided that I didn't want to be dragged into the gutter like some of the girls, they turned to drugs and sold themselves only because they needed money to pay for their drugs. Life's too short, so I decided this route of employment and became my own boss. I went for courses and tried to learn as much as I could." I kept opening up, little by little.

"You've done well considering what you have been through," said Lloyd sounding sincere.

We continued chatting about our lives until 2 am, but then I felt too exhausted.

"Lloyd, I need my bed," I mumbled waiting for him to move.

"Oh I didn't realize it was that late," said Lloyd pushing himself up to give me a hand. Ten minutes later, we were in bed together, our naked bodies entwined. He kissed me on my cheek saying thank you for today before he fell asleep after which I dozed off too.

I was awake at 6 am, but with it being a Sunday I thought I would give work a miss and have a lay-in. Lloyd had wrapped himself around me with his hand firmly on my breast. His hand felt so soft as I closed my eyes drifting back to sleep. It was nearly 10 am when I was woken up by Lloyd who had cooked breakfast and brought it upstairs on a tray.

"Hi I thought you would like breakfast in bed," said Lloyd placing the tray on the bed and slipping himself in between the sheets. I prized myself up, covering my breasts.

"Lloyd you're a diamond," I said, taking a sip of coffee before tucking into the full English breakfast Lloyd had cooked.

"I could get used to this." I blurted out without thinking.

"I don't mind. I love to cook; Emma was always out in the garden, so I always did the cooking," said Lloyd.

"That means you've got some hidden talents?" I jested. We finished our meal in bed while chatting.

"Thanks, that was lovely," I said, putting the last mouthful in my mouth.

"Good, so what plans have you today?" asked Lloyd sounding perky.

"Nothing really, I'd probably sleep." I stretched before sliding down into the comfy bed. Lloyd picked up the tray, taking them downstairs while I snuggled back down to dose off.

It was after 2 pm before I rose still feeling tired as though I hadn't benefited from the extra lay in, I had for a while. I could hear a motor running; I slipped out of bed to look out of the window. Lloyd was cutting the grass on a grass mower leaving lines of stripes in the grass. I slipped on a pair of joggers and a vest deciding to make some coffee to take out to Lloyd. I hadn't noticed the garden furniture before, but there again I hadn't seen all the grounds of the area the house was set in.

I placed the mugs of coffee on the garden table, waiting for Lloyd to come back up with the grass mower. Lloyd had seen me as he was heading back with his perfect stripes on the grass. As soon as he approached me, he cut the engine of the mower climbing over to a much-needed drink of coffee. He had a nice smile, quite sexy.

"You must have been reading my mind, I was about to come in and make it," said Lloyd picking up his mug of coffee and taking a sip. "How was your lay in?" He asked.

"I feel more tired than if I had got up at 6 am, but the breakfast was nice," I said yawning. We sat in the swinging hammock drinking our coffees and taking in the view of the grounds.

"What made you choose this area to live in?" I asked as it was an expensive area to live in.

"I was going on the statistics of crime, and this is one of the best," said Lloyd sipping his coffee.

"Yeah, but it can happen anywhere." I shrugged. We chatted for a while until the sun went in and the clouds started to darken.

"I better get a move on before it starts to rain," said Lloyd getting up to walk over to the grass mower.

"I'd nip out to the flat while you finish off," I said, picking up the empty mugs.

"Yeah ok, I'll see you later," said Lloyd giving me a wave.

It was about 4.30 pm when I arrived back at the flat; I could hear rock music playing as I opened the flat door. Russ was obviously at home in his bedroom. This time I wasn't going to be quiet like I was when I came back finding a pair of heels and the smell of cheap perfume in the flat. I banged the door shut, making it obvious I was back and walked into the living room to find tins of beer and takeaway cartons strewn over the floor and coffee table.

What the fuck had he been doing? I marched out of the living room heading for his bedroom, not bothered if he had a woman with him or not. I shoved his door open, finding him wearing a towel wrapped around his waist while drying his longish hair.

"Oh, hi sweetie, how are you?" He approached to kiss me on the lips. Seeing him nearly naked with his muscular, tanned body made my arousal kick in. I needed a fuck. Russ took hold of my breasts as he started to kiss slowly down my neck, whispering that he had missed me.

That was a fucking lie. I thought about seeing the heels in the living room, the smell of cheap perfume and the moaning coming from his bedroom yesterday, but I needed a fuck. Within seconds I was naked with Russ fucking me hard releasing himself inside me. He wasn't the Russ who had made love to me a few nights ago.

"Oh, Caz, I've missed you," said Russ kissing my neck and massaging my breasts.

"Hmm," I said, it was all I could muster. He was using me, so I was using him. We spent over two hours making out as his playlist blurred out sounding good.

After our couple of hours of sex, I told Russ I wouldn't be back for a while only to collect a few clothes maybe and that I was staying with a friend who needed a friend to talk to.

"But sweetie what am I going to do without you?" said Russ kissing my neck.

"I'm sure you'll manage." I started to moan with his touch. I didn't say anything about the state of the place. At the end of the day he had to live with it, plus he had lied to me saying he was tidy when he first moved in. Now he was showing his true colours. As long as he paid up the end of the month, I wasn't bothered.

Chapter Eight

It was around 7 pm when I arrived back to Lloyd's home. I walked into the living room only to find him stretched out on the sofa watching TV. He had changed his clothes from when I last saw him cutting the grass on the mower.

"Hi Caz, everything ok at the flat?" asked Lloyd sounding in good stead.

"Mm I suppose so," I said. To be honest, I was a bit disappointed with Russ not being who I thought he was.

"You sound a little down." Lloyd looked at me with concern.

"Well it's my flatmate, he's not the person who I thought he was," I said, sitting next to Lloyd as he got up from the sofa.

"Oh, you share your flat with a guy?" asked Lloyd, surprised.

"Yeah, and he's not the person I thought he was. He's sort of conned me in a way." I sighed. I then started to tell Lloyd my problems with guys in general. I told him about Russ turning up on my doorstep hours after Shaun had left, spinning me a yarn about sofa surfing and trying to rent a flat in the area where he had started working on a large development across the city.

"So, I gave him a chance and let him in. the trouble was I let him into my heart, and I shouldn't have done that." I massaged my temples, and then I realized it. "Oh, sorry Lloyd, I'm babbling on about my love life. I'll go and make coffee." I said apologetically, standing up to avoid eye contact with Lloyd.

I was in the kitchen only a few minutes when Lloyd came through.

"Caz have you ever had a serious relationship with anyone?" asked Lloyd sounding serious.

"I thought I was going to, with Russ. I thought we had that connection, but he's conned me when I called in yesterday morning to pick a few bits up, I could hear him in his bedroom with a woman and saw her heels laid in the living room. It hurts Lloyd, I'm nearly 28 years old, and all I do is fuck to be loved. Sorry, Lloyd, it didn't mean to come out like that." I said, feeling embarrassed about what I had just said.

"Oh, Caz these guys are taking advantage of you, you are caring, and a beautiful woman and very fit," said Lloyd hugging me.

"Why can't guys see me for the person within and not my body? It's always been like that since I went into the care home. I just want someone to love me, that's all. Is it too much to ask for?" I started to sob on Lloyds shoulder as he hugged me.

We drank our coffee in the kitchen.

"Do you fancy a swim Caz?" asked Lloyd changing the subject.

"Hmm yeah, I need a distraction." I sighed, putting my empty mug in the sink to wash.

"I'll do them Caz you get off into the pool I'll be with you in a minute."

I dived in, swimming under and coming up to the other end of the pool. Lloyd had just dived in and was heading toward me. I needed to get these thoughts out of my head, keeping my heart inside and not get hurt. Lloyd followed, and after a few lengths, he caught up with me.

"You're on a roll tonight," said Lloyd smiling.

179

"Yeah, I'll be ok once I've done a few more lengths," I said, swimming off.

After my work out in the pool, I jumped out, wrapping the towel around me, and Lloyd jumped out behind me. We headed off upstairs to dry off, slipping into our short robes before going downstairs to the kitchen.

"Hey, Caz, what would you like to eat?" he asked me, looking into the fridge.

"I'm not really all that hungry, with having that nice breakfast this morning," I said, switching on the coffee machine.

"I'll make something light like a sandwich then." Lloyd grinned at me.

"Ok, you win thanks." I grinned back.

We lay on the sofa in the living room, eating out sandwiches and chatting.

"Lloyd I have a job to finish off next week it shouldn't take too long, they've asked if I would finish off and paint the room out and fit the wooden flooring down." I went on, hoping Lloyd would understand how my job worked.

"Yes, that's no problem, but you are coming back, here aren't you?" he asked with a little frown.

"Er yes if that's ok with you," I asked, assuming he wanted me there.

"Yes, of course, I do," said Lloyd bluntly. He hugged me as we lay on the sofa, watching the huge TV screen. Despite having a lay in I was tired and it was after 10 pm.

"Lloyd I'm going to bed I need to be up early in the morning," I announced, moving so he would let me get up.

"I'll come up with you, I just need to unlock up first," said Lloyd moving off the sofa.

I was nearly asleep when he came up, sliding into bed next to my naked body. I wondered how long was it going to take for him to start living again. I rolled over my back to him as he pressed his naked body next to mine, enveloping me with his arm and leg over my body, his hand resting on my breast. His touch was sending a tingle down my body. How I wished he would do something as I drifted off to sleep.

The following morning, I was up just after 6 am. Lloyd got up with me making me some breakfast before I left, he was so refreshing, but it was early days, and I didn't want to keep my hopes up. By the time I got to Alex and Jess's place, it was nearly 7.30 am. The 4x4 was in the driveway when I arrived. I just hoped that she wasn't going to ask me to do something else.

Having the keys to the building, I unlocked the bi-folding doors, sliding them back to step in. I took a good look around appreciating what a good job I had done. I measured up for the tiles and the wooden flooring I needed, setting off to the merchants to pick up the tiles and have the flooring delivered due to the weight. It was due to be delivered the next day, but I didn't need them as yet as it was the last job to be done.

When I got back, the 4x4 had gone. She must be taking the kids to school; I thought as I started unloading the van. But within minutes of my arrival, I heard a vehicle pulling up to the house with Jess clicking her heels over the hard surface of the yard towards the building.

"Oh fuck, what does she want now?" I thought.

"Morning Caz you're doing a good job for us, and I have recommended you to one of my friends, and she would like you to go and see her," said Jess talking to me like a child who was going to see the headmaster for a cane.

"Oh, what does she need to be done?" I asked, sounding interested.

"Well she was over last Friday when you weren't here, and I showed her what you had been doing, she was so impressed. She is going to have her outbuilding done like this for the kids now," said Jess sounding like she had started this outbuilding idea first.

"Ok, when does she want me to go around to have a look?" I asked.

"Well, I'll take you there this afternoon, she'll have a few friends around, but it won't take long," said Jess tottering off back to the house. I just hoped her so-called friend was not like Jess pushing for more and who changed their minds often.

By the time the afternoon had come, I had stuck the few tiles on the walls and the floor in the toilet and basin area waiting to be grouted in the following day. I was just tidying up as I could hear her heels clicking over the yard.

"Caz, are you in a position to go?" asked Jess sounding as though she wanted me to drop everything and go.

"Yes just give me a couple of minutes," I said, clearing the last few broken tiles up off the floor. I had to nip to the loo and wash my hands before we left.

We set off to Jess's friend's house which took about half an hour, the traffic wasn't too bad as the schools hadn't finished and Jess was picking the kids up from school later, hence not spending much time at her friend's house. Jess started chatting about her friends going into great detail that one of her friend's husband was having an affair, but she wasn't that bothered because she saw a bit of hot totty herself.

"How do you feel about that?" I asked Jess sounding her out if she was seeing someone.

"Well Alex is only at home weekends, and he's so bloody dull, no sex drive in him, but I love him, yes I would need some sort of stimulation though," said Jess grinning not saying yes or no to my question.

"Fucking dull, I don't think so." I thought. They seemed like two ships passing in the night. We approached the long driveway up to her friend's house. The driveway had large tall trees shadowing over. The main house was enormous, having several outbuildings, with the grounds mainly laid to lawn and borders of bedding plants throwing out bright, vibrant colours over the area.

We pulled up alongside a row of 4x4's.

"Hmm, I didn't think Angela would be here," commented Jess having a sound of sarcasm in her voice. I didn't say anything I wasn't interested in her life the stuck-up bitch trying to be lady muck and be first to do something and showing it off.

What a fucking snob I thought, but still, if it passed business my way I wasn't going to complain. We walked around to the back of the house onto a sun terrace where there were quite a lot of expensive garden furniture dots about on the terrace including a couple of large swing hammocks.

There were drinks and food spread on a table as the women helped themselves picking over the dishes on display.

"Hi Jess." said a slim tall woman with short blond straight hair approximately the same age as Jess.

"Oh, hi Eve I've brought Caz who has been refurbishing our outbuilding you saw last Friday," said Jess sounding rather proud.

We went through all the introductions before Eve took me over the outbuilding that she wanted refurbishing for the kids. While Jess stayed behind chatting to the other women. Eve explained what she wanted having the bi-folding doors with the one-way glass-like Jess's. I explained that they would have to be paid separately being exceptionally expensive with a lead time for delivery of approximately three to four weeks. Eve was the same as Jess having no indication of monies; she just wanted it done no matter the cost. This was definitely snobbery at its highest.

The building needed clearing out before even starting on the building itself.

"So when could you start?" said Eve sounding desperate for me to start straight away.

"I'm just finishing off at Jess's, and I have the council, I will have to give you a ring near the time," I said, not giving a definite answer.

"Ok, I'll just have to wait for won't I?" said Eve sounding a bit miffed.

We walked back to the crowd of women on the terrace where Jess was in deep conversation with a busty petite dark-haired woman. As I approached Jess, I overheard her say. "And keep your mouth shut, or you will regret it, bitch." and then Jess walked off.

"Come on Caz I have kids to pick up." She sounded snappy. I didn't speak on our way to the school to pick up the kids. Jess was driving rather erratic since I overheard her heated conversation with the other women. I assumed she must be Angela. We arrived on time as the kids were coming out of school. The kids pushed and barged their way through getting out of the school quickly, wanting to play on their computers.

Jess got out of the vehicle walking over to the gate as the two kids ran over to her. It brought memories back of the time when I was at school with my mum waiting for me and eventually catching the school bus when I moved onto secondary school. Joanne was six with her mother's mannerisms, and Charlie aged seven so laid back nothing really fazed him.

When we arrived back, the kids jumped out in a hurry to go and play, while Jess tottered off into the house ignoring me altogether after her heated discussion with Angela. Had Angela got something pinned on her? I had a quick look at the tiles I had stuck on assessing my handy work.

"Not bad." I thought, turning around to go, but I was stopped in my tracks as I spotted Alex standing there watching me. He had closed the bi-folding doors.

"Oh, you are not working?" I asked, trying to sound casual.

"Yeah, I'm working from home this week," replied Alex moving towards me.

"Jess will be pleased," I said as I tried to avoid eye contact.

"Caz I need you to let me touch you." He pleaded

"Alex, Jess and the kids are in the house, why don't you talk to her tell her how you feel?" I suggested trying to get him off my back.

"No Caz I want you. I need to be inside you." Alex grabbed my waist, pulling me towards him. He pushed me against the wall kissing my neck, hand lifting my top to access my bra to unleash. He pushed my top and bra right up, exposing my breasts as his mouth sucked my nipples while he squeezed them.

"Oh, Caz I'd been so desperate to see you again. I can't stop thinking about you." He breathed. I could feel his hardness pressed on my body.

"Alex Jess might come over," I said, try to neutralize the situation.

"She won't come over; she is not interested in me," whispered Alex as he pulled my trousers and undies down pushing my legs apart to lick my wetness. My moans grew louder as he started to fist me, making me explode for him to drink me. I ran my fingers in his hair as I could feel his movements.

"Alex, fuck me," I ordered. He took me down, releasing his length and sliding it inside me slowly. He kissed my neck, and then he pumped me hard to release inside me.

"Caz that feels so good." He murmured as he stayed inside me a couple of minutes, kissing me hard all over my neck and face. We pulled ourselves together after Alex had fucked me.

"Alex, I need to go," I said, picking up my bag and taking out a bottle of water drinking it down in one go.

The bi-folding doors opened as Jess walked in.

"Oh, I was wondering where you had gone Alex, the kids want you to fix something," said Jess oblivious to what had happened between her husband and me a few minutes ago. That was too close for comfort. I said goodnight and left leaving Alex and Jess in the building they had a spare key to lock up.

Lloyd wanted me to text him when I was leaving work; he wanted to cook having a meal ready for me when I got back. The traffic was heavy, taking me nearly an hour to get back. I texted Lloyd just in case anything was spoiling. By the time I got in it was nearly 7 pm. The smell from the kitchen was divine.

"Something smells good," I said as I gave Lloyd a quick peck on the cheek and a hug.

"It will be ready in 5 minutes," said Lloyd continuing to stir the contents in the pan.

"I'll just go up and have a quick shower before dinner." I patted his shoulder.

"Yeah no problem," said Lloyd checking the oven. I quickly run up the stairs needing a shower to get rid of the sweat, dirt and the unexpected sex I had had with

Alex. As the water ran over my body I thought, why do I do this? Giving myself to men so easily? Probably because it was the only kind of love in my eyes, but not the love in my heart. I washed myself well to take away Alex's bodily fluids and his smell on my body.

By the time I had finished and dressed in clean clothes, I was feeling more refreshed, Lloyd had dished up our meal.

"Oh Lloyd, you shouldn't have gone to all this bother, but I must say it smells lovely," I said, taking a seat at the table.

"It gives me something to do and to cook for two again," said Lloyd seating down opposite to eat the meal.

"Well, it's very good of you," I said, leaning over to squeeze his hand. Lloyd opened a bottle of wine, pouring me a glass and one for himself. Wow, this was like I was dining out. I told him I had another job for another client, a similar project like the one I was just finishing off.

"I haven't forgotten about finishing your job, Lloyd. I would like to finish it off at the weekends if that's ok with you." I said, looking at Lloyd's reaction.

"Great, yes no problem at all, just fit it around your work," said Lloyd smiling brilliantly. His smile was warming; I wished I could get into his heart; he was the sort of man that wouldn't fuck you around.

I helped Lloyd to wash the dishes before we entered into the living room with our coffee to settle down on the sofa together in our positions of Lloyd being laid between my legs and leaning on my chest.

By 10.30 pm I was starting to doze off, so I told Lloyd I was going up. Lloyd followed after locking up, and we were laid together entwined as he pressed his naked body against mine. I slowly drifted off to sleep.

The following morning, I was dreading going back to Alex and Jess's place to finish off, with Alex being home.

I just hoped he kept out of the way and left me alone to get on with the job. I turned into the driveway, making my way down to the house and seeing that Jess's 4x4 parked outside was ready to take the kids to school. Alex's vehicle was also parked outside. Fuck I wished he would be called back to his company so I wouldn't be disturbed. I was sure he was doing this to wind me up.

I started to grout in the tiles I had stuck down yesterday. They looked pretty impressive, making me feel proud of my work. By 8.30 am, I had completed the grouting, finishing off and wiping down, making it look perfect.

I washed my things from the outside tap at the back of the outbuilding that faced onto the gardens. Jess didn't want the bi-folding door this side of the building as you wouldn't see if anyone was coming up the driveway. But I personally would have had them this side showing the view across the wooden and grass area.

I heard a vehicle engine starting up and moving off down the drive. It must be Jess taking the kids to school. After I had finished washing out, I walked around back into the building to start to apply the first coat of paint to the ceiling. I had brought some water around with me to thin the paint out, with new plaster you had to give it a thin coat first. The bi-folding door was slightly ajar when I felt my breasts being cupped underneath my vest top. Fuck it was Alex again.

"Alex, you have to stop this, your wife nearly caught us yesterday," I said, sounding miffed.

"I know, but I enjoyed your body next to mine," said Alex undoing my bra to release my breasts. I turned around to face him.

"Alex stop I need to work," I said as Alex started to lift my top to suck on my bare breasts, making my arousal roar. Alex pushed me to the side of the wall, kissing my neck as I moaned with pleasure. Alex knew I would give in to him as soon as he had his hands on my body. He slipped my joggers and undies down parting my legs to fist me as his mouth consumed my wetness as he kept me coming over and over again.

"Alex, you know how to please me," I whispered as the sensation grew intense.

"I need to be inside you." He whispered back as he pulled me down onto the floor, pulling his joggers down. He slid his hardness in, and with a couple of pumps, he had come inside. His length stayed inside me while he kissed my neck to my breast sucking hard on my hardened nipples.

"I need to see you after when you have finished this job," whispered Alex.

"Alex I can't, you are married with two kids, you can't keep doing this." I protested. We heard a vehicle coming up the driveway.

It was Jess coming back from taking the kids to school. Luckily the glass in the bi-folding doors was one way. We saw her driving in with no notion of her seeing us on the floor half naked having just had sex. We quickly dressed and brushed ourselves down, making out that things were normal. We heard Jess go into the house as Alex disappeared out through the bi-folding doors.

"God, why I'm drawn to him as soon as he touches me, I melt in his arms and let him take my body." This shouldn't go on forever. I had to get a grip on myself. I thought as I let out a sigh before getting back to work.

Chapter Nine

I set up the work platform to start painting the ceiling now I had watered the paint down. I could hear a pair of heels coming over from the house.

"Good morning, Caz, how are you today?" asked Jess sounding chirpy.

"Yeah ok. Thanks." I said, thinking that her husband had just fucked me, how could I be?

"Oh good, I thought Alex would be in here seeing that he is not in the house," said Jess a little disappointed.

"Oh," I didn't say that he had already been in and serviced me.

"Hmm, he must be in the garage or the other side of the house," said Jess tottering off back through the bi-folding doors.

It took me until nearly 3 pm to give the ceiling and walls a thin coating of paint, so I decided I would have an early day and join Lloyd in the pool for a workout. But as soon as Jess disappeared down the driveway, Alex was back taking me by the waist kissing my neck as he released my bra and lifted my top to suck my nipples.

"Alex," I moaned.

"Mm?" hummed Alex with my nipple in his mouth.

"Alex, you have to stop, Jess was looking for you this morning," I said, as his hand slid down, inserting his fingers inside me.

"Yeah, she found me around the other side of the house," said Alex as he started fisting me. My legs parted further gaining more depth as I exploded with pleasure.

Alex knelt drinking my wetness as I moaned more and exploded again. Alex took me to lay down with his joggers wounded around his knees, his length hard and ready to pump inside me. He was like a piston for a few seconds and then came inside me. He held his length inside me while kissing my neck.

"Caz, we need to arrange to meet," said Alex as he slowly kissed me on the lips. I melted in his touch. "Don't take this the wrong way, but I will pay for your time." he continued, kissing me on the lips again.

"Oh, Alex, you're so persuasive." I sighed, giving in to his needs and mine. Why not?

I left before Jess got back with the kids. Lloyd was in the garden as I drove up to the house. Lloyd was surprised to see me this time of the day being so early.

"Hi," I said, giving him a peck on the cheek.

"I was going to make coffee." smiled Lloyd.

"Ah, good timing." I smiled back as we both started walking back to the house. "I'll just nip upstairs for a quick shower and change," I said as Lloyd started to head for the kitchen.

"Ok, I'll see you in a few minutes then," said Lloyd walking off towards the kitchen.

I needed to wash off the smell of Alex and the sex we had earlier. Why was I doing this to myself? I was like a bee drawn to the hot pot needing my fix of sex and wanted to be loved the only way I knew. I showered and changed into clean clothes and went down as Lloyd was pouring the coffee.

"Ah just in time again." I picked up my mug of coffee.

"So what made you finish early today?" asked Lloyd sipping his coffee.

"Well, I finished the grouting and applied a thin coating of paint to the walls and ceiling." I went on,

"I suppose I could have stayed on with the weather being so warm drying the paint. I could have put another coat on, but I thought I'd come back and have a work out in the pool if you would like to join me." I said, smiling at him.

"Obviously, I'll join you," said Lloyd with a smile. "I'll go and get a couple of towels, and I'll be with you in a minute," said Lloyd gulping the last mouthful of coffee.

The water was soothing as I dived in, swimming to the other end before coming up for air. I needed to de-stress, so I started to swim hard back and forth. I hadn't notice Lloyd slipping into the pool as he started to swim with me at my speed. I swam hard for half an hour; I needed it. Lloyd kept up with me stopping at the same time.

"Caz are you ok?" He asked, sounding concerned.

"Yeah, why? I frowned.

"You were pushing hard, I thought I was strong; I nearly had a job keeping up with you," said Lloyd touching my arm. I felt his touch as though it meant something, but was I reading this wrong as I did with Russ, but Lloyd had a good reason with the death of his late wife in a horrific attack in the burglary.

"Hmm, I have these bursts of energy now and again," I replied, setting off back to swim another length. Lloyd followed catching up with me as he grabbed hold of my ankle, pulling me down. I escaped his grip, making it to the side; he came up grinning as I tried to dunk him. For half an hour, we played in the pool splashing and dunking each other until we had had enough play and energy released.

Lloyd cooked steak for the meal, which was delicious.

"Lloyd I must pay you for the groceries, I can't stay here for nothing." I started clearing the empty dishes.

"No, you will not," said Lloyd in a stern voice.

"I can't stay here for nothing." I protested.

"You don't know what this means to me with you being here," said Lloyd not elaborating any further.

"Well, I am not going to charge you for my labour doing your shower then," I said.

"Caz I am paying you for the job whether you like it or not and that's the end of it," said Lloyd as he started to wash the dishes.

"Hmm, we will see," I said, slightly miffed.

"Shut up." teased Lloyds as he showered some dishwater at me.

"You know, two can play at that." I laughed, dunking my hand into the bowl and flicking the water back at him. We finished getting wet through despite the dishes being washed. But we had a bit of fun. After another change of clothes, I went to make the coffee while Lloyd finished off in the kitchen tidying up and changing out of his wet clothes.

I took the coffee into the living room, switching on the TV and laid on the sofa. Lloyd soon arrived lying in his usual position between my legs as I put my arms around him. This seemed to be the norm now after we had eaten and settled down for the evening. I was happy with his closeness. By 11 pm I was ready for bed with Lloyd following me shortly. Despite our nakedness in the bed, Lloyd still pressed his body next to mine with his hand on my breast and a leg over my body. At least he was now sleeping well having me to support him in any way I could.

For the rest of the week, I continued to try and finish the job at Alex and Jess's, but with Alex being at home that week and Jess nipping out to take the kids to school and fetch them home Alex would come in to seduce me, as I gave in to his advances before Jess came back from the school run. The job was going to continue into the following week due to the floor not being levelled for the wooden flooring to be put down.

"I hope you're coming over Saturday, Jess is away with the kids again, so I want you here tied to the bed again," announced Alex after he had come inside me, laying there kissing my neck.

"Alex, I am supposed to be finishing another job tomorrow." I protested.

"Yeah, but I bet they don't pay as well as I'm going to pay you for your time," said Alex kissing my breasts as he cupped and squeezed them.

I moan as I whispered, "no, they don't."

Seeing that I was coming back the next day to entertain Alex, I decided to leave early and start back on Lloyd's shower room. At least that was straight forward as the drainage needed looking at and the walls were ready to be tiled. I was surprised to find that Lloyd wasn't in seeing that the garage door was open. So, this was an ideal time to soldier on with the shower room. After further investigation,

I found that the drain was blocked. Luckily, I had some rods in the back of my van. It turned out that part of the drain had collapsed being outside the building. It was old pipework that had not been changed when the building was renovated. I had some offcuts of pipe in my van but no couplings and would have to go to the merchants. I would pick those up tomorrow on my way to Alex's. I already had the tiles waiting to be stuck on, so I set to it and started the job. Seeing that Lloyd wasn't around, I switched on my playlist of music, turning the volume up as I started applying the tiles to the floor singing along with a wriggle of my butt.

I had just finished when the song 'Living on a Prayer' by Jon Bon Jovi started. I started singing with the song as I got up and gigged about clearing up when it had nearly finished, I turned around to find Lloyd stood there dressed in a suit; his designer stubble and blue eyes watching my moves. I stopped dead just as the music had finished.

"How long have you been there?" I asked him feeling a little embarrassed.

"Long enough," said Lloyd smirking. It was the first time I had seen him in a suit looking rather sexy and handsome. God, I wish he would fuck me, I thought. I do have my moments of madness.

"Would you like coffee?" I asked, taking the rubbish out with me for the bin.

"It's already made," said Lloyd following me through.

We sat in the kitchen as we sipped our coffee.

"So, you've been out today?" I said, being nosey.

"Yes, I had to go into work for a meeting," said Lloyd, not giving any more explanation.

"Oh, so have you been out all day?" I asked, fishing for information without asking too much.

"Yes, I left soon after you did and I haven't been back that long, but long enough to see that butt of yours dancing to the music and the singing, but I wouldn't give up the day job for your singing," said Lloyd grinning.

"Less of that cheek." I punched him lightly on the arm.

"I thought you might fancy fish and chips from the chip shop tonight," said Lloyd changing the subject to food.

"Eer well yeah, I never thought about eating." I hadn't realized the time; I glanced at my watch. It was after 7 pm.

"I'll go and get them while you go and get a shower," said Lloyd standing up ready to go.

"Hang on a minute; I will pay for these." I pulled out a twenty-pound note from my back pocket.

"No, you won't," said Lloyd firmly.

"Yes, I bloody well will." I shoved the note in his jacket pocket.

"Caz no." He shook his head, taking the note out and stuffing it back in my back pocket. We argued for a few minutes over who was going to pay for the fish and chips with Lloyd winning.

While Lloyd went off to the fish and chip shop, I had a shower and changed into clean clothes for the next day. Lloyd had been doing my laundry not that I mind, but I felt a little different staying in someone else's home. At least Lloyd was domesticated. Lloyd was back with the fish and chips as I came downstairs. I could smell them, and it was making me hungry. Lloyd took off his jacket while we ate our meal in the kitchen.

"You look so different wearing a suit," I said, looking into his blue eyes.

"I don't like wearing them, but you have to make an effort for work," said Lloyd shrugging it off.

"Just as well you work from home then," I said, taking a mouthful of chips.

"I'll put the coffee on and go and get changed out of this suit." Lloyd walked over to switch the coffee machine on. I cleared away the papers having eaten from them and tidied up the tops before making the coffee. By the time I brought the coffee through, Lloyd was coming downstairs following me into the living room. I switched the TV on, and we both lay in our usual position.

During the evening I mentioned that I would be out most of the Saturday but would hope to complete the rest of the tiling on Sunday.

"There's no rush," said Lloyd feeling content. I wanted to tell him, but I didn't want to lose him. By 11 pm we were in bed with Lloyd pressed against me in his usual position with his hand and leg. But at least he was sleeping.

I arrived at Alex's place around 9 am. Alex was pacing up and down, waiting for me to arrive.

"I was expecting you earlier," said Alex being sharp. "Jess and the kids have been gone over an hour," said Alex guiding me into the house. We approached the bedroom we were in last. Alex had the tie straps ready to restrain me for the time he had me for that day. He was chomping at the bit, eager to strip me off quickly to restrain me to the bedposts. As soon as I was tied he went into a frenzy entering me straight away to release himself before playing with my body with his mouth and tongue making me explode, the more I exploded, the more he drank from me. Having a little helping hand from a tablet, he took he had a permeant hard on. He was fucking me in between playing with my body. As the sweat poured off my body, he continued licking the sweat off my body and giving me a drink through a straw, so he didn't have to release me. By 6 pm, he was fucked and released me out of my bondage.

"Oh, Caz you taste so nice I love drinking you in when you come. We have to make arrangements every week," ordered Alex not asking what I wanted.

"Alex, I need to work." I protested again.

"Well, you'll be working for me." He bluntly said.

"Alex, I am not a whore. Find someone else." My voice raised this time.

"I don't want anyone else I want you and I will pay more for your time despite you not being a whore." Alex sounded so uptight. "I need your body to play with you smell and taste so good since you came into my life, I can't stop thinking about you." Alex slid off the bed to cup my breasts.

"Alex, I need to go," I said, trying to put my clothes on.

"Caz before you go, I need one last suck from your wetness and to fuck you hard." He pushed me down back over the bed.

I was back with Lloyd by 7.30 pm he was in the kitchen making coffee.

"You look tired, have you had a busy day?" Lloyd was concerned.

"Hmm, you could say that." I sighed deeply as I sat on the stool in the kitchen.

"So, what have you been doing today?" I asked, making a conversation.

"Oh, the usual gardening." piped Lloyd.

"I'm going for a shower." I needed to get the smell and sex of Alex off my body.

"I was going to make an omelette if you would like one?" asked Lloyd waving a fish slicer and a frying pan in front of me.

"Yeah, that would be nice thanks; I won't be long." I waved my hand, running upstairs to shower while the thought struck me hard. God, what had I got myself into now? Alex was now starting to get obsessed with me.

I finished showering and changing into clean clothes and headed back down to the living room where Lloyd had brought in the coffees. We lay in our positions on the sofa until 11 pm until went to bed with Lloyd lying in his normal position over me.

The following morning, I was up at 7 am and needed to get on with finishing Lloyds shower room. Lloyd was still asleep as I slipped out of bed trying not to disturb him. By the time it was 9 am, I had completed half the side of one wall when Lloyd brought me a mug of coffee.

"Oh, thanks I was just going to make one seeing I had got this far," I said thankfully, taking the mug of coffee from him.

"Hmm, its looking good." Lloyd sounded impressed.

"Good, as long as you're happy with it." I smiled, sipping my coffee.

"I was going to nip to the flat if you wanted to come with me," I asked.

"No, I'll give it a miss I need to do some work in the study today," replied Lloyd.

"Oh, ok, I'm just going to finish this wall, and then I'll nip off."

It was after 11 am by the time I arrived at the flat, music was blurring out so Russ must be in. I unlocked the flat door with the same smell of cheap perfume hitting my nostrils. I wondered if he'd got a woman with him as I walked into the living room. There were empty cans and discarded take away dishes on the coffee table as though they had been there from last night. I couldn't see any shoes this time. I checked the post-rack in the kitchen where all the post was dumped. I picked them up flicking through to see if there was anything relevant to reply to. Most of it was junk mail until I came across an envelope looking rather official.

I opened the envelope to unfold the letter inside. It was from a solicitor, 'fuck! Who's suing me?' was my first thought until I read it further. They had been trying to track me down regarding the death of my uncle who lived in Italy, and would I contact them as soon as possible with more details to be discussed. My parents had never spoken about my uncle; I didn't even know he existed until my parents died when I was fifteen years old going into a care home because he was too busy to take me on to be my guardian. I was intrigued to find out more about him despite going into care all those years ago. I pushed the letter back into the envelope and put it into my bag. I flicked through the rest and dumped them into the bin.

I started clearing away the mess in the living room banging around, making it evident that someone was in the flat apart from Russ. There were a few mugs and dishes to be washed, so I took them into the kitchen to put them in to soak. There were papers and magazines spread on the floor as I started to pick them up with one, partway under the sofa. I got onto my hands and knees to pick it up, and as I pulled it back towards me, there was a screwed-up piece of paper.

I was curious, so I unfolded it and was shocked to find that it was the letter that Shaun had written to me explaining why he had left. My heart sank, feeling so gullible and naïve being taken in by Russ's charm. I wondered how long that had been under the sofa. I quickly shoved the note into my back pocket hearing Russ coming out of his bedroom.

"Hello my sex goddess, how's your friend doing, and when will you be back? Asked Russ, coming up behind me as I lifted myself off the floor with a handful of magazines.

"Yeah not too bad, but I don't know how long I'm going to be," I said, walking off around the sofa to avoid Russ touching me. "I need to remind you that the rent's due so if you have some cash on you for this month you can start paying directly into my account," I said putting the magazines on the side.

"Yeah, no problem. I've got some cash you can have it." Russ went back to his bedroom.

At least that was a good start, Russ paying his rent. I gave him my details, so we both didn't have to worry about the rent.

I was in the kitchen, washing the dishes when Russ wrapped his arms around me. Was I a fucking mug or what?

"So what's with all this?" I said, with a little sarcasm in my voice.

"I had a few mates around last night, and they didn't leave until 4 am this morning, so I left it and was going to tidy up later, but you've beaten me to it," said Russ kissing my neck as his hands slid under my bra cupping my breasts to massage. I had no will power; his touch kicked in arousing my wetness. I started to moan as I tried to finish the dishes but was overcome by my weakness of closeness needing a body next to mine.

"Mm Caz I've missed you," said Russ sliding his hand down my front into my undies. I was trying to resist, but it was futile my arousal now had gone too far to stop. Russ unbuttoned my trousers, slipping them down as I stepped out, parting my legs for him to fist me as he drank my wetness.

"Oh, Russ, I missed you," I whispered, twisting my fingers into his messy blond hair.

"Come on, Caz lets go to my bedroom for a change." he swept me up in his muscular arms heading for his bedroom.

Nothing was going to change, was it? My insatiable hunger for sex was causing me great damage, and I wish I had control over it.

Chapter Ten

We were both naked in Russ's bed, his lips kissing my body while he massaged my breasts. I kept exploding with pleasure as he entered me hard driving his length with urgency to find his release inside me. He then laid a few moments with his length inside me. I came down from my moment of pleasure slowly until I noticed a bra under the chest of drawers across the bedroom.

"Why do I do this to myself and get so weak?" I questioned myself. Russ was bringing women back to my flat while I had been away.

"Russ, I need to go," I muttered, pushing him off.

"What's the rush, my sex goddess? He asked.

"I've got to finish a job. I only called in here to check the post." I made an excuse.

I collected a few more pieces of clothing before leaving, fighting back the tears before I got into my van to drive off further down the road. I pulled over at the side of the road to sob my heart out. I used to be so strong, but now I was crumbling down, needing men to love me as a person and not for my body.

It was after 3 pm when I got back to Lloyd's house, running straight upstairs with the clothes I had brought back from my flat. It was not only that, but I needed to wash my face and apply a little make-up to hide that I had been crying as I didn't want Lloyd to worry and ask me questions.

I went into the kitchen to make coffee, assuming Lloyd was in the study. I had never asked him about what line of work he was in as I would feel embarrassed with me being a builder and having the muck and dust to contend with most days. Although that was my choice from day one, not being cooped up in an office or a factory, at least I worked for myself. I loved being my boss with only the clients to deal with.

I knocked on the study door and walked in to find Lloyd sitting at his desk typing on his laptop. Lloyd gave me a quick glance as I approached his desk with a mug of coffee and placed it on a coaster.

"You've read my mind," said Lloyd smiling as he continued to finish what he was typing. I sat on the corner of the sofa until Lloyd finished his work. I wanted to talk to him about the letter I had received from the solicitors seeing I had no one to confide to. Lloyd knew something was up as he closed the lid of his laptop swinging his chair around to face me.

"What's the matter, Caz?"

Lloyd asked, looking concerned.

"Well I've received this letter from the solicitor asking me if I would get in touch with them, it's to do with my uncle," I told him.

"Oh, the one you mentioned that lived abroad?" asked Lloyd surprised.

"Yeah, he's dead," I whispered, sounding unsure of the situation.

"Are you going to phone them tomorrow and make an appointment to go and see them?" Lloyd was curious.

"I suppose so, but why now when he is dead? He could have been in touch with me all those years being in the care home," I said slightly disappointed.

"Hmm, I see your point," says Lloyd coming over to hug me.

"Anyway, enough of doom and gloom lets go for a swim," I said, taking Lloyd's empty mug off him and started to head off to the door.

"Yes, that's a good idea," said Lloyd following me. Lloyd went off to get the towels while I peeled off my clothes diving in until I surfaced at the other end. I needed to de-stress having had sex with Russ a couple of hours ago and seeing the bra under the chest of draws in his bedroom afterwards. I pumped my strokes out doing several lengths before Lloyd dived in joining me with the lengths I was doing. After half an hour of work out and de-stressing, I felt I little better.

"You were going for it," said Lloyd as we stopped for a breather.

"Told you, I have my moments." I splashed water at him. He started to grin and dived down, grabbing hold of my ankle to drag me down, but I wriggled out of his hold swimming away to the other end of the pool. Lloyd caught up with me.

"You put up a good fight," said Lloyd surprised I escaped his clutches.

"Umm, you have to learn quickly. When I was in the care home, I learned a lot." I said, not giving much away. I started to dunk him as we both played flight for twenty minutes before giving up.

Lloyd cooked dinner for us; steak, he was getting to be a dab at cooking, and I wasn't used to this after years of living in the flat with various partners, being waited on except for Russ. We followed our routine; taking our coffees into the living room to lie on the sofa together to watch the TV until 11 pm before going to bed with Lloyd's naked closeness next to my naked body and his hand over my breast; Oh I wish he would take me.

The following morning I was up early needing to get the job finished over at Alex's place so I could get paid. Apart from that, I got the council phone, asking me to fit in some work they had started doing on one of the houses down the same street I worked on before, now that the next lot of monies had been released from the finance department. Plus, I had Jess's friend Eve wanting me to start the renovation on her outbuilding for the kids.

I pulled into the driveway; both vehicles were parked at the front of the house.

"God, why hasn't Alex gone back to working away like he usually does on a Sunday afternoon until Friday?" I thought. I had to leave this job for the rest of the week to work with the council; as it was my main work and paid regularly. I was glad I had the bags of level compound delivered in the week ready to crack one with the job in hand. I dragged my mixer from the back of the van, positioning it at the back of the building, next to the outside water tap and started to mix the compound to level the floor.

I was around the back of the building when Alex grabbed my breasts and started necking me.

"Oh, Caz I've been waiting for Jess to go. I'm so desperate to touch you." He moved his hand down inside my trousers and undies, feeling my wetness as my arousal kicked in.

"Please, Alex, you need to stop this." I protested, but as usual, I let him seduce me. I lay over the bags of levelling compound while he gorged my wetness with his mouth before he entered me pumping hard as he exploded inside me. His hand squeezed my breasts with excitement sucking hard on my hard nipples. We heard a vehicle pull in. Jess was back from taking the kids to school. I tried my best pushing Alex off me before Jess would start looking for him.

Within a couple of minutes, before Jess came looking, we managed to get a grip of the situation.

"Oh, you're here," said Jess in a stern voice.

"I was just telling Alex that I wouldn't be here for the rest of the week. I'm needed on the council, so it should be next week hopefully. I should be finished then." I made my excuse in front of Alex.

"Well, that's a pity. I was hoping you would be finished this week, I've organized a party over the weekend and would have liked to have it in here," said Jess sounding disappointed. Alex looked at Jess.

"You never said anything about having a party this weekend," said Alex sounding pissed off.

"Yeah, I decided when I took the kids to school this morning. I spoke with Eve and some other of my friends, so it's set," said Jess adamant, it was going ahead.

I continued with the levelling off the floor before having a quick break to phone the solicitors about the letter I had received. They wanted me to go into their office to see them about my uncle but wouldn't discuss anything over the phone. I would have to wait, but at least they worked until 6 pm so I could leave after 4 pm working with the council for the rest of the week.

By 3 pm, Jess had gone to pick the kids up from school. Alex soon came around to seduce me again. After pulling me down on the floor, he pulled at my clothes and fucked me hard until he came. He then took hold of my breasts squeezing hard to make me quince a little with pain.

"Ouch, Alex you're getting rough," I yelled, needing to get up.

"I thought you were here all week," replied Alex sounding miffed.

"I was, but the council rang so I have to go. They are my bread and butter." I said, getting up to brush myself down.

"I'll pay you extra," said Alex, sound desperate.

"No, I can't I'm on a contract to them." I lied.

"Mm I'll have to sort something out," said Alex tidying himself up. I didn't say anything, needing to clear up before leaving for the week. I could see Alex pacing up and down, thinking when he could seduce me next. I started to walk off to the front of the building as he grabbed hold of me looking miffed because I wouldn't be in the rest of the week. He pulled my vest and bra up, revealing my breasts. He pushed me to the wall his hand squeezing my breasts so tight I squeaked in pain, pushing him back.

"Alex you're fucking hurting me, what's got into you?" I said as I pulled my bra and vest back into position. "Just go." I shrugged off his hand as I walked off to the front. Luckily Jess had just come back with the kids. Alex said no more and left. Once I had finished, I left the place, when I would be back to finish off, I didn't know.

I was relieved to get away. Alex was starting to get too obsessed with my body, and I was now regretting it. I shouldn't have let it happen in the first place. May be some space between us was needed, and his urges might subside. Lloyd was in the study as I could hear him speaking to someone on the phone with the door being slightly ajar. I was going upstairs to have a shower before destressing in the pool. But I suddenly stopped dead overhearing his conversation on the phone.

"Yes, I love you too, Lara and I'll be down at the weekend, ok?" said Lloyd sounding defeated.

My heart sank, he loved someone called Lara, and he was going down to see her this weekend. I was gutted. Walking off to go upstairs for a shower, my world seemed to be falling apart. I was starting to get fond of Lloyd while helping him with the death of his wife, but now he seemed to be involved with someone called Lara. My tears fell while in the shower. Why was I doing this to myself?

I dived into the pool swimming hard for half an hour testing my limits. I needed to harden up, be strong and refuse the opposite sex's advances. Then my mind thought about the letter from the solicitor. I was going to see them after I finished at 4 pm with the council. I decided I was going out for the evening to give me some breathing space, so after destressing in the pool, I dried myself and slipped on a pair of jeans and a long-sleeved top.

Lloyd was still in the study as I popped my head around the door to say I was going out for the evening.

"I thought we might have a swim together," said Lloyd sounding surprised.

"I've already been, but you were on the phone when I came in," I said, making a pretend smile.

"Going anywhere nice?" asked Lloyd curious.

"Just to see a friend of mine," I said, hoping Tina was going to be in despite sending her a text message.

"Ok, I'll see you later then," said Lloyd carrying on with what he was doing.

It was nearly 7 pm by the time I got to Tina's flat being on the other side of the city and the traffic-heavy in places. I couldn't believe it as I pulled up. I just received a text back saying she was on holiday and was away until next week.

"God, what do I do now?" I decided to go back to the flat and see what Russ was up to.

It was another hour before I pulled up outside my flat. I could hear the music blurring out. Well someone was in, whether it was Russ or his so-called mates or lady friends. I walked in, hearing laughter and shouting. What the hell was going on? I walked into the living room to find Russ with three other guys drinking cans of beer and being jovial. One of the guys saw me coming in.

"Hey, we've got a fit bird come in." whistled the guy. Russ turned around surprised to see me standing there.

"It's my sex goddess," said Russ, slightly drunk. Russ stood up, staggering a little to come over to give me a bear hug kissing me on my lips.

"Russ, you're drunk," I said, pushing him off me.

"Only a little, why don't you join us?" asked Russ reaching for a can.

"Oh, fuck it, why not?" I thought, grabbing a can off the coffee table and peeling the tab back to take a sip. The guys moved over a bit for me to squeeze on the sofa as they all started chatting about working on the site and being jovial with passing comments of workmates on site.

Over the next couple of hours, cans of beer were consumed, and I was starting to feel slightly drunk. Then one of the guys suggested we played strip poker. We moved the coffee table out of the way giving us more space to play the game with all of us sat on the floor. The more we drank, the more sexual comments came out as clothing had started coming off.

We were now all down to our underwear playing the next round when someone would have to show their bits. We were all laughing and joking when I turned the card over. Fuck it was me having to take off my bra. The guy's tongues started hanging out as I released my bare breasts in front of them.

"Phew what a good pair of knockers." said one guy, while another asked, "are they real?" I started laughing and said;

"Do you want a feel?" pushing my chest out. Within seconds I was groped. "Ok, guys you've had a fumble," I said, brushing their hands off me. We played the next few hands with the rest of the guys stripping off altogether. I noticed despite them being slightly inebriated, their lengths were half erected and would not take much to make them hard. I was the last to take off my undies as I stood up with eyes watching me, their lengths getting harder.

"Yeah, why not? fuck it." I was relaxed being with people of my sort.

"Well, guys, how about playing truth or dare?" There came some gears and laughter all agreeing to play. Tony was asked to kiss me. He came over enveloping me kissing hard on the lips. Jonathan was asked to suck my nipple as he came over, grappling my breasts to suck hard on my nipple. I was starting to get aroused having four guys naked in my flat. I had drunk too much, but what the hell?

"Come on, guys!! who wants a blow job?" I offered, grinning at the guys. Russ was looking daggers at me and butted in saying that I had too much to drink and that I didn't know want I was saying.

"Russ let me give you a blow job," I said with a hiccup.

Russ took hold of me, "Caz, you have had too much to drink, I'm taking you to bed."

"Hmm, are you going to fuck me, Russ?" I said hiccupping. The guys started to disagree with Russ taking me to bed and wanted a blow job.

"You're no fun, Russ. We thought we could have a gang bang," said Tony taking another gulp of beer from his can.

It was after midnight before Russ's mates left, leaving the two of us together. Russ came in with a black coffee to see if I was ok once they had gone.

"Here drink this," said Russ handing me the mug of black coffee. I sat up, revealing my bare breasts taking the mug of black coffee. Russ slipped into the bed along the side of me, holding on to his coffee.

"Caz, I didn't like you offering blowjobs to my mates." He sounded jealous.

"Well, what about the woman you had with you the other day? I could hear moaning in your bedroom. I also saw the bra under the drawer." I said, flinging it back at him. Russ went quiet for a few minutes, not knowing what to say. I put my coffee down on the bedside cabinet. "I'll tell you what Russ let's forget it and just fuck me, will you?" I said, sliding down to his hard length.

Russ started to moan as he leaned back on his hands as I moved the covers back to suck him hard. Russ stopped me, kissing me on the lips sliding down my neck as my arousal kicked in with his touch; his mouth was on my wetness as I exploded.

"Russ, fuck me hard," I whispered. My demand was granted by fucking me hard until he released himself inside me.

Russ was up at the regular time for work, bringing me a coffee, as he used to and a couple of pain killers for my head.

I had missed this, but I would have to see him as my fuck buddy and nothing else. Still, that was my life at nearly thirty and still single. I still had some work clothes in the flat luckily; I hadn't taken them all with me.

I was parked up waiting for the council guys to arrive to unlock the house we were renovating. It was nearly 8.30 am by the time I started. The council guys were renowned for being so laid back and stopping for cups of tea nearly every hour. Looking at the job I needed to do and if everything went smoothly, I reckoned I could have it wrapped up by Thursday. Les was grumbling wanting me to finish before 4 pm for the day, but it needed to complete what I was doing having a new start in the morning. It was just after 4.10 pm as I climbed into my van to head off to the solicitor's office in the city. The traffic was heavy stopping and starting at the traffic lights. I finally found a parking space but with having to walk some distance to the office.

I had to bring some identification with me as proof of who I was before seeing the solicitor. I sat waiting in the reception area, looking at tall green leafy potted plants. The receptionist was a plump middle-aged woman wearing make-up that looked as though she had been trowelled to go on stage; she seemed a little snooty looking down on me as though she had trod in something brown and soft. After fifteen minutes, a young woman in her early twenties came through wearing a smart grey suit and heels from the far end door and walked up to me.

"Hello, are you Caroline Jones?"
A young girl asked me.

I stood up, "yes, that's me." I said, waiting eagerly.

"I am Jill, Mr Johnson's secretary, have you brought some identification with you so I can photocopy them?" asked Jill. I handed over my driving license and national insurance card. After ten-minutes Jill came back with my id and said that Mr Johnson was running late and it would be another ten minutes. I had been there over half an hour and was parked in a limited parking zone having only half an hour left; I just hoped I wasn't going to get a fine if I was over my time.

Five minutes later, Jill came back. "Mr Johnson is ready to see you now if you would like to follow me," said Jill. We had only two flights of stairs to climb; Jill seemed to take the stairs in her stride, probably climbing these hundred times a day. It was the first time I had ever stepped into a solicitor's office with folders and piles of papers packed in every nook and crevice in the room.

Mr Johnson's was about sixty with a slight bulge around the waistline sat in a comfortable looking black leather chair with a chunky dark mahogany desk piled with files. He stood up smiling as I walked in.

"Please take a seat. Miss Jones." He acknowledged the chair opposite his desk. I sat down waiting for him to start explaining why I was there.

"Firstly, I would like to give you my condolences regarding your uncle." I sat there not saying a word, I didn't know the guy or even seen a photo of him. "Your uncle, Garth Jones, lived in Italy had built up a lucrative business and a few substantial properties. Unfortunately, he was killed with further investigation going on. I can't give you many details of his death due to the enquiries, but they have released his body so arrangements can be made for his funeral."

I gasped with the thought that my uncle was killed despite not knowing him.

"You are needed over to Marina di Camerota Italy to arrange his funeral. There will be someone to meet you at the airport taking you to your uncle's house with someone to help you with the language barrier," said Mr Johnson looking over his spectacles at me. I was silent. I didn't know what to say.

"Is there anything you would like to ask me Miss Jones?" asked Mr Johnson putting the piece of paper on his desk and sitting back in his chair.

"Er, it's a lot to take in," I said, numb with disbelief in what I was hearing. "So when am I supposed to go over to arrange the funeral?" I asked, thinking that I had only been abroad a couple of years ago on holiday with a friend.

"As soon as possible, preferably the end of this week if possible. Just let me know the flight time, so I can let them know at the other end. Once your uncle has been laid to rest you will need to make another appointment to come and see me." said Mr Johnson sounding slightly pushy for me to go as though he either had another appointment or waiting to go home.

I walked back to the van in a daze, why hadn't he been in touch with me before and now it had come to this? I had forgotten the time of day until I got back to the van. There was a ticket stuck on my windscreen of the van. Fuck, I was only ten minutes late, and now it cost me sixty pounds. I pulled the tickets off the windscreen and flung it on the passenger seat of my van, fuck!!!

Chapter Eleven

By the time I got back to Lloyd's house, it was nearly 6.30 pm. As I walked in, I could hear the TV in the living room. Lloyd was laid out on the sofa watching TV.

"Hi," I said, walking in. Lloyd suddenly got up with me walking in on him.

"Caz, where have you been? You didn't come home last night," asked Lloyd sounding concerned.

"My friend Tina was on holiday. I should have phoned her instead of texting her. Then I went around to my flat and had a few drinks with my flatmate and his friends. With having a little too much to drink, I stayed over."

"Oh, you have a guy living with you?" said Lloyd picking up what I had said.

"Yeah, we share the bills." I shrugged, not making much of it.

"Have you eaten?" I asked, changing the subject.

"Well, yes, but I can make you something," said Lloyd, feeling guilty for he had already eaten.

"No, it's ok. I'll just make something quickly," I said as I turned around to head for the kitchen.

"I'll make coffee." offered Lloyd.

"No, I'll make it," I shouted back, wanting Lloyd to stay where he was. But no, he followed me into the kitchen, switching the coffee machine on while I made myself egg on toast.

"So, how's your day been?"

..5asked Lloyd, making conversation.

"Oh, the usual, I'm back with the council this week having one of the houses to refurb. I have to work their hours so I won't be going as early, and I'll be coming back early. I sometimes think about how they get any work done with the time they work." I didn't mention I had been to the solicitors and about having to go over to Italy as soon as possible to arrange my uncle's funeral.

By the conversation I overheard the other evening, Lloyd wouldn't be in over the weekend, so probably I would try and get a flight late Friday night or early Saturday in the hope that I could finish the job with the council in time.

We took our second mugs of coffee into the living room and lay in our usual position on the sofa. I missed these moments Lloyd lying between my legs, having my hands lying on his chest.

"I missed you last night," said Lloyd sincerely.

"I'm sorry, I should have texted you, but I had too

much to drink, and it slipped out of my mind." I hugged him. We lay there until 11 pm before going to bed.

Lloyd was last up to as I was about to doze off. I could feel him slide in between the sheets pressing up to my body.

"Caz, mm, can I hold you?" asked Lloyd.

My eyes opened wide. Had I heard him correctly? I turned over, "are you okay?" I asked, looking at him like a shadow cast across the room, throwing a little light in the room.

"I need you, Caz," whispered Lloyd sounding as though he needed comfort.

"I'm here for you, Lloyd," I said, holding him as his head rested on my breasts with his arm and leg draped over my body.

"I missed you, I didn't sleep well last night," said Lloyd hugging me. I wished he would take it further and make love to me. We both slept all night as Lloyd hadn't moved during the night.

As the week went by, I made enquiries on flights to Italy with one due to fly out early hours of Saturday morning. Lloyd mentioned that he would be away for a few days over the weekend and just to treat his home like mine, but I didn't tell him that I was going to Italy for a few days and wasn't sure when I would be back. I thought I could text him when I knew more once I was over there. Luckily, I managed to complete the job with the council by Friday and made arrangements with the flight and the solicitor to notify the other party in Italy that I was coming over.

After I had finished work the Friday afternoon, I went straight to my flat to pack a case for the journey; it was going to be hotter there being in the high 20 C for September. At least I had missed the peak temperatures, which would have reached nearly 40 C. It was bad enough working on some days with the temperatures reaching 25 C. But this time, I wouldn't be working. I thought I would book a hotel for the night next to the airport, which included parking for the period of time I was going to be away. Not only that but if Russ were in, we would probably be having sex all night and miss my flight with it being the early hours of the morning.

I arrived back at my flat just after 4.30 pm. Russ wasn't home, so I made myself a coffee before taking a shower with a change of clothes. I sat down in the living room with my coffee to have five minutes before I showered. My mind was racing, thinking about what could have happened to my uncle? Was it an accident, or was he murdered? If he was murdered, what did he do to cause his death? I would have to go to the police and find out who was dealing with the investigation and more details about his death.

I had nearly dropped off to sleep, spilling half of the mug of coffee on my lap and woke up with a start.

"Oh, fuck!" I swore, standing up sharply with the empty mug in my hand. Now the time was to take a shower after taking the empty mug into the kitchen. I had been in the shower about five minutes washing my hair at the same time when I felt a presence behind me, causing my playlist to blur out. A pair of hands cupped my breasts with the naked body of Russ pressing against mine. I knew his touch blindfolded.

"Hello my sex goddess, what are you doing home?" asked Russ kissing my neck as I could feel his hard length needing to be inside me. I moaned as I leaned back for him to take more of my neck.

"I'm going away for a few days," I whispered, moaning as he slid down, lifting my left leg onto his shoulder to have maximum fullness of my wetness. I twisted my fingers through his hair as he made me explode.

"Oh Russ, you know how to please me." I moan while I explode again. The water ran over our bodies while Russ started to fist me, I keep exploding, digging my fingers in his hair with the pleasure he was giving me. He was

ready to fuck me hard but lasted a few seconds as he kissed me hard against the shower wall.

"Caz, I love fucking you," whispered Russ, still locked inside me kissing down my neck, pressing my breasts.

"I suppose you're my fuck buddy," I whispered as I moaned with his lips skimming my neck.

"I'm sorry about the woman in my bed. I love fucking different women, but you're so different to the others," said Russ as he sucked my nipple.

"Well fuck buddy, you are then," I whispered, on the brink of exploding again.

I stepped out of the shower, knowing where I now stood with Russ and women in general. Fuck buddies it was, but I had to leave my heart cold; just take the moment of closeness we would have together. That's how I copped in a care home; having someone close to you meant just sex since I lost my virginity soon after my parents died. A lot of girls went into prostitution, beaten, made addicted to drugs stuck in a vicious circle and had to prostitute themselves to earn money to pay for their next fix.

I could see this and always told the girls what they were doing to themselves, but they wouldn't listen. I knew a couple of girls in the home who died by an overdose at only seventeen. At least I was in control with only have to be in the home just under three years, and for having a family life, a least I had my head screwed on knowing where I wanted to be.

I started to pack, sorting light wear clothing to take with me with a suitable outfit for the funeral. Russ came into the bedroom wearing a towel around his waist, showing off his fit muscular, tanned body. No wonder women wanted to fuck him, he was sex on legs, but he lived with me, leaving me with more time to fuck him.

"Russ, if you're going to fuck other women, can you do it elsewhere and not in my flat?" I said, feeling slightly jealous I had to share him. But I shouldn't be, with Alex sharing my body with him.

"Hmm, ok, my sex goddess." He came up to me, kissing my neck.

"Russ, I need to get on, I don't want to be late." I didn't mention that I was staying in a hotel before the flight.

"Yeah, but before you go, can I make love to you?" Russ dropped his towel in front of me. Resistance was futile. I enjoyed our last lovemaking, with Russ being so gentle. He made me moan with multiple explosions and eventually coming together.

I arrived at the hotel airport around 9 pm, parking my van in their car park. I did mention over the phone that it was a work van I would be coming in, but they were very nice about it saying it didn't matter the form of transport I turned up in and wished me a happy stay. They also gave me a call in the morning to take me to the airport for my flight to Italy, all being part of the deal I had booked with the hotel.

My flight was at 5 am with the taxi picking me up at 4. It was going to be a long tiring day, but the time I got there, I would be meeting Davide at the airport. I wondered what he was going to be like as the Italians were known for being studs in the bedroom. The flight took nearly three and a half hours, with over half an hour waiting for my luggage and clearing customs. I was looking out for someone with a sign. Wow, he was sex on legs being about thirty years of age with dark curly longish hair and fit. He wore tight-fitting jeans and a tee shirt. Mm, I've got to try him out, I thought, making my way towards him as he saw me approaching him. He hugged me and gave a peck on the cheek, which I found out later was the normal thing to do when greeting someone.

Davide spoke very good English being a godsend as we walked out of the airport to a waiting car parked out at the front of the building. The weather was in the early 20 C and due to peak by midday to nearly 30 C, but at least I wasn't working in these temperatures for a change. Expecting to be either driven by a taxi or Davide, we approached a dark 4x4 vehicle. A guy jumped out of the driving side door to take my luggage and to open the door for me to get in as Davide jumped in the front with the driver. I found it overwhelming, who was paying these people? I thought.

Davide explained that I would be staying at my uncle's villa on the coast, being quiet and slightly remote, but it had a sea view and a private beach. The drive took us nearly an hour to the villa as we turned off the main road onto various smaller roads until we came to a dead-end with thickly set trees and shrubs hiding an entrance with double gates. Davide presses the fob button to open the electric gates, which opened quickly as we started to move forward up the drive to the villa. I couldn't believe what I saw as we approached the villa; it was massive.

"So, this was my uncle's place?" I asked with my eyes wide open, not believing what I was seeing.

"Yes, he also has another property on the east coast of Italy; he used to travel between the two while doing business," said Davide, not making much of it.

We pulled outside the front of the villa; the driver got out to open my door and to take out my luggage.

Davide took my luggage while the driver got back in the vehicle and drove off back the same way we had just come. The door was unlocked as Davide opened the large solid front door. We stepped into a huge hallway, making Lloyd and Alex's hallway look small. With light oak, solid wooden flooring throughout the eye could see and white painted walls and ceilings, making it clean and fresh looking.

The hallway had a large staircase similar to Lloyd and Alex's, where the upstairs split. The villa had left and right-wing. Davide put my luggage down and started to show me around the villa. It comprised of three huge reception rooms, a huge kitchen with all the mod cons, a gym having the most up to date equipment and a fancy bathroom with an oversized shower area; Mm was I missing something here? We followed out onto the back of the villa to a large pool and terrace, which overlooked onto a lawn area overlooked out to the sea, which led down to the private beach at the bottom of the cove.

"What line of business was my uncle in? I asked eventually after trying to take in the size of the villa.

"He was into fine wines and antiques, owned a vineyard bottling his wine, owned a few night clubs and dabbled in other business dealings, so to speak," said Davide readily, giving me my answers.

"Hmm, do you know how he died?" I asked, seeing that he seemed to know my uncle.

"Well we are not sure if it was an accident or deliberate, he was driving himself one night with his chauffeur having the evening off. He skidded off the road, falling twenty metres into some trees and wasn't found until the next day when his chauffeur was concerned. But he was dead when they found him. He was a nice guy, and those who worked from him were loyal as he paid very well." said Davide sounding sad.

"What was he like?" I asked, wanting to find out more about my uncle.

"Well, he was one for the ladies, probably why he never married. He threw a lavish party every month; he enjoyed life but unfortunately was taken from us too soon," said Davide sounding depressed.

"Yeah, how long have you known him?" I asked, being inquisitive.

"I should say about ten years; I was in one of his night clubs with my boyfriend when I overheard him chatting to someone about needing a male PA, so I boldly asked him, and that was that," said Davide smiling.

"Fuck, the guy is gay, so good looking and fit what a waste." I thought.

"But why did he want a male PA?" I asked inquisitively.

"Well, if he had a female, it would have been complicated with his lifestyle, so with me being a guy, it suited him nicely," said Davide smiling.

"Hmm, so he was a bit of a womanizer then?" I said, smiling back.

"Yeah, apparently he always had been since building his business," said Davide raising a brow. I wondered if it was in my genes with the high sex drive I had.

Davide showed the rest of the villa; it had ten spacious bedrooms with en-suite bathrooms and balconies. By the time I had just about seen everything apart from going down to the beach, which I would explore tomorrow, it was getting late in the afternoon. Davide asked me if I would like to dine out or if I would be ok on my own with plenty of food in the fridge? In case, I wished to cook. I was getting a little tired having been up the early hours travelling to get here, so I said I would be ok on my own. Davide gave me a hug and a peck on the cheek before leaving, saying that he would see me on Monday to start organizing the funeral, but if I needed him before then, I could phone him. At least I was going to have Sunday all to myself to explore a little more of my uncle's villa.

Davide disappeared as I headed for the kitchen needing a coffee. It took me nearly half an hour to find where things were. While the coffee machine started its cycle, I made an omelette with a couple of tomatoes seeing that I hadn't eaten since leaving being on the flight over. It was around 6 pm when I had my meal and a drink, needing a shower feeling hot and sweaty from travelling. I headed upstairs with my luggage, choosing the best bedroom in the villa with a view overlooking the pool and the sea. I was thinking about my uncle while under the huge shower. I wondered what sort of parties did he throw? The oversized showers, mm was he having orgies? I wished I'd had known him.

My hair didn't take long to dry being so hot during the day, and the evening was still warm. The four-poster bed looked comfortable like Alex and Lloyd's; I sank into the mattress. I was so tired; and slept until 7 am but woke up with the sunlight shining through the window as I hadn't bothered closing the blinds before bed. The morning was getting warmer, I expected it would be similar to yesterday, so I was going to make the most of the day of leisure.

Shorts and a vest top with flip flops were the dress code for today. I decided to make some breakfast; with poached eggs on toast and a mug of coffee, I took my meal out onto the terrace and soaked the morning rays of the sun. It was so peaceful and quiet as I could hear the waves crashing on the rocks further down the cove. After eating and sitting for over an hour taking in the view, I thought I would explore the private beach and the cove. I washed my few dishes and started to descend the winding path to the beach and cove. Luckily, I brought my beach bag carrying a towel, sunscreen and a bottle of water with me; there was a feeling of a holiday.

The beach was clean with the water so clear, as I walked along the waterline of the shore, the water lapped over my feet. I must have walked half a mile down the coast following the shoreline until I couldn't go any further. The sun was getting hotter as I stopped for a drink of water and took out the sunscreen to apply to my skin. I sat down while observing the view out to sea, drinking my water, leaning back on my elbows when I heard someone shouting. I ignored it as I stayed in the same position blanking out any distraction. Within a few minutes, a shadow came over me; blinded by the sun, I had to shade my eyes with my hand to see them.

"You're on private property." said the voice bluntly.

"Oh, I'm so sorry, I didn't realize I was that far down the beach," I said, making an excuse. I stayed in my position, observing the guy stood next to me. He was tall and had dark curly hair with a fit body underneath his tight jeans and tee shirt. It must be a thing that the Italian fit guys wore their clothes, hugging their bodies. I wasn't wearing a bra under my vest as my nipples started to harden and poking through my vest, seeing his fit body.

"So where have you come from?" he asked, his voice was softer now.

"I've come from that way," I said, pointing in the direction of my uncle's villa.

"Hmm, you related to Garth Jones?" he asked, sounding interested.

"Yes, why?" I said bluntly.

"My father was a good friend of his, sorry, my name is Valentino."

"Caz," I said, standing up as he eyed my cleavage and the outline of my nipples showing through my vest. He hugged me and kissed both my cheeks as we introduce our selves to each other.

"Can I walk you back?" asked Valentino in his Italian accent. He sounded so sexy; I pulled on my vest, showing more cleavage.

"Yes, if you would like to," I said, thinking was I going to bed with him when we got back. He spoke of his brothers and their families, and his father being proud of his sons having children. He asked me about my family, which I didn't have much to say only that my uncle was my only family, but I didn't know him or knew about him until I was fifteen. He put his arm around me as I said I had no family and hugged me.

"I'm so sorry you are on your own," said Valentino kissing me on the cheek as he hugged me. His closeness felt good with his taut slim tanned body touching mine.

We were now at the bottom of the steps to the villa. I asked if he would like to come up for a drink before he went? Seeing that he had walked me back. I couldn't leave him, not only that I needed to see if he was going to take advantage of me. By the time we were in the kitchen, it was after 2 pm with the sun at its peak.

I was starting to glisten with the sweat; I could feel it trickling down my neck into my cleavage. I stood next to the coffee machine preparing the mugs as Valentino wrapped his arm around my waist before he started kissing my neck.

"You are so beautiful; I would like to make love to you," whispered Valentino sliding his hands under my vest to cup my breasts. I tilted my head back as I moaned with his touch. Fuck he was not hanging about. My wetness started to kick in. After a few minutes of massaging my breasts and kissing my neck, he slid his hand down to my shorts, unbuttoning them as they dropped to the floor, his hand slipped underneath my undies sinking his fingers inside me as I let out a moan. He knew I was aroused.

"Caz, we go to bed to make love," said Valentino with his sexy accent.

We were soon in bed both naked making love; he was so gentle and caring, making me explode with his

269

lovemaking. From the time we were in bed, the Italian stallions live up to their reputation. I was enjoying every moment as I lost track of how many times he entered me, and we both came together. We were both sweating from the heat of the evening and loving making, so we headed off to the huge shower to continue our loving making.

It was nearly 2 am when I was making coffee in the kitchen standing naked next to the coffee machine to finish its cycle, while Valentino massaged my breasts kissing my neck as I moaned, feeling his hardness needing to enter me. He pushed me to the table, laying me over, entering me, massaging my breasts as they hung loose. I was exploding with desire.

I finally made the coffee taking it back with us to the bedroom as he continued making love to me.

"Caz, you have a beautiful body, I need to make love to you until you tell me to go," whispered Valentino.

Fuck it, at this rate; he wasn't going anywhere; I would keep him until he gave in, I thought to have my moment of love.

Chapter Twelve

I could hear a vehicle approaching the villa, fuck it was nearly 9 am with Valentino still in my bed fast asleep.

"Valentino, wake up, Davide is here. I have to get up." Valentino mumbled, lifting his head, and his hand touched my breast gently. I wished I could stay in bed with him, but I had to sort out my uncle's funeral, and that's what Davide was here for. I jumped out of bed, scooping my short robe, and wrapping it around my body.

Valentino sat up in my bed, "Caz come to bed, I need to make love to you." said Valentino in his sexy accent.

"Valentino, you have to go. I have my uncle's funeral to sort out." I said, sounding desperate for him to go before Davide came in to find that I wasn't alone. 'But come and see me tonight, okay?" I said, kissing him on his lips.

"I will," said Valentino in his sexy accent.

Davide had walked in as I ran downstairs in my short robe.

"Someone's had a long sleep," said Davide raising a brow as he walked towards the kitchen.

"Yeah, you could say that I said wishing I was still in bed with Valentino. "Davide, will you make some coffee while I nip off for a shower? I shouldn't be too long." I said, running off upstairs for the bedroom to see if Valentino was still there. He had gone; I hoped he would be back tonight to continue our lovemaking. After a quick shower and a change of clothes, I was soon downstairs in the kitchen with Davide and a mug of coffee in my hand. Boy, I needed this, with a lot more depending on how the day went.

"Aren't you having any breakfast it's supposed to set you up for the day? Asked Davide, Surprised.

"Yeah, I suppose you are right," I said, making an effort to pull out the pan to make poached eggs on toast.

"Are you eating with me?" I asked, offering to cook him some.

"No thanks, darling; I've already eaten," said Davide sipping his coffee. While I made myself breakfast, we chatted about the funeral arrangements and what I wanted. I didn't know how many people would be at the funeral, but as we chatted, I guessed that there were going to be a lot, especially his lady friends.

After breakfast, we set off to look at a couple of churches that would be suitable and available. He was being cremated, so the church and the crematorium would have to be booked. I was in luck that there was a cancellation at the church on Friday of that week with the crematorium. It was booked easily as the majority of deaths in Italy were buried due to their religious belief. I was starting to yawn as the lack of sleep was starting to catch up with me. It was after 1 pm with another hot day beaming down on us. I needed some sleep, so I told Davide that I had had enough for today and that I would see him in the morning. He was quite happy with it and dropped me off at the end of the drive for me to walk up to the villa.

I walked into the villa, needing a drink of water before going upstairs to bed. My head felt as though it would explode, but it was the lack of sleep. I flopped onto the bed, fully clothed, and slept off. I woke up with a start and opened one eye to look at the clock; it was nearly 9 pm.

Fuck, Valentino had said he would come around tonight, but there was no sight and sound of him yet. I was disappointed, yearning for his love for a few hours, but it wasn't seemed to be happening. Dragging myself off the bed, I undressed and stepped into the oversized shower.

I stood there thinking of the night before and the lovemaking, I was in a trance. All of a sudden, I felt a presence behind me, cupping my breasts and kissing down my neck I leaned back, moaning with his touch caressing my body. It was Valentino's touch; his body pressed next to mine; I was feeling his length hard and waiting to enter me.

"I am sorry, I'm late. I had some family business to sort out," he whispered.

"Mm, you're here now," I said as I moaned. He turned me around as the water sprayed over our bodies. He knelt, lifting my left leg and taking in my wetness in his mouth to make me come, I pulled his hair with my fingers.

"Valentino, I need you inside me," I whispered as I exploded again. He pushed me against the wall as I mounted him, shimming onto his length with my legs around his waist and his hand holding me by my butt. We rocked together until we both explode to our rhythm.

We made love all night; I had no clue how he kept going, I could hardly recall anyone having a constant erection apart from Alex with a little help of a pill for a few hours. But there again Valentino was a lot younger than me by five years, so was in his prime being the stud he was with all that testosterone. It was a good job I had asleep because I wouldn't be having these moments of love. It was another late night and early morning having only an hour of sleep before Davide turned up bouncing with energy.

Valentino disappeared as we heard Davide come in, with my short robe tight around my waist, I ran downstairs to greet him.

"This climate must be tiring you out; you look you've had a heavy night," said Davide walking into the kitchen to make the coffee.

"Mm, you can say that," I said casually as I hated lying to him.

After breakfast, we went to sort out the type of coffin for my uncle to rest in. I went for the light oak with the brass looking fittings. Davide took me for a little sightseeing and a break, stopping at a bar for a drink and something to eat. It was another hot day; I don't know how they put up with these sorts of temperatures for long periods of time. While we sat eating our meal, we chatted about my uncle.

My uncle was my father's younger brother, only ten years older than I was. That would explain why he wouldn't be my guardian when my parents died being only twenty-five years of age and not wanting a fifteen-year-old teenager around his feet. He had worked for a company making his way up the ladder until he was in a position to set up on his own and started dabbling in all sorts of commodities expanding his business over the years. He liked the night club life, which he had acquired a few of his own over the years. He had met many women, and he dated but never married for a free spirit that he was. He also liked to gamble a little being a very good poker player, but he did upset a few people playing for very large amounts of money, according to Davide.

"It was Enrico Caputo, he lives in the villa next door further down the coast, but I think it didn't go down very well as fingers started pointing, saying that he was cheating," said Davide sounding serious.

"So what happened after that? were they still friends?" I asked, seeing that I was sleeping with the enemy.

"Well, they still bear a grudge," said Davide pulling a face.

"Does Enrico have any sons?" I asked, now more curious.

"Oh yes he has four, the eldest is Franco, who's thirty and married with a family, Carlo who is twenty-eight and married with a family, Alberto who is twenty-six and has just got married, and the youngest is Valentino who is twenty-one and is a total stud, but Enrico lets him get it out of his system until he ready to go into the family business."

My heart dropped hearing this; I was getting involved with the enemy. But he was a good lover and made me happy for the time we had.

"What sort of business are they in?" I asked, wanting to know more about the family.

"Well, they say wines, similar to what your uncle was into, but there are rumours they dabble into drugs, but whether that's true or not, we don't ask questions," said Davide drinking his last drop of cola and placing it on the table. "Are you ready to move?" said Davide, waiting for me to answer.

"Er, yes, ok, can you take me back to the villa? I think I am tired." I got up from the table to go.

Davide dropped me off at the gate, and I walked up the driveway to the villa. It was nearly 2 pm, so I decided to take a siesta, as it was so hot despite the pool being so inviting. I laid on the bed naked drifting off straight away until I was woken by the weight of someone on top of me having their full length inside me as they came. It was Valentino taking me while I was asleep. God, this guy was really something. Considering he was only twenty-one, he was very experienced in the bedroom department, knowing how to please a woman with so much passion. I wished I could find the right man in my life with so much passion and to love me as a person and not for my body.

Despite what Davide had told me about Valentino's family, I still let him make love to me, taking me as many times as he wanted. I loved his touch and everything about him and was going to make the most of him until after the funeral.

I asked Davide to sort out the rest of the details, such as the number of people attending and the wake after for the caterers. Davide would have a better idea, knowing my uncle's friends and associates. I spent the rest of my week with Valentino making love day and night; he was so hot, and I was so ready I had never had so many orgasms in the few days I was with him. He would make someone very happy when the time came to be married.

The funeral was in the afternoon, giving time for the caterers to set up in the villa on Friday morning. I was due to fly back Saturday morning, but at least it was a reasonable time in the morning.

It was the day of the funeral as Valentino bid his goodbyes for the last time, knowing I wouldn't see him again. I was sad knowing his passion for love, but it wasn't from the heart and just from the need. Davide turned up at 9 am to start instructing the caterers of where to put the tables and chairs. I decided to go for a swim in the pool, spending a good hour workout now that all my pleasures were done and I would be going back to normality. It was another coping mechanism I did when I was on a low by going to the gym or swim, pushing myself to the limits.

I had a shower and washed my hair to get ready for the funeral. I applied a little make-up and added a few more curls in my hair. My outfit was a plain basic black sleeveless dress that showed off my figure—a pair of black wedge sandals with three-inch heels and a black clutch bag to match. I was debating whether to put on my hold up stockings as I looked at myself in the full-length mirror. My legs looked too white against the dress, so I slipped them on despite the heat, but at least they were stockings and not tights.

The time had come with the automobile and the entourage of cars coming up the driveway. I felt my eyes moisten remembering my parent's funeral; it was starting to come back to me seeing the hearse with my uncle's coffin in the back. The car behind stopped outside the door waiting for us to get in. There were only Davide and me in the car with other friends and associates following behind. My thoughts drifted back to my parent's funeral, the heartache that I would never see them again. My tears started to fall despite me never had known my uncle. Davide took hold of my hand, squeezing it for comfort.

The church was packed inside with people standing outside. My uncle must have been very well-liked. I was being stared at as I followed the coffin into the church, feeling so surreal and sad despite not knowing him. People were a blur as my thoughts were elsewhere, as we left the church for the crematorium. I sobbed my heart out, partially because I had never met my uncle and partially for the memories of my parents and my life in general. Davide sat with me in the car until I got it out of my system before getting out to head into the villa to meet my uncle's friends and associates.

There was a lot of hugging and kissing on the cheeks with their condolences. Some spoke good English while some broken and some, none, but I got through the day meeting his friends and associates.

I was in the kitchen when someone put their hand on my shoulders. I turned to look up to see a well-dressed dark-haired man in his fifties with a slight podge and wearing a couple of gold rings on each of his little fingers.

"Hello, my dear, my sincere condolences. I was a friend of your uncles. I live next door over the other side of the fence. My name is Enrico Caputo, your uncle and I used to play a little poker now and again with a little business on the side." said Enrico knocking back a mouthful of whiskey in his Italian accent.

"It's nice to meet you," I said, Enrico, hugged me and kissed me on the cheek.

"I know it's not the right time to talk about business, but I take it that you will be taking over his business," asked Enrico sounding serious that I was going to be the main benefactor of my uncle's estate.

"Er, I don't know, no one has said anything about it," I said, surprised by the question he had just asked me.

"Well, if you are, we have some unfinished business to finish. I need to go now so my condolences again," said Enrico as he placed his glass on the kitchen worktop before leaving. What a strange conversation? I thought, going back into the main living room.

Once the funeral was over, and everyone had gone, including the caterers, Davide arranged to pick me up at 9 am the following morning to take me back to the airport. He asked if I would be ok being on my own. I said that I had been since I was fifteen, so I had to get on with it. Davide left just after 8 pm; the villa felt silent now I was on my own. The pool was lit up, so I decided to go for a destress in the pool for an hour to get my mind back on track before going home. By the time I had thought I had an hour in the pool, it was after 9.30 pm.

I dragged myself out of the pool to pick up a towel on the side when I saw a shadow cast across the path from the bushes overlooking the pool.

"Hello, who's there?" I shouted. I stood still and listened closely if the shadow would appear. A figure merged from the bushes, but I didn't recognize him. I thought it might have been Valentino, but this guy was taller with broad shoulders.

"Hello, have we met?" I asked, standing my ground. The guy didn't speak but started to walk towards me. "You don't speak English?" I said, again. His features were similar to Valentino's, was he related in any way? I stepped aside to walk back into the villa, but he grabbed my arm and started to run his fingers across my face.

"Sei a mareondoso ho bisogno di fare l'amore con te." said the stranger in Italian, smiling. I didn't understand a word he had said, but I should say I was going to find out. He kissed me on my lips, looking into my eyes, his arm wrapped around my waist, pulling me toward him as I could feel his hard length waiting to mount me. He started kissing my neck as I gave a little moan of pleasure to this stranger. If he was going to kill me, I might as well die in pleasure. He released me from my towel to reveal my naked body as he cupped my breast, kissing my hard nipple; my pleasure was bursting with his touch. Were all Italians like the in the lovemaking department, I wondered. He scooped me up, taking me to the bedroom, knowing where he was going. His loving making was as good as Valentino's. Was he one of the brothers? But they were married. I supposed, despite being married, they still strayed.

We made love all night until 6 am. I had fallen asleep when he disappeared the following morning, never to be seen again. Oh well, such is life.

I was already packed waiting for Davide to pick me up to take me to the airport. He was early by 15 minutes. The drive to the airport was quiet, my thoughts lingering around the week of loving making and my uncle's emotional funeral. Davide parked the car and walked with me to the airport, waiting for me to book in. My eyes became moist as we said our goodbyes, hugging and kissing each other on the cheek. My flight had been called as I started to walk off Davide shouted over, saying that he would see me soon. I was about to ask him what he meant by that, but I was ushered into the departing lounge, ready to board the plane.

Chapter Thirteen

I slept most of the way home on the plane and woke up only 15 minutes before landing. I needed it, seeing that I had not got much sleep making love to a total stranger most of the night. By the time I got back to the flat, it was nearly 6 pm. Russ was laid on the sofa watching TV when I got in lugging my luggage in the hallway. Russ jumped up, wrapping his arms around me, kissing me softly on the lips with a hug. He took hold of my luggage, bringing it into the living room.

"I'll make some coffee then," said Russ, happy to see me.

"Yeah, that would be nice," I said, flopping on the sofa tired from the journey despite sleeping on the plane.

"So how was your week away?" asked Russ coming back into the living room with the coffees.

"Mm, tiring," I said, not wanting to talk about it. Russ handed me a mug of coffee as he sat down on the sofa with me. I leaned back on the sofa tired and slightly depressed, having found out a little about my uncle's life, so young to die.

"Are you staying tonight?" asked Russ sounding me out.

"Why do you want me to go?" I asked him.

"No, I've missed you, and I thought we could spend some time together," said Russ, sounding convincing.

"Well I wasn't, I had just called around to pick up my phone. I forgot to take it with me." Russ's face dropped with disappointment.

We all can't have what we want in life." I thought, seeing Russ's disappointment.

"I'm sure you'll find a woman tonight," I said, getting up with my empty mug and taking it into the kitchen.

"Caz, please stay." Russ more or less pleaded.

"No, I can't, I need to get back to my friend who needs me," I said, taking my luggage into the bedroom to sort out.

Russ followed me in and started kissing my neck, sliding his hand over my body, his touch turning me into jelly.

"Oh Russ," I moaned, pulling my head back, his hand cupping my breasts. I couldn't resist him as he slipped off my clothes in between, kissing parts of my naked body. We are soon in bed, making love I didn't realize how much I needed him to touch me despite being no love from the heart I needed his body pressed against mine.

By the time I was pulling into Lloyd's driveway, it was after 10 pm. The living room light was on as I approached the house. I took a small bag out with the dirty clothes I had worn from the time I was in Italy that needed washing. I walked in, heading straight for the laundry room to put on a wash cycle before making a coffee. Lloyd was stood behind me while I was putting my washing in the machine.

"Caz, I've been worried sick wondering where have you gone all week," said Lloyd coming over to hug me. This wasn't like him at all.

"I had to go to Italy to sort out my uncle's funeral," I said quickly.

"Oh, Caz, why didn't you tell me?" asked Lloyd sounding disappointed.

"Well, I didn't want to bother you with my problems; anyway, you were going away," I said, walking back into the kitchen to switch the coffee machine on.

"Yes, but I could have told Lara I wasn't coming over, she would have understood," said Lloyd firmly. I was now curious to know who Lara was.

"Who's Lara?" I asked casually.

"She's my sister, why?" said Lloyd

"Oh, nothing," I said, shrugging my shoulders as the coffee machine completed its cycle. We took our coffees into the living room. So, Lara was Lloyd's sister, I thought. How wrong can you be over-hearing part of a conversation?

We lay in our normal positions on the sofa watching the TV for a bit.

"Caz, do you want to talk about it?" asked Lloyd being sincere.

"No, not at the moment, it's taking me some time to process it yet," I said, feeling a little numb. I needed a shower despite it being so late at night.

"Lloyd, I'm going up for a shower it's been a long day for me," I said, starting to move.

I kicked off my clothes, turning the shower up a tad, while I was under it, I could feel the water burning my skin. I stood firm, feeling the burn as my skin turned red with the heat, but the heat felt nice too, in some way. I stood in the shower for five minutes letting the hot water burn my body all over-consuming the pain. I just didn't know what I needed anymore. As I turned off the shower, I stepped out to see myself in the mirror with red blotches over my skin from the hot water. I quickly dried myself and slid into the bed, where I soon drifted off to sleep.

I was drifting in and out of sleep dreaming a little of Lloyd making love to me and telling me he loved me, but it was only a dream. I could feel Lloyd pressed against my body with his hand cupping my breast with the occasional squeeze, and then his length started to get hard, was I imagining this? I didn't want to read this all wrong as I did with Lara. I pretended I was sleeping, letting him take my body how he wanted to. He started mumbling, saying he loved me, no he was talking in his sleep missing his wife, Emma.

The following morning, I woke up at 7 am Lloyd was wrapped around my body with his hand on my breast. I moved to turn over on my back as Lloyd stirred, laying more over my body.

"Mm morning darling," Lloyd mumbled, half asleep.

"Morning, sleepyhead," I said, ignoring the comment he had just made.

"What time is it?" He stared at me, waking up a little more.

"It's just after 7 am. I was going to do some more of your shower room." I said, making an excuse to get up.

"No, stay in bed with me, Caz. I've missed you so much." He pressed his body next to mine, his hand on my breast squeezing gently. And then he raised himself from his pillow looking into my eyes and said, "Caz, I want to make love to you." I couldn't believe what I was hearing.

"I have been waiting for you," I exclaimed, kissing him softly on the lips.

His lovemaking took me into orbit, giving me multiple explosions; his love shone through, I gave him my heart. Our Sunday was made of trips to the kitchen for coffee and breakfast with the odd stop off for a pee. But apart from that, we spent all day making love. Could I tell him that I had fallen in love with him since I had been staying with him? I didn't know not wanting to spoil the present moment. But did he feel the same way having to lose his wife so suddenly?

We lay on the bed for a breather; it was getting on for nearly 6 pm.

"Lloyd, we need to cook dinner," I said, feeling hungry.

"So am I." He slid down the bed, spreading my legs apart to eat my wetness.

"Oh, Lloyd, you're killing me." I moaned as I exploded with pure ecstasy. He ate and drank me in as I kept exploding, sweat running down my neck. He entered me slowly kissing my neck and breasts, I am on constantly on cloud 9, with pure pleasure from this man, I just couldn't get enough of him. Once we had come together, I slid down, licking his generous length and balls, sucking and kissing, caressing and squeezing, making him soon to rise, filling my mouth with his huge length.

I sucked him hard until he shot his hot salty liquid in my mouth, swallowing it in one. His moans, shouting my name as he came. I was pleased knowing I could take his generous length into my mouth for him to enjoy me pleasuring him. Lloyd pulled me up, kissing me hard on the lips as our tongues entwined.

"Oh, Caz, that was the best blow job I have ever had in my life," said Lloyd affectionately.

"Good, I want to please you," I said, kissing him softly.

That evening we had a take away brought in, saving us cooking and having time for making love. Lloyd seemed a different person like a switch had turned on; his high sex drive had kicked in all of a sudden together with his gorgeous package down below, he was all man, and I loved it.

I had put my phone on charge when I came back late Saturday evening, leaving it on charge until I was ready to go to work the Monday morning. It was nearly 7 am, and I needed an early start to catch up with my workload, with having a week off in Italy. Lloyd hung onto me as I tried to slip on of the bed, wanting to seduce me before I went to work and succeeded. I quickly showered, and after a coffee, I was out picking up my phone on the way.

I was on my way to finishing the job for Alex and Jess hoping to complete the job by tomorrow and to get paid. I arrived at 8 am with both the vehicles in the driveway.

"Oh fuck," Alex was at home. I drove around to the building, parking up outside, jumping out to unlock the building to continue to lay the flooring. I started unpacking the flooring in, ready to slide into place when I heard the clicking of heels come across from the house. Crap! What the hell did she want now? Probably going to give me a bollocking for not being there last week.

"We have been trying to phone you last week, but you weren't answering your phone," said Jess exasperated.

"I had some family business to sort out," I said, not elaborating any information to her.

"I know you have Eve's job to start, but we were wondering if you could refurb the building on the other side of the house for the kids to play in?" asked Jess, pleading.

"Er, well, I don't know at the moment it may take a while," I said, making an excuse to see if they would get someone else.

"Hmm well, we will have to wait then, I need to take the kids to school," said Jess walking off, I could hear her heels clicking across to the house.

I saw Jess drive off through the one way glass in the bi-folding doors, soon after she had gone Alex came in grabbing hold of me. Pushing me to the floor and pulling at my clothing, exposing my breasts, his mouth eagerly sucked hard on my nipple while his hands cupped my breasts, squeezing them hard.

"Caz, where the fuck have you been? I was trying phoning you all last week, but your phone wasn't on?" He grappled with my trousers pulling hard to get inside me. He was in a frenzy, fucking me hard to release himself inside me; within seconds, he had and then laid there massaging my breasts hard and pulling at my nipples.

"Alex, stop it you're hurting me." I protested.

"Sorry I haven't seen you in a long time, I need you, Caz, and I have sorted somewhere to meet on Saturday," said Alex, desperate to tell me.

"Alex, this has to stop. I can't do this anymore." I yelled.

"Caz, I'll make it worth your while," said Alex trying to persuade me.

"Alex, I am not a whore, stop treating me like one," I said bluntly.

"Caz, you're not a whore to me. I am just paying for your time; that's all," said Alex, not understanding how it sounded.

"It's the same thing," I said as I started to get up, pulling myself together. "Just go, Alex. I need to get this finished. I'm behind as it is." I said as I continued working.

"Caz, I can't forget that first time you stayed the night with me, feeling your body and coming inside you, tasting and kissing your wetness," muttered Alex in his thoughts of fantasy.

"Alex, you just have to get over it, why don't you ask Jess to do it?" I asked, wanting him to go so I could get on with my work.

"She's hasn't been interested in me since having the kids," said Alex sounding miffed.

"So when was the last time you asked her?" I said, trying to convince him and to get him off my back.

"Oh, ages ago." snapped Alex going off in a huff. Thank fuck for that.

I saw Jess coming back after dropping off the kids at school. I wondered if Alex was going to ask her to get their sex life back on track, no doubt I would find out sooner or later. The job was going well, and I wanted to leave early to spend some time with Lloyd now that he had come out of himself, making love to me all yesterday. I have given him my heart and soul. By 3 pm, I saw Jess driving off to collect the kids from school; I just hoped Alex had tried talking to her on the subject of their sex life. I started to tidy up with only having about half a day's work to complete the job and to get paid.

I was about to go when Alex turned up, "Caz, you're not going, are you?" asked Alex looking surprised.

"Yes, I have something else on," I replied, picking up my bag ready to walk out.

"Caz, she's not as good as you, and she doesn't taste as good as you," said Alex taking hold of me kissing my neck.

"Alex stop it, who's not as good?" I asked, puzzled by his comment.

"Jess, she let me tie her up, but she wouldn't shut up," said Alex miffed. I pushed Alex off me, not letting him get to me. I needed to go.

I was soon out of the door, leaving Alex to lock up, but he caught hold of me, pushing me back inside against the wall.

"Alex fucking stop it; I'm not doing it anymore. I feel you are treating me like a whore." I ran out towards my van. Luckily Jess was coming up the drive with kids. I waved as I drove out, heading back to Lloyd's house. I was craving his love and giving him mine.

As I pulled up to the house, I saw a BMW sports car parked outside the house. It was the first time I had seen a vehicle outside the house; I didn't even know what type of vehicle Lloyd drove as I had never seen him drive because he was always in when I came back from work. I jumped out of the van, curious to know who it was heading towards the front door. I could hear raised voices coming from the study.

"What do you think you're doing having her living with you? Once she's got her claws into you, she'll bleed you dry." shouted a woman's voice coming from the study. Was she referring to me as a gold digger, and who was this woman shouting at Lloyd?

"She's helping me and keeps me company," said Lloyd trying to justify the question. Yes, they were talking about me.

My head started to spin as I ran upstairs with tears in my eyes. Why did good things go bad with me? Was I jinxed, stripping off my work clothes and switching on the shower; I stepped inside it as the tears ran down my face. It was first the guys needing my body, and now I was a gold digger. Fuck, why I did this to myself? I turned the hot tap a tad as the heat of the water burned my skin until my body adapted to the heat. With five minutes of heat on my body, I stepped out to dry myself, slipping a pair of jeans and a woollen top now, the weather had started to turn a little chilly. I needed to get out of the house.

I slipped out of the house as I could still hear raised voices in the study. I was gutted, jumping into my van I drove down the drive and headed towards my flat for no particular reason. The traffic was heavy with commuters leaving work and people spilling out of the offices, causing the traffic to stop at the pedestrian crossing. Then I remembered that I had to contact the solicitors to arrange an appointment to see Mr Johnson. Mm, I'll wait until I get to the flat. By the time I arrived at the flat, it was nearly 5.30 pm; I dialled the number hoping someone would answer the phone, but I was too late, bugger, I'll have to phone tomorrow.

Russ was in the kitchen when I arrived.

"Hello, my sex goddess," said Russ coming over to hug me. I wrapped my arms around him, needing some comfort to what I had heard early with the woman and Lloyd in his study.

"What's up, my sex goddess?" He asked, cupping my face and kissing my lips softly.

"Nothing, I've only come to see if there is anything in the post," I said, making an excuse.

"Yeah, you've come to seduce my body," said Russ jesting.

"You've caught me out," I said with a false smile, kissing him on the lips softly. Russ scooped me up, taking me into my bedroom, laying me on my bed as he slid off my jeans and top, revealing my underwear. Russ slipped off his clothes down to his boxers, revealing his tanned, muscular body.

He straddled over me as his mouth worked on my neck while unhooking my bra, sliding it off my body. I started to moan as my nipples hardened, his mouth working around my breasts slipping down to my undies, his hands sliding them off, parting my legs to take my wetness as he drank me. I exploded with pleasure.

"Hmm, you taste so good," said Russ sucking at my wetness, sliding his fist inside me, hitting the spot when I exploded again to release my wetness for him to consume. I was overwhelmed with the pleasure as he made me come multiples times.

"Russ, you are killing me with pleasure," I whispered.

Russ slid up my body to my mouth, tasting my wetness with him as our tongues entwined. He slipped his length inside me, holding on knowing he would come straight away. I clamped my legs around his waist, trying to stop him from coming, needing him to stay inside for longer.

"I can't stay in any longer." breathed Russ feeling his need to push. I released him.

"Russ, pump me hard as you can," I commanded. Within a second, he pumped as hard as he could. I could feel his hard length pounding inside me, it was rough, but I needed it. Russ released himself inside me holding it inside flopping on top of me with the energy he had put into it.

I drove back to Lloyd's, needing to destress in the pool. It was just after 7.30 pm; I just hoped that the BMW wasn't parked at the front of the house. My luck was in; there was just a light on in the living room when I pulled up to the house. Lloyd heard me coming in as he came out from the living room.

"Hi, Caz, have you had anything to eat?" asked Lloyd, sounding sincere.

"Yes, thanks," I lied, not feeling hungry. "I'm going for a swim," I said, going to head upstairs for a towel.

"I'll join you, but I'll nip up and get the towels," said Lloyd heading upstairs.

I stripped off diving into the pool, gliding through the water until I came up at the other end, as I started to swim hard to destress. Within a few minutes, Lloyd had joined me diving in catching up with my strokes as we swam together for a half-hour hard work out. We stopped together at the shallow end of the pool.

"Caz, have you got something on your mind?" asked Lloyd, sounding concerned.

"What makes you think that?" I asked curiously.

"Well, you always swim hard when you have something on your mind," said Lloyd putting his hand on my arm. I didn't want to ask him about the woman in the study and the conversation they were having, so I just said it was to do with my uncle and started to splash him to get off the subject of me being stressed.

We splashed and dunked each other for half an hour in the pool as our energy ran out of steam. I pushed myself up out of the pool onto the side as Lloyd grabbed hold of my leg, turning me over as my legged fell apart on the edge of the pool exposing myself in front of him. He came in, pushing me back as he put his mouth on my wetness, flicking his tongue, making me moan with his touch. I started to moan his touch so intense I come.

"Oh, Lloyd, I need you inside me," I whispered. Within seconds Lloyd jumped out of the pool his hardness ready to take me as I turned around to take him on the side of the pool. His thick hard length filled me with so much pleasure as he slowly pushed back and forth, I moved with him exploding with his gentleness as his pace increased when we both had our climax together.

"Oh, Lloyd, I love you being inside me," I whispered, panting with the love I felt for him.

"I love making you explode," said Lloyd kissing me softly on the lips.

Chapter Fourteen

Lloyd and I dried ourselves, slipping into our robes to make a coffee. We then took it into the living room lying in our positions on the sofa watching the TV for a while before bed. I chatted about my work and that it was nearly finished at Alex's place and that I was due to start at Jess's friend's place for a similar job. Lloyd seemed pleased that I was busy despite not finishing the job off for Lloyd. I must complete Lloyd's job; I made a mental note.

It was nearly 11 pm before we went to bed. I couldn't get enough of him. He was sending me into space and back with the intense orgasms he gave me. I was losing my heart to him and was slowly falling in love with him. Although

I had heard the conversation in the study with a woman telling him I was a gold digger. He was everything I had always wanted in a man. He was still a kid at heart; during our playful moments being a kid and a wonderful lover in bed. He had captured my heart.

I woke at 6 am with only having three hours of sleep, but it was worth it. I stirred to get out of the bed, needing to get the job finished at Alex and Jess's. Lloyd grabbed my wrist, pulling me back into the bed.

"Caz, stay with me today,"
asked Lloyd, sounding seductive.

"I wish I could, but I need to work Lloyd," I said, kissing him on the lips softly.

"I want to give you more orgasms." He tried to convince me as he rolled me overrunning his mouth over my body. I started to moan as I was on the tip of exploding with desire.

"Oh Lloyd, I have never met anyone like you," I whispered, moaning with intense pleasure as he tasted my juices. With waves of intense orgasms hitting me over and over again, I was shouting his name in pure pleasure. I floated down from the space.

"Lloyd, I need you inside me," I whispered, within seconds, he slid inside me slowly as I kissed him passionately with our tongues entwined as he paced himself, waiting for me to find my climax with him.

It was after 9.30 am before I arrived at Alex's place to finish off the job. I heard the clicking of heels coming across from the house. Oh there, she comes again, I thought as she opened the bi-folding doors.

"Good morning Caz, I take it will be finished today?" asked Jess sounding perky. I hoped Alex had been servicing her. I smiled, thinking he could always shut her up and stick his cock in her mouth; the thought brought a slight chuckle to myself.

"Yes, I should say in the next couple of hours. Would you be able to pay me today?" I asked, not wanting to deal with Alex.

"I'm sure Alex could write you a cheque out, or would you prefer being pay directly into your account?" asked Jess.

"Oh, the cheque would be ok, I need to go into the city later." I made an excuse as I needed to get this and out of the way.

It took me until lunchtime to finish the complete job. I was pleased with the work I had achieved, making the building looking larger inside with the colours being light with the light oak flooring. All it needed was the furniture and any soft furnishings that Alex needed as an office.

I had cleaned and wiped everything down as though it was a showroom. Jess should be pleased with what I had done.

I was now ready to go, so I walked over to the house to find Jess. I knocked on the door, waiting for a couple of minutes before she turned up. She was wearing her short robe and padded over to answer the glass door at the back of the house. I was grinning inside, knowing what she must have been doing with Alex.

"Oh, Caz, you've finished now?" She blurted out; she was slightly harassed and embarrassed.

"Yes, if you would like to have a look before you pay me," I asked, hoping I would get paid today.

"Umm, Alex had to go. There's a bit of a crisis on at the company and won't be back for a few days," said Jess tightening the sash on her robe. Fuck I did hear a vehicle, but I wasn't expecting Alex leaving the house.

"Mm, so could you pay me directly to my account then," I asked, not wanting to see Alex again.

"Yes, no problem." Jess wrote the details from my card down on the note pad next to the back door.

"Could it be in my account by the weekend?" I asked, sounding a little sheepish.

"Sure. I'll have a word with him," said Jess wanting me to go.

As I drove off, I noticed a car parked outside the house. I bet Jess was having her lumps felt; I was grinning with the thought. I was just about to turn out onto the main road when my phone rang. It was Tony from the council; they had released another six houses to be refurbed starting on the following Monday. I wasn't sure about starting the job Eve wanted me to do or having the rest of the week off with Lloyd and finish his job off.

I was back in Lloyd's house by 1.30 pm only to see the same vehicle as before with the voice of a woman in Lloyds study, giving him a lecture about me. I needed to see who she was and her purpose of interfering in Lloyd's life. I shut the door with a bang letting them know I had come back from work as I headed towards Lloyds study. The door was slightly open as I walked in, finding a slim tall woman in her late forties stood over Lloyd looking at his laptop screen.

"Oh, sorry, I was just going to make a coffee if anyone would like one?" I asked, seeing her turning up her nose at me.

"Yes, please, Lara will have one as well," said Lloyd. "And Caz, this is my sister Lara, Lara, this is Caz." He introduced us. Lara was looking at me up and down; her nose seemed to turn up with a bit of snobbery.

"Hi, I'll go and make it then." I turned around and headed off to the kitchen. I could hear Lara's voice rise in disapproval as I walked towards the kitchen. I just hoped she wasn't poisoning Lloyd's mind with her snobbery.

I was back, heading to the study, and I could tell the conversation about me was heating up, hearing clearly in the hallway.

"Why the hell have you got involved with the likes of her when Lucy has been after you for years?" said Lara disapproving of me and my financial status.

"Lara, she makes me laugh, and we have fun," said Lloyd coming back with an answer.

"She's only a bit of rough; Lucy has a good pedigree and refined," said Lara stating her case.

"Just leave it, Lara; if I want a bit of fun, I'll take it," said Lloyd raising his voice.

"I hope you are still coming down at the weekend for the party, Lucy will be there and she will be pleased to see you, and don't bring that trollop with you," said Lara implying that he had to be there.

"Ok, I'll be down," said Lloyd agreeing to her wishes.

I couldn't believe what I had heard; I was called a trollop and a bit of rough. I had to go back to the kitchen with the tray of coffees. I felt sick, Lloyd's sister slagging me off with Lloyd saying I was fun and Lara saying I am a bit of rough to him. It took me nearly 15 minutes before I took their coffees into the study as I needed to make my face presentable as though I hadn't been crying.

"You've been a while," said Lloyd smiling at me as I came in with the tray of coffee.

"Yeah, I had a phone call," I said, lying to him for an excuse for the delay.

"I need to go," I said, putting the tray on the desk next to Lloyd's laptop with a false smile before leaving.

I was out of the door as the tears started to spill out. I got into my van and sobbed my heart out, hearing those words on repeat in my head. Lara, saying that I was a trollop and a bit of rough, Lloyd saying I was a bit of fun. I had let my guard down caring for others' loss and had my heartbroken. I needed to be somewhere else, and then I thought of Davide in Italy. I had the rest of the week off as long as I was back to work on the following Monday. I started the van and headed off back to my flat; I was going to arrange to see Davide if he was happy for me to come over.

I managed to get a cancellation on a flight that evening as Davide was delighted, I was coming over and would meet me at the airport. The plane touched down just before midnight with having to clear customs and the journey to the villa; it was around 2 am. I was tired. I thanked him and said I needed some time to myself and would phone him. The villa was spotlessly clean as if it was waiting for the next batch of holidaymakers to move in. I dumped my bags just inside the door, going upstairs, stripping off my clothes and slipping between the sheets. I slept until late morning.

I woke up with the sun shining through the window, lighting the whole of the bedroom. For a moment, I wondered where I was. I then realized I was in Italy away from Lloyd, Alex, and Russ; I needed some space on my own to think. Then I remembered I hadn't phoned the solicitors when I came back after my uncle's funeral. I slid out of bed, wrapping a sheet around my body, padding off downstairs to bring up my bags.

I found my phone, and as I opened it up, I saw texts from Alex and Lloyd wanting me to get in touch with them. I ignored them ringing the solicitors to sort an appointment. I eventually got through to Mr Johnson's secretary. He was away until December, and I was told to wait, for he was the only person dealing with my late uncle's estate.

"Oh well, I suppose I'll have to wait until then," I said to the secretary. I made the appointment, setting a reminder on my phone for the date and time. Bugger, I had to wait nearly six weeks.

I pulled out a towel deciding to go for a swim, the pool was cold due to the time of the year, but this didn't faze me. I would soon be warmed up, giving myself a hard workout. I released the towel by the pool to dive in and came up as the cold water took my breath away.

"Wow, that's cold." I thought. I started my lengths, pushing myself hard until I could feel the pain. I needed pain in my body to feel better. It was a good hour non-stop until I was exhausted. I dragged myself out of the pool, lying naked on the side, breathing heavily.

The sun was radiating heat as I could feel my skin tingle a little, knowing I was burning. I lay there feeling the burn as I had turned the hot water up in the shower burning my skin before moving. I was feeling pain inside and wanted to feel the pain outside and torture myself for what was happening in my life. The only way I could cope was to work out hard by either swimming or at the gym. In my younger days, I would be fighting against opponents on courses from judo to kickboxing, showing my aggression.

I needed a coffee; Davide had replenished food stocks in the kitchen, knowing I was coming over, which I appreciated not wanting to leave the villa just yet. I made myself something to eat, seeing that I hadn't eaten since the flight. It was just after midday with the sun radiating heat at its strongest for this time of year, so I decided to go to the beach for a walk. I felt peace walking along the shore for over half a mile to the end of the cove further down the coast.

I sat down on the beach looking out to the sea, pulling out a bottle of water from my bag, gulping down nearly half its contents. I decided I should text Lloyd to tell him where I was. I texted him, making it brief, saying that I had to see a friend and wouldn't be back until Sunday. I just hoped Lucy hadn't got her claws in him. Lara had made it quite clear I wasn't invited to her party being a trollop. Is that what people saw me as? A good fuck and easy with it. But that was how I coped in the care home when my parents had died. Sex was the next best thing to have that closeness with anyone, but at least I hadn't turned to drugs like most of the girls did.

I could hear someone shouting, I ignored it thinking it was for someone elsewhere, but the shouting became louder as I turned around to find a tall dark-haired guy. He was casually dressed and was coming over, shouting and waving as if I shouldn't be there. I now realized where I was, facing the villa on the cliff. It was Enrico Caputo's villa, and someone was very protective of his property. The guy was now in my face, I noticed that he had a large scar down the side of his cheek, 'la vostra sulla proprieta private, si dovra venire con me' said the guy in a raised voice taking hold of my arm.

I understood the private bit of Italian, but whatever he had in mind, I wasn't going with him. I yanked my arm away from his grip to escape his hold, and I was about to set off to run back down the beach toward my villa, but the guy had rugby tackled me to the ground as the sand kicked up.

We started to struggle with each other as he tried to get a grip on me, thinking I was going to be easy to be bullied somewhere I didn't want to go. My instincts kicked in as I punched, kicked, and bit him to release me. I managed to get away from him running as fast as I could to get away. Luckily, he didn't follow. I slowed down to a walking pace, and then it got me thinking about Enrico speaking to me at the funeral, saying there was some unfinished business to be done that my uncle hadn't finished. I wondered if my uncle was involved in drugs with Enrico.

I got back to the villa and made myself a coffee and buttered a couple of croissants to take out onto the terrace with the sun starting to go down. It was so peaceful and quiet, no traffic or people in your face. The light started to fade as the sun went down; it was a lovely scene as the sun disappeared into the sea. I was feeling tired despite not having done a great deal of anything apart from the workout in the pool. I picked up my plate and mug, taking them into the kitchen to wash, after which I went off for a shower.

My muscles were aching from the workout in the pool plus the sprint from the guy on the beach. I slipped into the bed as my muscles started to relax, drifting me straight off to sleep. I was woken by a hand over my mouth, and I could feel someone's body weight on top of me. I was terrified, not knowing what this person was going to do; I could only see the silhouette of him in the light of the moon shining through the window. I was being dragged out of my bed as my instincts kick in to escape. 'Nessuna cagna sta per farmi vedere davanti al capo' said a male voice as we started to struggle. I recognized his voice as the same guy at the beach who had tried to take me to Enrico's villa. Despite being naked, I managed to wriggle from the sheet as he was trying to use it as a restraint to hold me. I shouted as my kickboxing came into practice. I planted a punch to the jaw and one to the mouth, making him shout out. 'Tu cazzo cagna, sis ta andando a rimpiangere quella cagna' said the guy shouting.

Whatever he had said, he wasn't very happy. I could see in the moonlight that I had made his lip bleed. He lunged forward as I kicked him in the groin, making him double up in pain. For a few seconds, he didn't speak with the pain I had given him. 'Cazzo cagn, sis ta andando a rimpiangere questo piu tardi,' he said, shouting in agony. I managed to escape the bedroom while he nursed his meat and two vegs; I grabbed my robe and disappeared into the night, waiting for the sun to rise.

I needed to speak with Davide, tell him what has happened; I wasn't going to be bullied by a man telling me what to do. The sun had started to poke through after having a chilly night. I tried to sleep down in the private cove in front of the villa with only wearing my short, thin robe. I gingerly crept up to the villa, being on my guard for any unsavoury visitors. I must have left the door unlocked, not thinking for him to attack me. I searched the villa with no signs of anyone apart from the blood splatter in the bedroom where I had punched him in the jaw and mouth. He would have a shiner this morning, I thought, glad I had still got a good kick in me from my early years.

I had cleaned up before Davide came round. He arrived early, having breakfast with me out on the terrace. I told Davide what had happened on the beach with the same guy attacking me last night in my bedroom.

"Mm, I would be careful,"

said Davide sounding concerned.

"Davide, tell me about them,"

I asked, needing to know.

"Well, it's only rumours, but Enrico Caputo deals in drugs, and he likes his privacy, so his henchmen guard his villa, including the beach. This guy that tried to take you back to the villa would have hurt his ego with you escaping his clutches, so he visited you. The only problem is that he will have it in for you now, so be careful." said Davide sounding concerned.

"Mm, I think I will move into a hotel until Sunday then."

"You will not; you're coming to stay with me said Davide firmly."

"Davide I don't want to put you out, what about your partner?" I asked, sounding grateful for the offering.

"I don't have a partner," said Davide firmly.

I repacked my things while Davide packed the supplies from the kitchen to take with us back to his place. We managed to bundle my bags and supplies in his Fiat Panda and set off to Davide's place, which was half an hour's drive away.

Despite the nights being chilly, the days were still warm, with the sun about to poke through the clouds. There were patches of greenery dotted about the side of the road, with the weather being dry most of the season, most of the land was brown. We travelled down the road leading to the town with a mountain range and trees in the distance behind the town. As we approached the town, the traffic started to build up; it seemed a busy town not being a tourist area.

Davide turned left at the traffic lights heading towards the riverfront. There was a mixture of pleasure and cargo boats tied up along the side of the front, with the cargo boats docked opposite large warehouses having cranes offloading the cargo from the boats and further down boats being loaded. It seemed a very busy area.

Davide pulled the car into a parking lot in front of the end warehouse along the front. I was curious where he lived, expecting to be a flat or a traditional old Italian house down a back street in the town. We walked around to the side of the building, where there was a metal door. Davide opened the door stepping into a wide corridor walking to the end to find a large lift. The lift took us to the top of the warehouse. I was getting more intrigued in where we were going as the lift reached the top of the building. The lift doors opened, facing a large window facing the riverfront. We stepped out, walking to a door on the left as Davide unlocked it, opening it for me to enter. I was gobsmacked. He was living in a penthouse above the warehouse, how could he afford to live here, I thought. I walked in with my mouth open with a window overlooking the riverfront with the backdrop of the trees and mountain range; it was beautiful.

"Just dump your stuff down, dear. I'll give you a tour of the place," said Davide sounding his normal self. I dropped my bags and followed him into the kitchen area near the door. It wasn't as large as I thought it would be with the size of the living room. But still, the kitchen was very modern with all the mode cons with light units and tiles. We walked through into the living room heading for the bedroom, was quite large with a bathroom but rather basic being the spare bedroom. We walked through into the next bedroom, it was Davide's I was surprised by the colour scheme being black and white, and this usually indicated a straight bachelor pad. Had I misinterpreted the understanding of him being gay?

Davide left me to nose around his pad while he went to make coffee. There wasn't any indication of anyone staying with him or had been the place was spotless, making my flat a bit of a hovel. I stood looking out of the huge front, drinking in the views of the mountain range and the river as Davide handed me a mug of coffee.

"Davide, how do you afford a place like this?" I asked him, sounding nosey.

"I don't; it comes with the job," said Davide sipping his coffee, looking for my reaction.

"Oh, so is this to do with my uncle's business?" I asked curiously.

"Yes, since your uncle died, business is as usual unless you want to change anything," said Davide interested to know what I was going to do.

"Sorry, Davide I don't know what you mean by me changing anything," I said. I was puzzled by his comment.

"Well, you are his next of kin; I thought you would have known about it by now that you're the main benefactor of your uncle's estate."

Wow, I had to process this information.

"I don't know anything only that I have to see the solicitor after my uncle's funeral, but I can't see him for another six weeks," I said, sounding that this cannot be true.

"Well, I'm sure you will be boss," said Davide grinning at me.

"Yeah, right. So would you like a grand tour of your estate madam?" said Davide smiling at me.

"Yeah, go on then." I had still not processed this information, but I was nosey and wanted to see what my uncle had been doing all his life before he died.

Chapter Fifteen

"So let's start with the warehousing along the river," suggested Davide taking my empty mug from me. We took the lift to the ground floor, walking to the front of the building. All along the side of the river were warehouses as far as the eye could see with boats being offloaded and loaded with various commodities and goods. Davide explained that the business varied from storage to selling wine, and dealing in fine arts and antiques. Your uncle had a good eye on that side, but his manager finally took over as he started to take a back seat and stopped getting too involved, he was planning to do some travelling.

I wondered if he would have come over to England to find me, but I will never know that now, I thought.

"Your uncle has a vineyard on the east side of the country, so tomorrow we can drive up there to have a look around," said Davide sounding like a tour guide.

We had to watch out for the forklift trucks moving pallets of wines in the warehouse as we walked through to the stairs to the offices above, which overlooked the warehouse floor. Davide opened the door to the open-plan office, and heads looked up to see who was coming in.

"Ciao a tutti: said Davide.

"Ciao." came a reply from the office.

"Questo e Caz Jones, Garth Jones nelce, lei sara prendere in consegna il business," said Davide sounding proud. I felt out of my depth, not understanding the language.

"Mm vorrei conoscere meglil il suo." said a guy sat next to us eyeing me up.

"'Hai il caso di sapere, lei e mia," said Davide grinning at the guy. It sounded as though they were having a bit of banter between themselves with a couple more butting in. All eyes seemed to be on me; I felt lost being in a foreign country, not knowing the language. We walked over to the large window overlooking the warehouse watching goods coming in and out through the doors. The phones were ringing while we stayed a few minutes as Davide was called over as a conversation started. I assumed it was worked related, which left me to overlook the warehouse.

I could hear raised voices, but this seemed normal with Italians as other colleagues were equally loud-speaking on the phones. We left the office walking further along the riverside until we came across the largest cruiser moored alongside the quay with other smaller boats. We jumped on board from the back, Davide unlocked the cabin climbing down a couple of steps into the living area of the boat, and it was quite large inside with the living room and a separate galley kitchen. The room had all the mod cons with soft furnishings matching the interior. There were three nice size bedrooms and a bathroom.

"Your uncle sometimes used to cruise around to the east side of the country in the boat instead of driving, but he never went alone," said Davide. This must-have cost a fortune, I thought, running my fingers along the side of the interior.

"Davide, what was my uncle like?" I asked, trying to find out more about his lifestyle.

"Well, sit down, and I'll tell you," said Davide patting the bed for me to sit down. I sat waiting for him to start. "As you know, when I first met your uncle, it was in a night club which just happened to be one that he owned. Like I said previously, he was looking for someone as a PA but didn't want a female, and I was cheeky and asked him. Well, he was one for the women, and quite often, I had to help him out when they started to get too serious, having to intervene and seduce them. I can love them and leave them, but your uncle was too nice a guy, so I had to do the dirty."

"I thought you were gay," I said, sounding surprised by what he was saying.

"Oh no, want makes you think I was gay?" asked Davide raising an eyebrow.

"Er well, when you said you were with your boyfriend in the night club when you met my uncle?" I said, thinking if I had misread this.

"No boyfriend is no different to you having a girlfriend as in a friend," said Davide putting his hand on my leg and patting it. Fuck he could have stayed with me at the villa all week making love to me; he was lush.

"Why did you want to jump on me?" he asked, joking with a laugh. I looked at him, grinning.

"I could have fucked you all week," I said with a laugh.

"I was thinking the same thing." his hand cupped my face as he leaned over to kiss me on the lips. I felt a tingle between my legs.

"Davide, make love to me." I breathed. He pushed my back onto the bed as he started to kiss me, his lips working down to my neck as I started to moan to his touch. Within minutes, we were both naked on the bed as he entered me slowly. I wrapped my legs around his fit body, holding him in place needing his length to stay inside me as long as he could take it while we necked each other as the intense pleasure made him come together.

We lay on the bed, breathing heavily from the intense pleasure. I surprised myself with having sex as I had come over to get away from it, but it was different. I was in a different country, and I knew Davide was a bit of a male whore with what he had told me. So what if I was using him as he was using me? Plus, I was supposed to be the boss according to him.

We dressed and walked back to his pad.

"Would you like to eat in or out and maybe go to one of your nightclubs?" said Davide giving me the option to decide.

"I don't mind. I suppose it would be easier to eat out; let's go to the club." I said, looking at his fit body needing him inside me again.

"Ok, let's have shower and change," said Davide giving me a sexy look as to invite me into the shower with him. I went into the bedroom, taking my bags to fish out something suitable for dining and clubbing. I could hear Davide calling me from the shower wanting me to join him.

I stripped off, wrapping a towel around me and padded off to the bathroom. Davide was in the shower waiting for me to join him as I slipped off the towel and stepped in. He enveloped me with his strong arms; I began feeling his hard length next to my body. His lips were soft as they glided over my body, my nipples hardened as his mouth sucked my breasts. I moaned with his touch the sensation started to kick in, my arousal was racing as I was about to explode.

These Italians seemed to be in a different league when it came to making love with high testosterone levels. As the water ran over our bodies, we made love again with him making me explode multiple times. With a final thrust against the shower wall, I gasped, feeling his hardness inside me as he lifted my leg high to gain maximum entry inside me. He then exploded inside me as he kissed me hard on the lips.

It was nearly 7 pm when we arrived at the restaurant.

"Ah, chi e questa bella creatura che hai con te." shouted a voice across the restaurant.

"Questo e Garth Jones, niece," said Davide shouting back to an older man in his sixties.

"I take it you come here often," I said, looking around the restaurant.

"Yes, Mario's pasta is 'magnifico'," shouted Davide as Joseph hugged him like a father. Joseph hugged me and kissed both my cheeks before letting me go. It turned out that Joseph was Davide's father as he explained about the family business being too small to sustain three brothers in the business with Davide following the path of working for my uncle.

We spent a couple of hours of eating and drinking. The food was delicious, including the wine which I found out later to be from my uncle's vineyard. I was enjoying Davide's company as we strolled further into the town to the nightclub. There were more greetings on the door of the nightclub as I joined in with the greetings, hugging, and kissing. I was slightly tipsy, having consumed a couple of bottles of wine with Davide. But I was enjoying myself and was going to make the most of it. We entered the main room that had two levels with the more modern stuff playing downstairs while upstairs was more of my type of music, ROCK.

As time went on, the club started to fill, Davide knew a lot of people as he was greeted with hugs and kisses from both male and female acquaintances. I said to Davide I was going to have a wander around the club and made my way upstairs to the sound of rock music. With another couple more glasses of red wine, I was away in my bubble dancing and singing to the music as guys joined me on the dance floor. I lost track of time as I felt an arm wrap around my waist, joining in with the music; it was Davide with another guy as they both danced with me, enveloping me. It was nice to feel their bodies next to mine. I could feel a sex fix coming on as I put my arms around both of their necks, bringing them both down for a kiss. They both sandwiched me holding me tight as I could feel they were both aroused while I was on fire ready to explode with the drink and good music to dance to.

Davide's boyfriend was Antonio. It was after 1 am as we walked back to Davide's pad. Antonio came with us, and I guessed that he lived further down the road. He was staying with Davide for the night.

"Mm, this is going to be interesting." I thought. Davide made coffee thinking that I needed to sober up, but I wasn't that drunk only a little tipsy and was having fun since god knows when.

"Come on, boys, I need some fun," I shouted as I sipped the coffee.

"What sort of fun would you like?" asked Davide running his fingers across my mouth.

"Hmm, now that takes a lot to think about." I grinned, looking at Antonio as he raised a brow. "How about both of you make love to me for the rest of the night," I said, standing up, kissing Davide on the lips softly as I floated across to Antonio, kissing him on his lips softly before disappearing into Davide's bedroom.

I was laid with Davide, and Antonio naked sandwiched between them, their naked bodies, and hard lengths ready for some fun. I put both of my arms around them with my legs apart over their legs needing to explode. Their mouths are playing with each of my breasts as their fingers entered inside me to the maximum penetration to explode. My moans were intense as they kept me pushing me to the edge. I was being sent to space and stars and back with the sensation.

"Come on, boys, fuck me, and I'll bring you both up again." We spent the rest of the early hours fucking and sucking. The Italian stallions kept it up until the sun came up. I was nearly flagging hot, sweating, and needed a shower with so much sex and the bedroom smelling like a brothel.

Antonio needed to go to work, leaving us in bed falling asleep until midday. When I woke up, the bed was empty, leaving me to stretch out, having to nurse a slightly bad headache. I could hear Davide banging about in the kitchen. I hoped he was making coffee, my mouth felt dry needing lubrication of some sort, as I had done a lot of sucking during the early hours with two guys enjoying my moment of madness with them. I had acted like a total slut. Fuck it; I didn't care after hearing the conversation between Lara and Lloyd calling me a trollop and a bit of rough.

Davide padded through into the bedroom, holding two mugs of coffee. I opened one eye seeing him placing them down on the bedside cabinet, jumping back into the bed with me. I groaned as my head started to throb from the amount of drink I consumed from last night to the early hours of the morning. But it was worth it, especially having two gorgeous men in bed giving me so much pleasure and sex. I turned over to sit up, asking Davide to pass me my coffee.

"Here you are, boss,"

said Davide passing me my coffee.

"I'm not your boss yet." I snapped, taking the mug of coffee from him, sounding half asleep.

"Well, in my eyes, you are," said Davide patting me on the leg. We both drank our coffee in silence for a few minutes.

"So what are we doing today?" asked Davide sounding upbeat despite having drinking wine last night.

"I need to get my head sorted, have you any headache tablets I can take?" I asked.

"Here, I thought you might need them." Smiled Davide, passing a couple of tablets across from the bedside cabinet.

"Oh, you're a darling, Davide." I swallowed them with a gulp of coffee. "I need a shower, Davide shower with me," I asked, groaning from my headache.

"I'll help you, boss," said Davide sounding sorry for my condition.

I got up and managed to get into the shower with Davide having the shower running ready for me to enter. He held me while the water ran over our bodies.

"Ah, Davide, you are a good person." I groaned, leaning on him.

"You need more coffee," said Davide ignoring my comment.

"Yeah, I suppose, you're right." I lifted my head to the showerhead for the water to pour over my head and face. It seemed to knock some sense into me. Davide started to wash my body with a sponge; I stood there as if I was being body searched for drugs, his hands giving me a thorough rub down. It was nice, especially on my breasts and wetness.

"Davide, you are arousing me," I said as my fingers started curling his hair further while he washed between my legs. My groaning turned into moaning with pleasure, and I spread my leg further apart.

I didn't have to ask as Davide's mouth was on my wetness, dropping the sponge to insert his fingers inside me. I kept moaning as he increased the pressure, his mouth coming up to my breasts, and his other hand cupping my breast.

"Davide, take me." I moaned. He lifted me onto his length, pressing me against the shower wall while holding me up by my buttocks. I shimmy a little to feel his length inside me, god it felt so good as my wetness exploded my headache felt so distant.

Davide made some more coffee while I finished off in the shower washing my hair. Fifteen minutes later, I padded through wearing a light robe into the kitchen as Davide poured out the coffee. I sat on the kitchen stool with my head in hands leaning on the countertop with a coffee in front of me.

"Do you feel up to going to the vineyard today? We would be stopping in the villa up there," said Davide testing my enthusiasm.

"Yeah, just gives us half an hour to get going." I groaned now. I was out of the shower.

Within the hour, we were on our way, travelling the East coast to the vineyard and the villa. I was looking forward to seeing the villa to compare it with the one on the outskirts of the town being next door to Enrico Caputo. We had at least a 4-hour journey stopping for a break halfway to stretch our legs with Davide's car being so small. It was dark when we arrived at the vineyard, with the villa being further down the track. We were greeted by a dark-haired woman in her late fifties.

"Ciao Davide sei un po in ritardo." said the dark-haired woman shouting.

"Si eravamo in ritardo partier, spero che ci hai fatto quell bel piatto di pasta che si utilizza per are per Garth." said Davide shouting back.

"Qualsiasi relazione die Garth avra rispetto e il miglior cibo." said the dark hair woman waving us into the villa.

With it being dark, I couldn't see the full size of the place as I was trying to compare it with the one down on the west coast of Italy but would have to wait until the morning. Davide introduced me to the woman as Maria being the housekeeper and cook when my uncle lived here. She had served up a delicious meal being pasta with red wine. I just had one glass needing a clear head for the next day. Maria showed me to my room. It was beautiful and airy, having a four-poster bed, which reminded me of Alex and Lloyd's bed.

I wondered where Davide was, as he had disappeared. I walked through into the living room, which was so spacious having three large sofas and open views from one side of the room, but couldn't see outside with it being so dark. I could hear Davide talking to Maria in the kitchen as I walked into the kitchen to find out what Davide was doing.

"Davide, I'm going to bed. Are you coming?" I asked, hoping to have his body next to mine.

"I will be gone for about half an hour. I need to go down to the office to check something," said Davide sounding a little concerned.

"Oh, do you want me to come with you?" I asked, concerned there was a problem.

"No, it's ok. I just need to check if an order has been dispatched for one of the new customers," said Davide coming over to kiss me on the cheek.

"Mm, ok, I'll see you later." I padded off to jump into bed.

I was woken by a mouth on my core and my legs apart. My arousal kicked in by the sensation as I started moaning with pleasure, I pulled the cover back as Davide started coming up, taking my breasts in hands, kissing and licking my nipples. I couldn't stop moaning; he was pressing all my right buttons of pleasure. He fondled my breasts and nipples for at least ten minutes I wriggled exploding with his touch moaning as I whispered Davide to enter me. His length slipped in as he held it inside me, kissing my neck and, eventually, my lips with passion as he pumped me, reaching my climax with him.

We lay there while our breathing receded.

"Davide, had my uncle ever thought about marriage?"
I asked, wondering.

"No, he couldn't stick to one woman long enough,
he was a ladies man; he loved sex too much," said Davide. I
must have some of his genes in me, I thought.

"You have a high sex drive like him," said Davide
turning over to touch my cheek.

"I suppose I do," I replied, thinking about it.

"These parties he used to have what were they like?"
I asked, now curious.

"You really want to know?"
asked Davide sounding surprised

"Yeah."

"They were mainly sex parties, orgies I suppose,
couples and singles mixed with plenty of wine," said
Davide smiling.

"I wish I was there," I whispered.

"Did you go?" I asked, even more curious.

"But of course I had to arrange it, and had to make sure everything ran smoothly," said Davide grinning.

"Did you participate?" I asked, feeling slightly jealous of women being pleasured by him.

"Sometimes, but I had to be on call all night," said Davide kissing me on my lips.

How I now missed knowing my uncle? His lifestyle, I would love it money and plenty of sex. But there was one thing missing, did anyone love him as a person and not for what he had, that was the question.

I turned to Davide, "I am going to give you a good blow job after which you can fuck me as many times as you like all night." I pounced on his length and started to tease his length ridged sucking so hard he soon came, his pleasure was so intense.

"Caz, I have never had anyone give me a blow job like you do." He commented as he came back down from his orbit. Davide pumped me every half hour making me come with him until 6 am until we fell asleep in each other's arms.

Despite it being morning, we both were showered and out for 10 am. I could now see the views from the living room; they were spectacular, overlooking the pool and vineyard as far as the eye could see. The villa was as large as the other one on the west coast but did not have the beautiful scenery of the vineyard with the hills far in the distances. It was the end of the harvest season; we strolled along the track down to the pickers and the machinery with last few grapes being picked for the factory, being processed on-site with some bottled and the remaining poured into vats to mature for a couple of years in temperature-controlled buildings.

Davide showed me around the factory; there was a strong fruity smell from the grapes being processed as wine bottles made their way along the conveyor to be filled.

It felt great knowing it all belonged to me. I inhaled the smell of fruit and the gardens. I would never miss home in a place like that.

Chapter Sixteen

Davide explained that there were a variety of grapes and the wine made from them varies from the cheap to the expensive end of the market; this also depends on the variety of the soil type to make quality wine. We spent a good four hours walking and talking about the business, how my uncle started small and managed to expand to the size he was today. I was so impressed now knowing why my uncle couldn't take me on when I was fifteen. He was only twenty-five at that time, and since then, he had worked very hard. But I wished I had known him before he died.

I had forgotten when I was there last time; I should have gone to the police station to find out about my uncle's death, instead of indulging in pleasures of sex. I must go when we get back to David's place; I made a mental note

Maria had made us a meal when we arrived back from the tour of the site. My stomach snarled as we walked in, smelling her cooking. I just had time for a quick shower and sex in there with Davide joining me. We sat and ate the delicious meal before we departed, making our way back, which would be late.

We packed our few things and hugged Maria goodbye before setting off for the long journey back. I was pleased Davide was driving, as not getting much sleep last night was catching up with me, sex was a tiring job.

It was after 11 pm by the time we got back; I was knackered despite sleeping on the way back. I didn't know how Davide was so lively with so little sleep. I supposed one must get used to it, not knowing what hours he worked. We were climbing into bed by midnight after having half an hour of rampant sex before settling down to sleep. God, I was becoming a total slut over here.

Davide was up early and made me a coffee before going into work. Fuck, he reminded me of Russ bringing me coffee in the morning before going to work, how surreal that was. Davide said he wouldn't be gone too long, probably a couple of hours, depending on if there were any problems. We kissed before he left, I laid back now having the bed to myself to stretch out in. I drank my coffee and got up for a pee before jumping back into bed, curling up to go back to sleep.

A mouth woke me over my wetness; I stretched out for Davide to consume more of me. It was a nice feeling waking up to being eaten and then exploding with desire; he just knew how to press the right buttons. My sex drive was on fire with Davide sliding inside me. I wrapped my legs around him, I couldn't get enough of his perfect lush lips, but I let him go releasing him to penetrate me harder.

"Davide, treat me like a slut." I whispered.

"I can't do that to you; you are a perfect lover to me," whispered Davide.

"Please, Davide, I need this." I insisted.

"Mm, your wish is my command." He pulled out and rolled me over, spreading my legs apart to enter me from the back in doggy fashion. He slid in hard and took hold of my hair, pulling it back as he pumped me harder. I moaned with ecstasy, enjoying the roughness he endured on me, finally finding my climax with him.

We spent the rest of the morning sucking and fucking until midday. I got up in a hurry, in need of a shower, washing the morning sex with a quick one in the shower before getting out to dry myself and dressed for the day. Davide made coffee as I sat on the kitchen stool, watching his perfect body, so taut and tanned and lush, he was sex on legs.

"My lover, what are we doing today?" asked Davide handing me a mug of coffee. I raised a brow grinning as I looked at him.

"I know what we are doing tonight." I flicked my brows, grinning.

"I thought so," said Davide kissing my neck as he sent a tingle through my body.

"I need to go to the police station to ask about my uncle's death," I said, sipping my coffee.

"Yeah, that's no problem; we can go when you're ready," said Davide hugging me. It was nearly 2 pm went we arrived at the police station. I was surprised how small the building was, sandwiched between two three-story high flats and with a metal gate for the police vehicle to enter around the back. Davide parked his vehicle further down the road due to a couple of police vehicles parked outside the building. The door was straight off the pavement going through double doors into a small reception area. I rang the bell on the counter for assistance, digging out my passport as identification, ready to ask the questions about my uncle's death.

An average built guy with short dark hair came through the side door looking rather miserable as though things weren't going well in the back office.

"'Si?" said the guy resting his elbows on the counter under duress. I turned to Davide.

"Davide, would you ask him about my uncle, please?" Davide explained with a few grunts and groans from the officer before walking back through the side door. Ten minutes later, the door opened again as a tall willowy guy with short dark hair came through smiling as he approached us.

"Hello, signora, my name is detective Dino Grasso; what would you liked to know?" asked the officer.

"Hi, er I would like to know about Garth Jones, I was told that the police were investigating his death with the possibility that his death may be suspicious."

"Aah, yes, I vaguely remember, he was found in his car off the road," said Dino rubbing his chin.

"Yeah, so was it suspicious?" I asked, desperate to know.

"No, he had some drug in his blood that would have caused him to run off the road." said the detective trying to sound convincing.

"No, that can't be true," I shouted. "He didn't take drugs." I was annoyed by his comment. "So is that it then? Case closed?" my eyes started to moisten.

"Sorry, signora, but yes." He looked at me as if to say just go. It sounded like an open and shut case to me, but what could I do about it. Without even knowing and meeting my uncle, I felt I knew him and the lifestyle he had. I was gutted walking out of the police station as tears started to flow. Davide put his arm around me, giving me some comfort as we headed back to his car.

"What do you think, Davide?" I asked, wiping my face with my fingers.

"Mm same as you, but what can you do?" said Davide shrugging.

We drove back in silence while my mind was thinking about what Enrico had said at the funeral about unfinished business. Would he be the sort of guy to have had my uncle killed, and if so, what for?

It was after 3 pm when I left the police station without really finding the truth out on my uncle's death. Davide asked if I wanted to go out to his father's restaurant and the night club after? Well, I didn't want to dwell on my uncle's death, so a drink was in order. By the time we hit the night club, it was after 11 pm; we spent some time with

Davide's parents as his mother could speak a little English and helped out a little as the restaurant became busy.

The night club was heaving for it being a Friday night. I had not drunk as much as previously but was merry and was enjoying the atmosphere. Davide was a magnet as the females were chatting him up and giggling as I was dancing and could see from a distance. If Davide was my man, I would have thrown daggers at them; the problem was that Davide knew he was sex on legs and could charm a snake. He was a total male slut, but I loved him for my closeness needs.

While I danced, someone grabbed my waist, knowing it wasn't Davide, I turned around to find Antonio. I wrapped my arms around him, kissing him on his lips as he hugged me closer, feeling the heat between us. His tight black leather trousers made him look sexy with his loose white shirt. I was wondering if he was going to come back with us to have another replay of all-night sex. Davide could see me with

Antonio and came over as they hugged each other with fist bumps. It was getting on for 1 am when Davide asked if I was ready to go.

We all went back to Davide's place to enjoy the rest of the early hours of pure lust of hot sex with two gorgeous male sluts, and I loved every minute with them. Antonio didn't work on Saturdays, so he stayed with us until noon, the bed smelt like a brothel with so much sex. We needed a shower; both guys joined me both washing my body from top to bottom.

My flight home was early Sunday morning, so the rest of Saturday was a leisurely walk along the riverfront and a little window shopping in the town centre. Davide had to go into the office to check that everything was ok and would catch me up later in the day. Antonio walked with me into the town city before I said my goodbyes to him for the last time before I departed to the airport.

Davide cooked as it was my last night with him. He was a good cook, but I suppose that would be expected with his parents having a restaurant business. I spent a romantic night of passion with him until it was time to go to the airport. I was gutted now, leaving him despite only knowing he was a straight guy for the few days I had stayed with him.

We parted at the airport as I started to shed a few tears, and promised him that I would phone him as soon as I had seen the solicitor about my uncle's estate. My memories wandered through my mind as I settled in the seat of the plane for over three and a half hours. It was an eye-opener seeing my uncle's business still running like clockwork despite my uncle gone. I just wished I had the chance to have met him. Now I knew why I had to go into the care home; he was young and had to make his way up the ladder. It was sad, but he must have thought of me in some way or another for the solicitor to be in touch with me.

After I had cleared customs, I headed for the car park, but where do I go? I thought. Either back to the flat or Lloyd's place. Seeing it was just after midday, I thought I would check on the flat to see if Russ was behaving himself having a ban on women in the flat. I pulled up outside the flat; it seemed quiet as I unlocked the door. The flat was tidy, considering I hadn't been around for a few days and with it being a weekend. There had been no signs of him having a woman in the flat, as I gave the flat a quick scan around the rooms. I wondered where he was, probably in some bird's bed he picked up during a night out with the lads. But I had to wind my neck in about him and let him go only using him as my fuck buddy.

By the time I arrived at Lloyd's place, it was nearly 4.30 pm; I just hoped his snobby sister wasn't lecturing him on his sex life. I pulled in the entrance as the gates opened, I drove up to the house. There was no car in sight, thank fuck for that I thought as I pulled up to stop the engine thinking about Lloyd. Then I remembered he was over at a party with his sister's crowd this weekend. I still had feelings for him, but what did he think of me? I jumped out and dragged my bags off the front seat of the van.

The door was locked. I was surprised thinking Lloyd would have been back from the weekend party. At least he did give me a key to the house, which was on the keyring with the gate fob. I needed some laundry washing, so I went into the laundry room to sort out my things for the wash, after which I went upstairs to sort out the rest of my clothes. The bed looked as though it hadn't been slept in. I was starting to feel a little unsettled was he with Lucy, the woman that Lara had mentioned to him at his sister's party? She had insisted he had to go knowing that Lucy would be there. My mind was working over the thoughts of the two of them together now he had come out of his depression but had sent me into one. I needed a work out having to destress hard in the pool.

I spent over an hour in the pool swimming hard until I was beaten with exhaustion, after which I took a hot shower turning up the heat to burn my skin. I needed the pain on my body to match the pain in my heart. After I dried myself off now having blotches of red skin with the heat; I slipped my short robe and scooted down to the kitchen to make something quick and a coffee. I switched the TV in the living room to watch expecting Lloyd to be home soon, but 10.30 pm had come around with Lloyd still not turning up, so I decided to go to bed. I felt lonely knowing I was on my own, tears fell on the pillow until I fell asleep.

It was Monday morning; I woke up hearing the rain beating on the window in the dark, it was 5 am, and the bed was empty, still no Lloyd. Where the hell was he? I wondered; Do I text him, asking him where he was? Or was that being too nosey? Mm, I'll just send him a text to say that I am back, I decided. I couldn't start work until 8 am as it was with the council, so I decided to get up and stick a few more tiles on in Lloyd's shower room.

Lloyd had texted me saying that he wouldn't be back the rest of the week, not giving anything away. My heart sank, knowing I was on my own in this house, so do I go home to my flat or stay to finish off Lloyd's shower room after work to finish his job completed and decide where I went from there? Alex had been phoning me every day, leaving voice mails as I didn't want to speak to him as the week went by.

By Friday, the work with the council had been completed on time, leaving early Friday at 2 pm. I just had a little bit more to finish off Lloyd's job in the shower room to complete his job. I had to speak with him regarding me staying not feeling comfortable with the situation when I next saw him. I had just remembered I hadn't checked to see if Alex had paid me for the office space that Jess needed for him, so I scrolled through my account to find he hadn't paid me as Jess said he would. Oh fuck, I would have to speak with him now since I had been avoiding him all week.

It was nearly 8 pm by the time I had complete Lloyds shower room. He should be pleased with it as I had added a little colour with the tiles, so it didn't look too clinical. By now my phone was ringing, it was Alex.

"Hi, I was about to phone you," I said, sounding surprised he had rung.

"Caz, where the fuck have you been? I've been phoning you every day," said Alex slightly miffed but relieved that he was speaking to me now.

"Yeah, I know I've been that busy," I said, lying to him but sounding convincing. "I was about to phone you anyway; you haven't paid me for the job, Jess said that you would sort it out and would be in my account last weekend."

"Yeah, I'm sorry about that, but 1 will pay you tomorrow, but would you spend some time with me?" asked Alex sounding as though this was blackmail.

"Alex, we have been down this road before. I give you an inch, and now you're taking a yard." I said, exasperated.

"Look, Caz, just one more time, and I will pay you generously," said Alex trying to persuade me.

"Alex, I need paying, and I am not a whore." I said, raising my voice a little.

"Oh, Caz, don't take it the wrong way, please, Caz, just one more time," pleaded Alex. I hummed and thought it was the only way I was going to be paid and could get Alex off my back.

"Yeah, ok, then just this once and pay me as soon as I arrive," I said, being firm with his demands.

"Yes, no problem, just come around on Saturday at 9 am," said Alex sounding pleased.

"What about Jess?" I asked.

"Oh, she is doing something else, don't worry about her," said Alex.

"Mm, ok, I'll see you then." I ended the call. I wondered what Jess was doing, especially this time of the year as the holiday season had finished plus the weather was a lot chilly and wet.

I had a late workout in the pool, and by the time I had eaten, it was nearly midnight. Lloyd was still away. I was getting lonely now and was glad in one way that I had agreed to see Alex Saturday morning for a day of pleasuring despite being slightly blackmailed into it.

The following morning, I woke up hearing the rain beating on the window panes as the wind howled. I turned over, eyeing the time on the clock; it was only 6 am. I stretched out, thinking what the fuck am I doing with my life? I had to prostitute my body to get paid.

"Oh well, it's only today, and it should be the end of it, I'd be more careful in future with these posh clients," I promised myself.

I turned up at Alex's house just before 9 am wearing black leggings and a baggy navy jumper and knee-high boots. Alex had seen me arrive and waited for me at the door. He whistled at me and slapped my butt as I walked in.

"Ouch, that's a bit hard." I protested.

"You'll be getting something harder in a minute." Alex grabbed hold of me, pushing me against the hallway wall and started pulling at my clothing while kissing me hard on the lips.

"Alex, Alex, wait." I pushed him back, "before we start, you said you would pay me for the job."

"Yeah, ok, I'll sort it out now." He went off to grab his laptop to have the money transferred.

Within a few minutes, he was back having had transferred the money over. I checked my account on my phone.

"Alex, are you sure this is right?" I asked, puzzled by the amount he had transferred across.

"Yes, why?" Alex asked, surprised.

"You have paid me too much," I said.

"No, I haven't; you have turned my sex life around," said Alex grinning.

"Oh, so this is the last time?"
I asked double-checking.

"Hmm, but you're in for a treat," said Alex, smirking.

"Yeah? so what's that?" I asked curiously.

"Don't worry, you will enjoy it," said Alex taking my hand, pulling me towards the stairs.

We entered the same bedroom where we had our first encounter. As soon as we were in the bedroom, Alex pushed me onto the bed, fully clothed. Resistance was futile as he was bursting to seduce my body.

I was soon naked, and Alex had restrained my wrists and ankles, Alex soon dived in fucking me hard in a frenzy. It felt good after not having sex for a week. His hands and mouth, pressing hard over my body. My wetness kicked in as he went down to drink it in savouring every drop of me. For nearly three hours of pleasuring and fucking me, he said that he was going to blindfold me. I was a little concerned about not seeing what was going to happen. But I had no option being restrained. It felt a little scary, especially being naked and vulnerable. Alex continued pleasuring me as I could hear the bedroom door open quietly, but no voices spoke.

I could feel Alex get up off the bed, but within a few seconds, a mouth was on my wetness. It wasn't Alex's; it felt lighter as the tongue worked around my entrance as a fist entered me. I soon climaxed as the mouth drank my wetness as I moaned with the new sensation. The mouth travelled up to my breasts, sucking my nipples massaging gently, and finally, the lips were on mine. The person kissed me as their tongue entered mine while massaging my breasts. Suddenly a mouth was on my wetness. Two people were seducing my body, but who was it? As they both seduced my body, I kept on climaxing, my wetness being sucked away, drying me of my juices. My entrance was being fucked, but it felt as though it was a sex toy. As time went on, they both fucked and sucked my body as sweat started to pour off me with the pleasure they subjected to me.

With breaks of drinking through a straw, with them not wanting to release me, I wondered how long this would last. I seemed to have been blindfolded for hours, not knowing the time of day. But still, I had no one to go home to.

"Alex, what time is it?" I asked.

"Its late afternoon," said Alex.

"Alex, could you please take the blindfold off me?" I asked, now feeling a little suffocated.

"Mm ok, but don't be annoyed when I take it off," said Alex as he untied my blindfolds while a mouth circled my wetness, making me climax.

I was gobsmacked to find it was Jess drinking me. She had turned a corner sexually; also looks can be deceiving I would have thought she would have been the last person batting for the other side so to speak. I must say women feel different than men being gentle with a soft touch.

"Caz, I'm sorry we had to do it this way you wouldn't have had agreed otherwise," said Jess kissing me on the lips. I was lost for words. "Would you stay the night with us?" asked Jess kissing my neck down to suck my nipple. Mm, why not? I had no one to go home for, I thought, saying yes I would but needed something to eat and a shower.

Once my restraints were off, and I had been refreshed, fed, and watered by 7 pm, we all were back on the bed without the restraints, now to be a total slut with her husband as Jess watched and learned. It was a good thing Alex had a little helping hand with his erection, making him hard for most of the night while Jess and I worked him. Alex eventually ran out of steam around 2 am, so I continued to seduce Jess using her sex toy, making her climax multiple times, taking it in turns until Jess could not take anymore. I had fucked them both senseless. What a result.

I left the following morning around 10 am, having an invitation to have a threesome again. I said I would think about it; now I had been paid for the job which got me in this mess in the first place. Jess had asked me about refurbishing the other outbuilding at some stage, but I said it would be quite sometime before I could get around to doing it.

I was in the living room with my feet up on the sofa watching the TV when Lloyd turned up. I jumped up, looking excited to see him.

"Hi, Lloyd, long time no see?" I said, kissing him on the cheek.

"Oh, Caz, I am so sorry I haven't been here for you, but I'm here now," said Lloyd sounding apologetic kissing me on the lips softly enveloping me in his arms as his kiss turned more passionate. I felt tingles going through my body; his smile looked so refreshing in his black polo sweater and jeans. I just hoped Lucy hadn't stuck her claws into him last weekend at the party.

Chapter Seventeen

After making coffee, we laid on the sofa with Lloyd, asking me about my week. I told him I had been over to Italy to find out more about my uncle's death. I told him that I was suspicious about his death but couldn't prove anything with the police not being particularly helpful. I did not mention about my uncle's businesses and the type of lifestyle he was leading out there. Lloyd sympathized with me about the police being unhelpful as with some of the police was being run by the drugs cartel, according to him. Lloyd mentioned he had been to his sister's party that weekend staying a few days with the rest of the week sorting out a few things at work, but not going into any detail about the party or his work, so I didn't push it.

"Fancy a swim?" I asked, needing to destress now he was back.

"Yes, I'll nip up and get the towels," said Lloyd as he lifted himself off the sofa. By the time he had jumped into the pool, I had swum six lengths. I continued to swim hard with Lloyd half a length behind me. Half an hour later, I stopped to have a breather while Lloyd caught up with me.

"Caz, I know something is troubling you, tell me," asked Lloyd sounded concerned as he stroked my cheek.

"No, I'm alright," I said, giving him a false smile.

"Caz, you're not; I know that you only swim like this when you have something on your mind," said Lloyd coming over to hug me.

"I think I have outstayed my welcome here," I whispered, avoiding eye contact with him.

"What's brought this on?" asked Lloyd, his hand cupping my chin to look into my eyes.

"Your sister doesn't like me, does she?" I asked in a neutral tone.

"She doesn't know you," said Lloyd kissing my lips softly.

"I heard what she was saying about me when I went to make coffee last week. She thinks I'm a gold digger and a trollop and a bit of rough." I said, my eyes started to well up, and a tear managed to escape the corner of my eye.

"Oh, Caz, don't take any notice of what she says, she says that about everyone," said Lloyd, wrapping his arms around me.

"So, what about Lucy?" I said, sniffing a little as my tears started falling.

"She's a friend of my sister's, and she wants me to take her out, but she is such a bore and only thinks of herself, not only that I'm not interested in her. You, on the other hand, are beautiful, caring, and thoughtful and so much fun," said Lloyd trying to convince me. I hugged him, wanting him to say more to convince me, but he didn't.

What did I expect? Was I a stop-gap until he found his perfect partner again to be by his side for always? I suppose I could always go back to Italy to be a total slut for Davide and Antonio, but I wasn't getting any younger with time moving on what would happen to me then?

I pulled away from Lloyd, splashing him to get his attention for a bit of fun, swimming off to the end of the pool, but Lloyd was quick in grabbing my ankle as he dragged me under the water. I struggled managing him to lose his grip as I made it to the end of the pool. I waited until Lloyd caught up with me.

"You have a good kick," said Lloyd sounding surprised that I had managed to escape his grip.

"Hmm, I used to do kickboxing, it does come in handy sometimes," I said, giving him a peck on the cheek.

"You are full of surprises," said Lloyd, now pressing his body against mine on the side of the pool kissing my neck. I started to melt and was about to wrap my leg around his waist, feeling his length hard waiting for my entrance, but I was distracted by him touching my body. He caught me unaware, grabbing hold of me, pushing me under the water hard as he swam off to the other end of the pool. I came up gasping for air, taken by surprise. Lloyd was grinning at me as I came up. This was war; I swam to him diving under to pull his feet off the bottom of the pool. We finished playing fight with each other for nearly half an hour before we both gave in exhausted.

Lloyd cooked for the both of us having replenished stocks in the kitchen when he had returned home after over a week. I was spoilt having someone to cook for me while I made the coffee and sat on the kitchen stool watching him.

"So, what did you do while you were over in Italy?" asked Lloyd, making conversation. I couldn't tell him that I had been a total slut and bedding two gorgeous Italian studs in bed at the same time having constant sex for hours. So I opted for my encounter with the attack in the villa and how I had to use my kickboxing experience from my younger days to survive my ordeal with my opponent, clinging to his meat and two vegs.

Lloyd was astonished to hear what had happened to me and was impressed to hear that kickboxing had helped in the situation.

"Caz, why didn't you let me know? I would have come with you if you had asked me," said Lloyd hugging me.

"It was something I had to do on my own," I said, knowing I couldn't face him at the time and needed to get away.

After a delicious meal, we took our coffees into the living room to settle down for the evening to watch TV on the sofa. By 9 pm we were in bed making love; I had missed him for over a week. I gave him my heart and soul and was in love with everything about him. He said that he had missed me while he was away; he just wished that he had been with me when I had gone. I felt more relaxed, did he have any feelings for me? Time would tell.

The only problem I had was my sex life in general; my need to be close to people would be interpreted seeing me as a slag. It would probably catch up with me at some stage in my life.

6 am had soon come around, I could have stayed in bed making love to Lloyd all day, but I had a living to earn, so I made an effort to get up. Lloyd had his naked

body wrapped around mine as though he did not want to release me. I stirred to get out of the bed, but Lloyd held onto me, he was awake.

"Caz stay a little longer," asked Lloyd, gently cupping my breast and kissing my shoulder.

"Lloyd, I need to get up for work," I said half heartily. But resistance was futile as he straddled over me, making love to me passionately.

It was after 9 am when I arrived on site. I had told Eve I would be there before 8 am when I had phoned her after getting back from Alex and Jess's place.

"Sorry I'm late, something came up," I said, making my apologies and grinning within.

"Oh, it's ok you're here now," said Eve, accepting my apology.

The skip was due to arrive at lunchtime, giving me a chance to make some space inside the outbuilding. It was going to take two skips, and the next day to clear the building before starting the primary job, I was employed to do. I was back at Lloyd's home just after 5 pm with a meal ready for me as I had texted him before leaving work. I didn't have time to shower as the meal was hot, and he had already served it up on the plates. I was covered in dust and dirt, needing a shower desperately, but Lloyd sat with me around the kitchen table to eat.

After my meal, I thanked him, kissing him on the cheek before going upstairs for a much-needed shower. My hair needed washing with all the dust thrown into the skip. I must have been in the shower for at least 15 minutes before I felt a presence behind me. Lloyd had stripped off to join me, I had nearly finished, but with him in the shower, I could never have enough of it.

Eve's job was taking longer than I thought, and I had to put a halt to it with the council phoning me to say that they had released another house to refurbish. I was pleased in one way mainly because I could spend more time in bed with Lloyd having to go to work for 8 am and finishing at 4 pm. Over the weeks, it felt like we were newly-weds making love as soon as we were together. I had started to fall in love with him as our loving making was so intense and explosive. I couldn't get enough of this man. I had never had feelings for anyone like this before.

My appointment with the solicitor had soon come around. I sat in the reception area, flicking through the magazines but not taking anything in. Jill, Mr Johnson's secretary, came through after half an hour of waiting.

"Sorry, Miss Jones, but Mr Johnson had to go home in a hurry; I can't apologies enough. Could we phone you when he is available?" asked Mr Johnson's secretary, sounding apologetic.

I was a little miffed now that I had to wait again.

"So how long will that be? I had to wait six weeks for this one." I said with a sigh.

"His wife has had a car accident and has been rushed to the hospital," said Jill sounding concerned for her boss.

"Oh, I'm sorry, yes, no problem. I'll just have to wait," I said, picking my bag up to go. I phoned Davide on the way back to my van, explaining I was no further forward with the solicitor not knowing what was happening to my uncle's estate. Davide said that he missed me, and so did Antonio. I bet mainly because I was a total slut with them both, but I still enjoyed the pleasure of them both together. I said that I would let him know as soon as I had found anything out and would phone him. After a quick chat, I ended the call, finding that I had gained another parking ticket on the van.

After waiting for half an hour and then being told he had to leave and to top it all, I finished up with another £60 parking ticket and had to fight my way through the city traffic. You could say I was a little pissed off. I banged the door shut; still uptight over the last wasted couple of hours costing me £60. I needed to take it all out in the pool. Lloyd was in his study typing on his laptop when I entered. He looked up, seeing I wasn't thrilled and stopped typing.

"Caz has something happened?" asked Lloyd, standing up to hug. I explained what had happened that I how, I had waited six weeks for the appointment and finally finished with a £60 parking fine.

"I'm going for a swim," I said, turning to walk off.

"I'll join you shortly, I'll bring the towels," said Lloyd as he continued typing.

By the time Lloyd had joined me, I had done twenty hard lengths of the pool; I had continued working hard until

I was exhausted. Lloyd could see I had things on my mind and came over, cupping my chin kissing me on the lips. He melted my heart, wrapping my body around him my tongue down his throat; I needed him inside me.

"Lloyd, make love to me," I whispered. He spun me around, pushing me against the side of the pool his length hard and waiting to enter me.

After a delicious steak and chips, Lloyd had cooked, and a leisurely evening in the living room on the sofa watching the TV, we finally went to bed at 10 pm. Despite my work out in the pool, I needed to feel pain. We had just made love as we lay there in silence.

"Lloyd, when you are ready, could you fuck me as hard as you can?" I asked, wanting to feel pain inside. Lloyd turned onto his side, his fingers touching my cheek.

"Caz, I don't want to hurt you, why do you want me to fuck you hard as I can?" asked Lloyd sounding concerned.

"Please, Lloyd, don't ask. I need it." I said, not wanting to explain to him that it was all about him. Lloyd hesitated, not knowing whether he could do it, being well endowed in that department, and knowing it would probably hurt me. "Lloyd, please do it for me," I begged him.

We lay together for another half hour in silence.

"Lloyd, are you ready?" I asked, sounding desperate.

"Yes, but tell me if it hurts you, I will stop," said Lloyd compromising.

"Hmm, ok," I said, knowing that I wouldn't. Lloyd slipped over me as I parted my legs for him to enter me.

"Are you sure you still want this?" asked Lloyd, still sounding concerned for me.

"Yes," I said, my voice slightly raised. He pushed his hard well-endowed length inside me, waiting to pump me hard.

"Lloyd fuck me hard," I shouted, feeling his length inside me, and he started to pump. "Harder, harder." I kept on saying as his speed went into top gear, I could now feel slight pain, but it wasn't good enough, "harder Lloyd, I need it harder." I yelled as he pushed harder. He was pushing hard, causing me to slide up the bed slightly. The pain was intense as he pumped me hard, his thick length filling me inside to the max. Lloyd was about to come. "Harder!" I shouted the pain so intense I felt as though I was bleeding. Lloyd climaxed and kissed me on the lips. "Stay inside me, Lloyd," I asked despite the pain I endured. I loved him so much he could have done anything he wanted to me; I needed his heart.

"Caz, are you ok?" asked Lloyd sounding concerned that I didn't stop him.

"Yeah, I am now." I kissed him gently on the lips. Lloyd rolled off me as I turned over, his hand resting on my breast with his leg over my body snuggling up to my back.

His body radiated heat after his vigorous work out inside me until we both fell asleep.

The following morning, I was up early, I was surprised to see Lloyd still fast asleep. I was lucky; I was not bleeding with the hard sex. It reminded me I was due to start my period, which he had been very understanding about since I had been here.

It was running up to Christmas as most of the building trade finished for Christmas. I still hadn't finished Eve's refurbishment due to the council releasing monies for several houses to be completed by the end of the tax year.

I wondered what Lloyd was doing over the Christmas period; he hadn't said anything as yet. So I approached the subject and asked him.

"Sorry, Caz. I didn't know how to tell you, but I have to go to Emma's parents as we used to when she was still alive," said Lloyd sounding uncomfortable. I didn't know what to say but tried to keep a brave face on.

"Oh ok, no problem, my friend Tina asked me what I was doing because she wanted me to stay over," I said, lying to him. I was going to be on my own I was gutted I thought Lloyd had got over the death of his wife and hearing this was about to tip me over the edge.

"When are you going?" I asked curiously, thinking of where I could go over the Christmas period, I wasn't too sure about Russ knowing that he would have a woman in tow somewhere. Then it came to me; I would phone Davide to see what he was doing. Davide was pleased to hear from me saying I was welcome to stay over as long as I wanted and would pick me up from the airport as soon as I had my flight booked. I could have finished Eve's refurbishment and get paid straight away or go and spend some time with Davide. It was a no brainer; I was soon heading for the airport I needed closeness.

Davide was waiting at the airport with a broad smile on his face. We hugged and kissed r as Davide took hold of my bag as we walked to the car.

"I hope you don't mind me coming over," I said, sounding apologetic.

"I'm glad you have come over. I miss you, and so does Antonio," said Davide sounding genuine.

"Mm, thanks," I said, hugging him once more. It was late Thursday evening; we arrived back at Davide's apartment. Davide asked me if I wanted to go to the restaurant for something to eat, seeing that I had only eaten a little on the plane over.

"Yes, why not."

I could have Davide all to myself later.

Davide's father managed to squeeze us a table in the far end of the restaurant with it being more romantic with the lighting dimly lit by a candle glowing from the table. After we wined and dined, we chatted for a while before heading back to Davide's apartment. I sat on the kitchen stool while Davide made the coffee.

"I would have thought you would be partying over the Christmas period," said Davide wondering why I had come over.

"It's a long story, Davide. I have fallen in love with someone, but I don't know how he feels about me," I said, sighing putting my elbows on the table with my chin in my hands.

"Oh," said Davide, not sure what to say. "I love you, Caz, and so does Antonio," said Davide.

"Yes, but you both would love other women and won't stay with the one," I said, trying to justify the situation.

"Yes, but you love other men, too,"
said Davide explaining.

"Davide, I do it only because he has not committed his love to me, then it would be different," I said, going into more detail.

"So you say if Antonio and I committed our love to you and we didn't have anyone else, would that be enough?" said Davide kissing my neck.

"I suppose so," I said, thinking about my options. With two men, I have only known a few months in Italy, saying they love me to Lloyd, who was caring, thoughtful, and pressed my buttons to send me to space and back, but I didn't know what he thought of me. Was I a temporary stop-gap until he found someone else in his league?

It was nearly midnight when we went to bed after Davide had said he and Antonio loved me. But I could imagine they would stray over a period of time, but could I accept that situation having other lovers, I just didn't know. The Italians seem to have their own rules, like the night when one of Valentino's brother came to visit me despite being married. I just didn't know at this moment in time; I decided that I would just live the moment over the Christmas holidays.

"Davide," I want to suck you dry." My hands travelled down his taut body, his length already hard waiting to be sucked. I sucked him hard within seconds he was empty. He moaned loudly as I pleasured him and leaned back while I played with him. My tongue sucked, licked, and flicked his tip. He kept coming as I kept on pleasuring him, his hot salty liquid kept coming all night long.

"Oh, Caz, you are killing me, but I love you," said Davide moaning as he came. "Caz kiss me," asked Davide pulling me up to his lips, his tongue played in my mouth while he rolled me over. "I need to taste you." He said, sliding down to play with my wetness making me explode.

We sucked off each other most of the night into the early hours.

"Davide, fuck me like a slut, will you?" I asked as we lay on the bed, catching our breath.

"Caz, I don't want to treat you like a slut." said Davide protesting.

"Do it," I said, raising my voice. Davide was reluctant at first, but suddenly he had my face down, ramming his hard length inside me from the back. He grabbed my hair tight, pulling it hard. I felt the pain.

"Fuck me harder, Davide, harder." As Davide pulled my hair tighter, he thrust so hard I felt the pain I needed to feel, but only lasting a few seconds until he came.

It was nearly 9 am; the bedroom smelt like a brothel again as we lay on top of the bed with our sweaty bodies entwined.

"I need a shower." I murmured, opening one eye.

"Mm, so do I.," said Davide sitting up to roll on top of me.

"Oh, Davide, I don't know what I would do without you," I said, running my fingers across his lips.

"I have never met anyone like you," said Davide kissing my lips. Davide slowly made love to me before we headed off for a much-needed shower.

After a cup of coffee and a refreshing shower, Davide went out to check on the business while I stripped the sheets from the bed, putting them straight into the washing machine. I replaced them with clean, fresh sheets ready for tonight with more sex to come. I thought I would take a walk down into the town looking to see if I fancied anything that caught my eye. I went off to the office to find Davide just to let him know where I was going.

Chapter Eighteen

As I opened the office door, several heads looked up from their work stations, and I spotted Davide chatting to one of his colleagues at the far end of the office. Davide smiled as I went over to him and hugged me. The office seemed busy with the phones ringing and the buzz of people answering them.

"Are you ok?" asked Davide concerned, looking at my face,

"Yeah just came to let you know I was going into town to have a look around and to do some window shopping," I said, smiling.

"Oh, ok, I should be here a while so I'll see you later," said Davide kissing my cheek. As I walked out of the office, I could hear the banter going around the office, although I hardly had any understanding of the Italian language.

The town was busy with it being the festive season. I passed a bakery with delicious looking cakes displayed in the window. I couldn't resist and went to taste one as it was making my mouth water. I purchased a pastry and a takeaway coffee since I had noticed a park further down the road. I walked to the park spotting a free bench; sitting my coffee down I dug into my pastry; it was delicious; I had never tasted anything like this before. I sat for a while, taking in the scenery thinking could I live here with Davide by my side? But would he be faithful to me if I committed myself to him? I just didn't know, but if I could ask Lloyd his feelings towards me, then it would probably answer my question.

I was deep in thought when someone behind me put their hands over my eyes, which I could guess was Antonio.

"Hello gorgeous," said Antonio sitting next to me on the bench.

"Hi, my sex on legs," I replied, smiling at him.

"So how long have you been here?" asked Antonio.

"Er well here on the bench about an hour, but I came over late evening and staying with Davide," I explained.

"Yeah, he said you were coming over, I am glad you have come over. I missed you so much," said Antonio rubbing his fingers across my lips.

"Hmm for sex," I said, trying to trick him.

"Well, yes and no. You are my perfect woman, my love for you comes through heart," said Antonio pressing his hand over his heart.

"Oh, you Italians are all the same with romance," I jest.

"No, not me. I do love you very much, and so does Davide," said Antonio sounding serious.

"I can't believe you both love me, especially a short period of time you have known me."

"We know when it is right and when you turned up, it was love at first sight," said Antonio kissing my lips softly.

"We'll see." I murmured undecided by him declaring his love to me.

Antonio got up saying that he would see us both tonight. He kissed me on the lips before disappearing across the other side of the park. Were these two guys spinning a yarn, or were they genuinely in love with me? I wondered. Could two men love you at the same time and share you?.

I was back by 5 pm, Davide was in the kitchen making coffee.

"Just in time," I said, wrapping my arms around his waist. He poured me a cup asking how I got on in the town.

"Nothing caught my eye, but I met Antonio in the park while I sat down, eating one of those delicious pastries from the bakery," I said.

"Oh that's nice, I forgot to mention he is coming around tonight. We are all going for a meal at the restaurant and then onto the night club," said Davide sounding upbeat.

"Yeah, he did say that he would be seeing us tonight."

I was in the shower getting ready to go out when I heard the door open; it sounded like Antonio had arrived. I quickly dried myself nipping through into the living room in my short robe to see Davide and Antonio chatting in Italian.

"Hi my lover," I called out, coming across to kiss him. Antonio was wearing his sexy black leather tight trousers with his loose white shirt; Davide had showered early and had just changed also in black leather trousers and a white shirt. They looked fucking hot, they could have fucked me senseless, and I would have sucked them back up. My arousal was on fire, no wonder why the ladies were always around them. But could I put up with that despite them saying they both loved me? Would they be loyal and not stray, that was the big question?

We all had a romantic meal by candlelight as the wine and chat flowed over our meal. It seemed odd having two guys taking me out at the same time and eventually bedding me with explosive sex and pleasure. I explained to Antonio about Lloyd not committing his love to me despite me being in love with him. Antonio said the same as Davide, insisting that they both loved me and would be committed to me. I was stuck for words as these two gorgeous guys confessing their undying love to me.

413

By the time we hit the night club, it was heaving, and even though we had consumed a couple of bottles of wine between us, I still had room for more. Davide nipped behind the bar to serve our drinks, seeing a large queue at the bar or we would have to wait a while for our drinks. Davide and Antonio greeted several partygoers being hugged and kissed, especially the ladies kissed them both on the lips. I thought to myself, would this work having two guys looking so hot would they soon get fed up with me?

I didn't know, so I decided to live in the moment and ignore it. Two guys in black shirt greeted me; they took hold of me by the waist pushing me onto the dance floor. I lost sight on Davide and Antonio while being pushed to the dance floor as they both danced with me sandwiching me between them. Both the guys were making seductive jesters running their hands over my body. I drank it in as the women were around Davide and Antonio like bitches in season.

One of the guys had their hands on my butt while the other on my breasts as we danced moved our bodies with the music. I was on a high as I had drunk my glass of wine down in one, feeling the buzz. I wrapped my arms around the guy holding my butt as the guy behind pressed his body next to mine, squeezing my breasts, making me come alive; my wetness was on fire. My eyes were closed enjoying the music moving in rhythm as my body was being played with. Suddenly, there was some shouting, and I could feel the party-goers moving, I opened my eyes to find Davide and Antonio in conversation with the two guys as they released me and departed.

"Caz we are going home," said Davide grabbing my wrist as Antonio put his arm around my waist guiding me off the dance floor and out of the night club.

Davide and Antonio were slightly annoyed with me for letting the two guys sexually touching my body. It wasn't as though I had fucked them. It was only 11 pm and the night was still young. We were soon in the apartment; as we entered, Davide had shut the door with a bang. Yeah, he was annoyed.

"Davide, what's got into you?" I asked, raising my voice slightly.

"It's you, Caz; I don't want guys touching you like that," he shouted.

"Well, what about you two having the women kissing you on the lips?" I shouted back in defence.

"That is fucking normal here, they are not at my crotch sucking me off," said Davide walking off into the kitchen where Antonio was making coffee.

If we looked at it like that then yes, I had to try and get my head around there way of culture being so different back in England. I went into the kitchen as Antonio poured the coffee in the mugs with Davide handing me a mug. Antonio came over and stood behind me as I sat on the kitchen stool, holding my mug of coffee.

"Davide I'm so sorry. I was jealous of seeing both of you being kissed by other women." I said as my voice turned into a whisper. Antonio enveloped me from the back, hugging me.

"Nothing is going on with any woman in the club," said Antonio kissing my neck.

"Can I make it up to you both and suck you both all night?" I asked, sounding sorry.

"No, but you can get in that bed, and we will show you how much we both love you," said Davide sounding a little dominant.

I kissed Antonio on the lips before I left for the bedroom; I undressed, slipping into bed and waited. They both came in a couple of minutes later, so handsome and sexy I melted needing them both inside me.

Their love-making was so intense; I could feel their heart beating inside me. Their kissing was so passionate, their touch so gentle and their lips as lush as they skimmed all over my body making me explode. My breathing was heavy in lust being sent into heaven and back, which made me sweat with the constant tension of love-making.

We lay there in silence while our breathing came down.

"Guys, can I suck you both in return?

"No, Caz, we are both making love to you all night even if we have to restrain you," said Antonio bluntly. Mm, the thought of being restrained brought back memories of Alex and Jess.

"Well, you'll have to restrain me then," I said as I started to move down the bed. Antonio grabbed hold of me, pulling me back while Davide found some belts to tie my wrists to the bed headboard. I loved this; they started playing with my body making love to me as my wetness kept on exploding.

We had been asleep for a couple of hours when I woke; my body was still covered by their bodies. I tried to move, but I was still restrained, I needed to pee.

"Davide, Antonio wake up. I need a pee." I wriggled my body to wake them. They both woke but were half asleep. "I need a pee, can one of you untie me, please? Davide pushed himself up to untie me. I had marks around my wrists where the belts had been tied. I quickly nipped off, picking up a robe on the way to the bathroom. After I had peed, I needed a coffee and something to eat, so I padded off into the kitchen. While the coffee machine went through its cycle, I searched in the cupboards for something to eat and found a pack of croissants and butter from the fridge.

I took a tray of buttered croissants and three mugs of coffee back into the bedroom where Davide and Antonio were laid out in the bed, half-asleep.

"Come on; sleepyheads breakfast is served," I said, placing the tray on the bedside cabinet. The guys moved slowly as I jumped back onto the bed, sliding in between the two guys now woken up. We ate breakfast in bed, after which there was more loving making until midday. How two guys can give me so much love, it was beyond belief. But was I doing the right thing by keeping my options open, now seeing them being so protective towards me.

Over the festive period, we dined with Davide's family after the whole family went to church for mass being a catholic. I decided to take a walk into town to the park for a couple of hours. There was hardly anyone about being most of the Italians at mass. Coming back, I walked along the riverfront which was also quiet for the festive season with the warehouses closed, and the cranes stood still. There were cargo boats moored up despite being the season of goodwill which would soon be over and business back to normal. Then something caught my eye in the distance. There seemed to be someone on my uncle's boat. I was curious knowing it wouldn't be Davide who was at mass with his family.

By the time I had arrived at the boat, the guy dressed in casual trousers and jacket was about to leave.

"Hello, can I help you?" I asked, making it clear that he had no business being here.

"No, I am just checking the boat for Mr Caputo." said the guy jumping off from the boat.

"Sorry but this belongs to my uncle," I said, slightly confused.

"So, you are the niece?" asked the guy as he approached me. I could see he had a gun in a shoulder hold underneath his jacket. "You have some unfinished business to sort out with Mr Caputo; also Nico is not happy with you and owes you one." said the guy walking off to his Mercedes car parking next to the mooring. I was about to ask him something else, but he drove off in a hurry.

Who was this guy? He must work for Enrico and who was Nico? I wondered if he was the guy that attacked me that night, but what did he mean by his comments? I walked back thinking about what the guy had said by unfinished business. What the hell had my uncle got himself into? I thought.

Davide was home, making coffee when I arrived back from my walk and the disturbing encounter and comments from the guy on my uncle's boat.

"I'm ready for this," I said, picking up a couple of mugs from the stand.

"How was your walk?"

asked Davide sounding casual.

"Hmm good, but I went down to the cruiser and found a guy looking it over saying he was checking it out for Mr Caputo, what was that all about?" I asked curiously.

"Well I don't know, Garth did do business with him, but I wasn't privy to that," said Davide shrugging his shoulders. I thought I would find out at some stage and picked a mug of coffee Davide had just made.

After the festive activities were overrunning up to the New Year, there was going to be a party to celebrate the New Year. Antonio stayed with us in the apartment, and they both took me out for walks in the forest and a leisurely cruiser down the river. They were so affectionate with me while chatting and play fighting with each other. We all wined and dined at Divide's restaurant, having no meals to cook with early nights as they both made love to me. I could have stayed here forever, but I thought of Lloyd and his late wife, could I ask him how he felt about me?

It was New Year's Eve, and I had to get ready for a party, I was excited wanting to celebrate with my two gorgeous sexy guys who loved me and who I loved in my way, but still had Lloyd at the back of my mind. I had just had a shower deciding what to wear for the party.

I decided to wear my short black sleeveless dress showing maximum cleavage, and that fitted like a glove hugging the body in all the right curves. I added some more curls in my hair and applied my make-up. I usually applied some eyeliner, but this time I did the full work bringing out my blue eyes to their full potential looking like come to bed eyes with a sparkle. Davide and Antonio were already waiting in the living room.

"Hi guys I'm ready," I said, walking through into the living room. Davide and Antonio looked up, and they stared at me in silence.

"What, I have done something wrong?" I opened my arms out, shrugging my shoulders, waiting for a response. They looked at each other and grinned, within a few seconds they had jumped off the sofa picking me up and heading for the bedroom dumping me on the bed. But before I could say anything, they were undressing me and started making love to me with urgency. It made them both breathless, and I also lost my breath with the tense feeling of love I had for them both.

We all redressed and headed to the restaurant first before moving onto the party in the night club. Davide and Antonio were looking so hot in their black leather trousers and black shirts, making their dark features stand out. It was only 10.30 pm, but the club was heaving being New Year's Eve. We were greeted by many party goers hugging and kissing, so I joined in kissing the women as well thinking back that I had done more with a woman then kissing. Davide and Antonio were glued to me, not letting me out of their sights, as guys were very friendly having my butt grabbed and squeezed.

`Davide went off to get the drinks in while Antonio held me around my waist as he nuzzled my neck. I was feeling good with the music blurring out and the wine I had drunk with two gorgeous sexy Italian stallions who loved me. Davide pushed his way back through the crowd as a woman kissed and hugged him; I had to ignore this being the norm. As I looked at it logically, many countries had their mannerisms in greeting people. Davide handed the drinks out as Antonio released me and Davide slipped an arm around my waist and kissed me on the cheek. I was being overwhelmed by their protectiveness; I felt like the crown jewels, being protected.

The New Year went with a bang as everyone hugged and kissed each other, with Davide and Antonio keeping an eye on where I was. There were fireworks to be set off for a 25-minute walk down to the riverside as people started filtering out of the night club to watch them being displayed after which they fell back into the night club to dance the rest of the night away until the early hours of the morning.

After watching the fireworks; we walked back home calling it a night. I was ready for a coffee as we opened the apartment door, walking straight into the kitchen to put the coffee machine on. I could hear Davide and Antonio talking between themselves in Italian, which annoyed me not knowing why they had been speaking to me in English since I had known them all this time. But I did pick up the word 'bambino'. I was sure that meant baby, but why were they discussing babies?

"Coffee's ready,"

I shouted, pouring it into three mugs.

"So, what was that all about?"

I asked, curious to know.

"We were talking about babies,"

said Antonio kissing my neck.

"Oh someone's having a baby?" I asked, having no idea. Davide and Antonio had their arms around me as they sandwiched me between them kissing my neck and shoulder.

"Caz, we both love you deeply and would like you to have our baby?" said Davide kissing my neck.

"What?" I screeched, "what did you say?" I asked, needing to hear those words again.

"Antonio and I would like you to have our baby to be a family," said Davide looking me in the eye. I couldn't believe what I was hearing. I did love them both but this? It was insane.

Chapter Nineteen

"Davide, Antonio, I love you both, but the baby is a large commitment," I said, trying to process what they were asking of me.

"Why? We are here for you." Said, Antonio, smiling at me.

"Well, for a start, I don't know what is happening with my uncle's estate as yet," I said, giving an excuse to delay the question.

We drank our coffee in silence. I debated in my head why two handsome guys would want a baby with me when my life was a total disaster, and they could have any woman who would fight their high teeth to be with them?

I had sobered up slightly when I got into bed. Davide and Antonio joined me soon.

"Guys, why don't you both find a girl to marry and have kids with?" I said, sounding them out.

"Italian girls and families are different, not loveable, fun, so serious and not as beautiful as you," said Antonio sincerely.

"But I haven't known you both all that long," I said in a matter of fact tone

"Caz, the day I picked you up at the airport was love at first sight for me, but with it being your uncle's funeral, I didn't think it would be appropriate to tell you," said Davide kissing me.

I felt so guilty now for asking Davide to finish sorting the funeral arrangements while I was fucking the youngest son of Enrico Caputo.

"But I thought you were gay." I blurted out. Antonio started laughing at the thought, and both of the guys started to banter in Italian.

"Had I said something I shouldn't?" I started to laugh as Davide slid down, pulling me down slightly annoyed and fucked me hard, followed by Antonio. I loved these guys. Once my uncle's estate was sorted, 'do I take the plunge and enjoy them both and have their baby?' I asked myself; I wasn't sure yet.

New Year's Day was spent in bed with both of them making love to me. They wouldn't allow me to suck them as I wanted to for pleasuring me so much. Making love was the Italian way of true love. I was due to go home the following day, but I was not happy about going back home. However, I had to go back and ask Lloyd if he had any feelings for me.

I had an 11 am flight home with Davide and Antonio taking me to the airport. Their love shone through as we departed with hugs and passionate kisses from both of them after my flight was called for departure. My tears flooded out, my heart not really wanting to go, but I had a living to earn until I knew what was happening with my uncle's estate. I told them both I would speak to them as soon as I knew something.

By 7 pm, I was pulling up outside Lloyd's house, not really knowing if he would be in after the festive season. There were no lights on, which indicated that he wasn't, so I pulled the keys out of my bag together with my luggage dragging it to the front door. I unlocked the door having that sinking feeling of knowing Lloyd still had feelings for his late wife, despite my love for him. Could I still live with that thought even if he confessed to loving me knowing he loved his late wife? I didn't know anymore so I thought that I should move out back to my flat.

I sorted my dirty laundry and put a wash on while I sorted my other clothes and toiletries out upstairs. It looked as though Lloyd hadn't been home since I left over a week ago; I could guess it with the groceries rather sparse in the fridge and cupboards. Being a Friday, I thought I would head out for fish and chip, taking them around back to my flat to check on Russ.

I unlocked the flat door; the flat was warm with the heating still on, there were no signs of Russ, he was probably fucking a bird somewhere. I switched on the kettle to make a coffee while eating my fish and chips. I enjoyed them, as I hadn't had them for a while. I switched the TV on and sat down with my coffee flicking through the channels until I found something of interest. I tucked my feet up onto the sofa, ready to settle in for the night drinking my coffee. Over the week, I had so much lovemaking with two gorgeous guys without having a lot of sleep; it was catching up with me as my eyes started to get heavy soon. I finished the last mouthful and headed off into my bedroom, undressed, and fell into my bed, drifting off to sleep.

It was nearly midday before I woke up; I must have been so tired of sleeping so long without any disturbance. I needed coffee. I slipped on my robe and padded off into the kitchen to make a coffee.

Russ must still be out for the flat being so silent. After I had made my coffee, I went through into the living room to switch the TV on more or less for some background noise with the flat so quiet. I sat on the sofa thinking about Davide and Antonio and their love for them and me being so protective. Yes, they would be my perfect men, but to have two of them would mean I would not be able to marry.

Would that matter? I guess not these days. But then there was Lloyd, I loved him but did he love me? His sister hated me and called me names, could I put up with her if Lloyd wanted me? I was so confused, but I had to process this new information from Italy. I knew my decision would be made more clearly once I had seen the solicitor.

The flat needed a good clean with me being away for over six months, Russ kept the flat reasonably tidy, but it needed a deep clean, so I set to and started to clean the flat throughout including stripping the beds and cleaning the kitchen cupboards out. I didn't find any evidence of Russ having a woman in his bedroom, which I was pleased about seeing that I asked him not to. The flat now smelt fresh and clean, with the beds having fresh sheets. I put on a washing cycle for the sheets while I was in the kitchen and made a much-needed cup of coffee.

It was nearly 8 pm when I had finished the thorough clean of the flat. I then decided I would nip out for a takeaway and find a bottle of my uncle's wine. I found a wine store in the city, where I walked up and down until I found the Italian selection. I couldn't believe the prices, even the cheapest was expensive, but it was the one that Davide's father sold in his restaurant, so I purchased it knowing it was quite good. I picked up my take away on the way back— good thing that I had phoned my order through so I didn't have to wait.

By the time I got back, it was after 9 pm, and still, there was no Russ in the flat. He must be having a whale of time somewhere, I thought settling in for the night with my wine and take away, but as I had just sat down, I heard the key in the lock, and Russ came in with his large bag.

"Hello stranger," I shouted, knowing it would be Russ. Russ came through, looking surprised to see me.

"Hello, my sex goddess." He enveloped me, kissing my cheek.

"Have you eaten?" I asked.

"No, I was going to nip out and get something," said Russ pinching a chip off my plate.

"You can have some of mine. There's plenty here for two people." I said, getting up to get another plate and fork from the kitchen.

"Oh, go on then," said Russ, not wanting to go out.

"Would you like a glass of wine?" I shouted through to him.

"Yeah," said Russ sitting down on the sofa.

I dished the meal up onto the plate handing Russ a fork and poured him a glass of wine. We ate in silence until we had finished.

"This wine is good," said Russ knocking it back.

"Yes, it is, isn't it?" I said, not telling him the story behind it. I leaned back on the sofa.

"So, where have you been over the festive period?" I asked, being nosey.

"The lads and I decided a boy's week away," said Russ grinning.

"Hmm, more like shagging all week,"

I said with sarcasm.

"No, how could I, my goddess? I missed you; we were mainly pissed," said Russ smirking.

"Yeah, right, cut the flannel," I said, picking up the plates and taking them in the kitchen.

Russ followed me into the kitchen, wrapping his arms around my waist, hugging me tight as he started to kiss my neck.

"Russ, stop it and put the kettle on," I said, trying to stop him arousing me, but it was futile. I was weak giving in as he pinned me against the countertop, his hand underneath my top to find my breasts. I could feel his hard length pressing against my body. Russ slipped off my top, undoing my bra with his mouth and hands all over my neck and breasts. I was moaning with the touch I had already come.

"Russ, take me now," I whispered. He pulled my jeans down; I stepped out of them together with my

undies. I unzipped his jeans, sliding them down as I jumped onto his length, shimming down, feeling his fullness inside me. We moved together, our kissing so intense we climaxed together. We were breathing heavily with tense sensation as we stayed locked together for a couple of minutes.

"I have missed you so much Caz, you make me feel I need to be inside you all the time," whispered Russ, sounding severe. I didn't know what to say.

It was nearly midnight by the time we were in bed. As soon as I was in bed, Russ was over me, fucking me hard as though he hadn't had sex for a while.

"Caz, when are you coming back to the flat?" asked Russ as he rolled off me.

"I don't know yet," I said.

"Are you living with a bloke?" said Russ curiously.

"Why do you ask?"

I said, wondering why he needed to know.

"Hmm, just curious," said Russ sucking my nipple.

"Russ, guess what?" I said.

"What?" I had dived down the bed to his limp length taking it in my hand. I started to work my tongue and fingers around his balls up and down. I took his full length and sucked as hard as I could; his pleasure was so overwhelming that he came shouting out my name.

"Fucking hell Caz, I've never had such a good blow job the way you do them," whispered Russ coming down from his explosive climax.

"Russ fists me hard, please."

"No, I can't; I'll hurt you," said Russ looking at me.

"Please, Russ, I'll tell you if it does," I said, knowing that I wouldn't. I needed to feel physical pain inside as I had in my heart. "Please, Russ." I pleaded.

"Mm ok, but shout if it hurts," said Russ.

But first, Russ started kissing my body down to my wetness, where he started to insert his fist slowly into me.

"Russ pump me." I whispered as he twisted his fist inside me, "harder Russ, harder," I started feeling slight pain but needed more. "Russ, harder." Russ pumped harder; I was now feeling the pain. My moaning was in pleasure and pain, but I was climaxing at the same time, it felt good in one way. Russ knew I had climaxed, so he pulled his fist out to taste my wetness. My body sweated with the intense sensation of pleasure and pain; it felt good.

"Are you ok, my goddess?" asked Russ coming up to kiss me gently on my lips.

"Yeah, good, thanks," I said as my breathing came down. We lay together arm in arm until I fell asleep in Russ's arms.

The following morning, I woke up and stretched out, feeling that the bed was empty, but I could hear movement coming from the kitchen. I hoped he was making coffee. I rolled over to check the time.

"Fuck, it's only 6.45 am, what the hell is Russ doing up at this time in the morning?" I mumbled. I could hear Russ coming back carrying a tray containing coffee and toast.

"Er, Russ, what are you doing up at this time in the morning?" I groaned.

"Because we are having breakfast and going to stay in bed all day to make love," said Russ kissing my lips.

"Mm, ok." I rolled onto my back for a few seconds to get my head into gear to eat breakfast. "Where did you get the bread?" I asked, knowing that both of us had been away.

"Oh, I went next door and asked if they could spare some slices," said Russ taking a slice of toast.

"Wow, you're in with the neighbours?"
I asked, surprised.

"Yeah, just had to show my body, and they couldn't resist," said Russ grinning.

"Just watch that ego of yours,"
I said, grinning at him.

We spent all day rolling about in the bed, Russ was brilliant, he did everything right, making me come time after time his sex drive had gone up another gear with our juices running all day until we lay on the bed and fell asleep with the intense sex we had.

"What time is it?" I murmured, opening one eye at the clock. "Oh Russ, it's nearly 7 pm. I need to go." I said, surprised at the time.

"Caz, when are you coming back for good? So I can keep making love to you," said Russ kissing my shoulder.

"I don't know, yet I'm just waiting for something at the moment." I pulled myself out of bed, heading for the bathroom in need of a shower.

Russ joined me in the shower, and we had another session of pure hard sex. I asked Russ to be rough with me so I could feel the pain and still come at the same time. It was nearly 8.30 by the time I left with Russ, not wanting me to leave him. He seemed to be a little clingy, wanting to see me next weekend to take me out to dinner. It wasn't as though we were dating; we were fuck buddies. I said I would text if I was free and left it like that.

I was back at Lloyd's place by 9, but Lloyd wasn't in. Where the fuck was Lloyd all this time? He was away for nearly two weeks. I unlocked the door going straight upstairs to check to see if the bed had been slept in, but it hadn't. I got my stuff ready for work starting the New Year with the council, but I still had to finish off at Eve's, and then I would get paid. I ran down the stairs going into the kitchen to make a coffee when I heard the front door open and close. I knew it must be Lloyd and I went to see him in the hallway. But it wasn't him; it was his sister Lara. My face dropped, seeing her dressed to the nines as butter wouldn't melt.

"I would have thought you would have gone by now. I don't know what you're expecting from him; he's only using you until Lucy's divorce comes through, then you will be out on your ear. He knows all about you with Alex and Jess and being paid for sexual pleasures. I told him you are a trollop and a slut, so I suggest you go before he comes back." said Lara coming out with so much venom.

I was gobsmacked by such venom coming out of her mouth; tears started to form in my eyes.

"When is he coming back?" I managed to say, keeping a brave face on and not wanting to have this conversation with her.

"What's it to you? He'll soon kick that backside of your out of this house," said Lara raising her voice in disgust. I didn't want to hear anymore, so I ran upstairs to the bedroom, banging the door shut as I slid down the door sobbing my heart out for a man that I loved.

It was nearly 4 am when I woke with a start remembering everything that Lara had said. Yes, she was right; I was a total slut I didn't deserve him. I should not have gotten involved and stayed in my flat and just do the work I was supposed to do. But I had to see him explain why I do these things; would he understand me? I just didn't know if he would. I needed a swim to destress, so I got up to collect a towel and headed off downstairs to the pool. I switched on the pool lights, dropping my towel and dived in. I came up at the other end of the pool and started to endure a painful work out for an hour. I pushed myself to exhaustion, feeling the pain I needed and deserved; I was a slut at the end of the day.

I was waiting outside the council house for the council workers. I had been there since 6.30 am thinking things over in my mind; I was having a total meltdown with my heart needing to know where I stood with Lloyd and if he wanted me out of his life. I was still in my thoughts when there was a knock on the van window; the council workers had arrived.

The day seemed to drag on with Lloyd on my mind and with what Lara had said to me last night. By 4 pm, I was ready to go. I didn't know if I should go back to Lloyd's place or the flat; I needed to know if Lloyd was back and to speak to him as I drove up to the house. The door was unlocked as I tried the handle, so I braced myself walking in expecting Lloyd asking me to leave. He was in the study on his laptop, typing away as I put my head around the door to say hello.

"Hi, would you like a coffee?" I said, being casual in my voice. Lloyd looked up and smiled, nodding his head in

447

acknowledgement that he wanted one. I was relieved that he was still smiling at me.

I was pouring the coffee into the mugs as Lloyd came through wrapping his arms around my waist kissing my neck, my heart melted with his touch wanting him to make love to me there and then, I had missed him so much despite my time in Italy with Davide and Antonio. I turned to wrap my arms around his neck. I kissed him so passionately, my heart beating fast, needing more.

"Lloyd, I've missed you so much, make love to me," I whispered. He scooped me up, taking me upstairs undressing me; his mouth was on my breasts with my wetness exploding. I grappled his belt, unzipping him as we fell onto the bed. He pulled my trousers off with my undies, undressing as he slid inside me, his length filling me with so much pleasure. My heart melted with the intense sensation he was giving me. Our mouths savoured each other's tongue as he pushed hard inside me. I had already climaxed as I came again with him. My breathing was erratic; I asked him to stay inside me as I hung onto him.

"I've missed you so much, Lloyd," I whispered, enjoying the moment as he laid on top of me.

"I've missed you too," said Lloyd kissing me gently on my lips. I wanted to say something, but I didn't want to spoil these moments of love I had with him as we laid on the bed.

"I'm going for a swim," I said after a while, kissing him on the lips as I got up from the bed. I needed a shower before going in, being at work all day with the dust and dirt. I quickly jumped in the shower and started to wash as Lloyd joined me, taking my breast in his mouth, his length ready to take me again. I jumped onto his waist, shimming down onto his length as he pushes me against the wall. I could feel him to the max; it felt as good as I moaned with pleasure. We cradled each other back and forth his mouth, taking mine devouring each other we couldn't get enough. With the tension so intense, I kept on coming with Lloyd, finally coming with me.

"Stay inside me, Lloyd." He pushed me against the wall, his mouth on my breasts.

"Oh, Lloyd, you keep making me come." I moaned, my fingers digging in his back.

I was in the pool before Lloyd, swimming four-length before he dived in. I swam hard, and Lloyd couldn't catch up with me. I was putting myself to the limit to feel the pain until I was exhausted. Lloyd finally caught up with me and enveloped me.

"Caz, there's something wrong, isn't there?" asked Lloyd, sounding concerned.

"No, I'm ok," I said, shrugging him off. I wasn't ready yet to ask the question if he had any feelings for me.

"Yes, there is, Caz," said Lloyd being persistent.

"I haven't heard any more from the solicitors since they cancelled the appointment in December," I said, making an excuse to avoid the real truth behind it. He hugged me, saying that these things take time.

Lloyd cooked that evening as he always did and served up a delicious meal with a glass of my uncle's wine. At least Lloyd had good taste in wines. We enjoyed each other's bodies all week until Lloyd informed me that he was going away for the weekend. I was gutted thinking that things were moving on to the next level.

"Oh, you're working over the weekend?" I asked

"I'm needed," said Lloyd, not elaborating any more information on the subject. I didn't push it, not wanting to upset the situation we were having.

"Oh well, I'll finish that job off at Eve's this weekend while you are away," I said casually but hurting underneath.

"I am sure you will be busy with something," said Lloyd hugging me.

Friday morning, I was late for work, not wanting to leave Lloyd in our intimate moments, but he did say he would be back Sunday sometime in the evening. I left for work that morning with tears in my eyes as I would be missing him for a couple of days. I was in no hurry to get back after work, knowing that Lloyd wouldn't be home. Russ had texted me, asking if I was coming over Saturday so he could take me out. I was in a dilemma whether to stay in on my own or have dinner with Russ. I didn't want to be on my own Saturday night, so I texted him saying I would see him Saturday after I had completed a job.

I spent the rest of Friday evening doing my laundry and having hard work out in the pool feeling drained at the end of my swim. I had pushed my boundaries to its limits as I kept on expecting more from myself to feel the pain. I felt so lonely in bed without Lloyd by my side and the intimacy we had. I was lost needing that closeness.

I was up early having a work out in the pool before I went over to Eve's to complete the job. She had rung me a couple of times, asking when it would be finished, but I managed to fob her off with excuses having to go back to the council being my main work. It was a cold winter morning; I had to scrape the ice off my windscreen before leaving despite the sun shining through. I had about six hours of work to finish off the job, but it was nearly 6 pm by the time I have finished. Eve came over to inspect my work and was delighted with the result.

I texted Russ. I was running late, and it was 7 pm by the time I would be at the flat. I was pleased that Eve had paid me straight away, giving me a generous size cheque for the job. I needed a shower as soon as I got in, luckily, I still had some clothes back at the flat which had worked out well with my mind being all over the place. Russ was in the kitchen when I arrived.

"Hello, my sex goddess, would you like some coffee?" asked Russ coming over to hug me.

"Mm, please, I'm going for a shower first, though," I said, making my way to the bathroom.

"I'll join you," said Russ following me into the bathroom. We had hard sex before showering the day's work off, Russ was on overdrive with his high sex drive fucking me hard three times before we finished showering. I loved the hard penetration with my legs wrapped around his waist, feeling slight pain with the hard thrusts he subjected me to against the shower wall.

Russ was in the kitchen making coffee as I came through wrapped in a towel and my hair wet.

"So, where are you taking me tonight?" I asked, picking up my mug of coffee.

"I've booked an Italian, I thought it would make a change from having Chinese," said Russ sipping his coffee.

"Ok, that's good." I nodded, thinking of all the Italian food I had over the festive period. I went through into my bedroom to dry and curl my hair. I slipped leggings and a loose-fitting low-neck top showing maximum cleavage with my thigh boots on. I hadn't worn any make-up since the New Year's Eve party in Italy, so I applied my make-up, making myself look like a person and not a builder. Russ was ready, waiting in the living room watch TV while I got ready.

"Right, I'm ready," I announced, walking through; Russ got up, switching the TV off and turned around, seeing me waiting for him to go.

"Caz, you look exceptionally gorgeous, my sex goddess," said Russ, his eyes staring me up and down. "Fuck the Italian I want to ravish you," said Russ as his hand cupped my cheek while he kissed me on the lips so gently.

"Cut the flannel Russ I'm starving," I said, walking off, picking up my coat and bag.

After our meal, I asked Russ if we could go to a night club in the city centre. Russ seemed to be a little reluctant, but I managed to twist his arm. I had a bit to drink and was feeling I needed to dance. The club was heaving; it brought back memories of my uncle's night club in Italy having two dance floors with two eras of music playing.

"Come on, Russ, let's go upstairs; they are playing rock music; we can get a drink up there," I said, grabbing his hand and dragging him upstairs. I pushed my way to the bar as I felt someone grab my butt and give it a squeeze, but I ignored it until I got to the bar. Russ had disappeared in the crowd as I turned around to ask what he wanted to drink. I decided for him with a beer and a red wine.

I pushed my way through the crowd looking out for Russ as an arm enveloped my waist, pressing their body next to mine. I had a knowing this wasn't Russ; I turned around as a tall guy with short hair hung onto me

"Do you mind?" I said, trying to elbow him in the chest.

"No, but I could fuck them tits of yours/," said the guy ogling them.

"Fuck off." I tried to wriggle out of his clutches and pushing him back. He lost his balance, grabbing hold of me, pulling me down on top of him, spilling the drinks over the both of us. A bouncer soon turned up to see what the commotion was as I picked myself up off the floor with a couple of guys giving me a helping hand.

I looked around to see if I could see Russ in the crowd, pushing myself towards the door to go downstairs for the exit of the club. I saw Russ talking to a couple of guys I didn't know.

"Russ, can we go?" I asked, grabbing hold of his arm.

"Caz, what the hell have you been doing to yourself?" asked Russ, starring at my front.

"Oh, some knob jockey put his arms around me, and I pushed him. He lost his balance-taking me and the drinks with him." I explained slightly miffed. The two guys ogled me as I stood there waiting for Russ to move.

"Come on my sex goddess, let me take you home." He said, putting his arm around me and heading for the exit. We walked down the road to find a taxi but without any luck. So, we started walking towards home, hoping to find one along the way.

We could hear someone shouting, but we ignored it, thinking it was someone causing trouble outside the night club, but the shouting came nearer as we both turned around to find the guy who wrapped his arm around me at the bar.

"Who the fuck are you shouting at?" asked Russ being protective.

"She's spilt her drinks on me, and I want to pay for the laundry." said the guy slightly intoxicated.

"Fuck off mate, you pulled her on top of you," said Russ walking up to him, ready to punch him.

"Russ, just leave it. Come on, let's go." I said, pulling at Russ's arm. We continued to walk on, but the guy wouldn't leave it and kept on mouthing off. Russ was about to turn around and punch him; I stopped him facing the guy and kneed him in the groin with a punch in the face. He doubled up as I walked away, knowing he wouldn't be following us as he was nursing his meat and two vegs.

"Fucking hell Caz I didn't know you have quite a temper," said Russ surprised by my actions.

"Russ, you don't know the half of it," I said, continuing to walk on. Russ found a taxi to take us home. It was only 11 pm when we got in; I headed straight into the bathroom to change out of my wet clothes and a rinse in the shower. Russ had made coffee when I came through dressed in my robe with the wet clothes, putting them in for a wash straight away, so the stains didn't dry on the fabric.

"How's my little fighter?" asked Russ, kissing the back of my neck.

"You better behave and do as I say," I smirked, taking hold of his crutch, giving it a gentle squeeze.

"I'd do anything for you, my sex goddess," said Russ slipping off my robe kissing my breasts as he squeezed them.

"Russ fucks me hard now," I demanded, taking hold of his belt to undo his trousers. I shimmed onto his length, feeling the hardness to his balls, fuck that felt so good. We moved in rhythm with Russ coming too quickly. "You're going to have it tonight," I said, looking him in the eye, raising my brow.

"Mm, I like the sound of that," said Russ kissing me hard on the lips.

We drank our coffee, and by midnight, we were in bed. "Russ, can I tie you up?" I asked, sounding him out.

"Eer, why what have you in mind?" asked Russ being a little cautious.

"Well, you'll find out, you can always tie me up if you want," I said nonchalantly.

"Mm, ok," said Russ. I jumped out of bed in search of some restraints. I tied his wrists first, then his ankles spreading his legs apart. Hmm, is this what it's like when you are vulnerable, I thought thinking of Alex and Jess. I started to kiss him gently on the lips slowly down his neck.

"I'm going to suck you until you can't take anymore," I whispered as I continued slowly down his body to his length, already waiting for attention. I ran my tongue down his length, his moans were so intense begging for a release, but I teased him as he seeped from his tip.

"Caz, you are fucking killing me," shouted Russ. I played with the tip flicking in with my tongue on his sensitive part as it seeped some more. Russ was starting to wriggle needing his release. I came up to his lips, kissing gently.

"Caz, fucking do something with it," shouted Russ, frustrated. He was seeping so much I relieved him, giving him two sucks, and he came. I played with his body most of the night, sucking his body all over, giving him love bites, marking him as though he was mine and no one else's. By the early hours, I had sucked him dry; he was fucked and sucked, so releasing him of his restraints, we fell asleep in each other's arms.

Russ was sleeping like a baby when I slipped out of bed for a pee and to make much-needed coffee. I came back with two mugs of coffee as Russ was half asleep, spreading himself out in the bed.

"Come on, move over," I said, giving him a slight tap on the side.

"Hmm, Caz, you've fucking worn me out." murmured Russ.

"Good now, budge up, or I'll suck you off again." Russ moved over, knowing he was beaten. "Here, get this down, you," I said, holding a mug of coffee. He slowly sat up, taking the mug of coffee from me as I started to sip mine.

"Oh, Caz, you're going to kill me at this rate," said Russ, his voice more like a moan.

"Yeah, well, you may as well die on the job," I said, pulling the cover back and patted his length gently with my hand. "You fancy another blow job, my sex god?" I said, looking him in the eye, raising a brow.

"You've fuck it, but I'll get my own back," said Russ placing his mug on the side as he slid down, parting my legs entering me with his fingers; until he started fisting me, then I exploded. He kept on fisting me until his wrist ached. It was when he gave up and started sucking my breasts and nipples. He was sucking hard, and I remembered Lloyd.

"Russ stop, stop, no, please stop," I shouted, pushing him off.

"What's up Caz, are you living with a guy?" asked Russ suspicious in my actions.

"It's complicated," I said.

"Caz, I was hoping we could be more than fuck buddies," said Russ, sounding disappointed by my reaction.

"I'm sorry, Russ, I have to go," I said, getting out of the bed, going to the bathroom.

"Fuck what I was doing? No wonder my life was so fucked up. I had a quick shower as Russ padded in just as I was getting out of the shower.

"Caz tell me, are you living with someone?" asked Russ pleading.

"Yes, but I don't know if he loves me," I said bluntly.

"So why do you let me make love to you if you are in love with this guy?" asked Russ, confused.

"As I said, it's complicated, Russ. Look, Russ, there are a lot of things going on in my life at the moment, and I am sure I'll find out soon, so could you not push me because I don't know anything yet?" I pleaded, kissing Russ gently on his lips. I dressed and left.

It was late afternoon when I get back to Lloyd's place, but he wasn't in, so a swim was in order. I must have spent a good hour swimming hard until the pain kicked in, and I was exhausted. I struggled to get out of the pool as my body ached with the fierce t workout I had committed myself to. After a quick shower, I made myself a coffee, I was feeling hungry but couldn't be bothered to make anything, so I went into the living room to switch the TV on and lay on the sofa in my robe. I must have fallen asleep on the sofa waking up feeling a little chilly; it was after midnight with the TV blurring out and no signs of Lloyd, so I switched the TV off and dragged myself upstairs to an empty bed.

It was Monday morning, I woke up again hearing the wind howling as the rain beat on the window, I was feeling cold, and my head throbbed, but I had to get up for work. I realized I must be coming down with a cold; I ached all over despite my hard work out in the pool yesterday. I dragged myself out of bed, getting dressed, and slowly made my way downstairs into the kitchen to make a coffee and a slice of toast.

I just made it to work for 8 am; the council workers were making tea as I turned up. They asked if I would like a cup? I didn't normally drink tea, but I was feeling like crap, so I had one. It was later in the morning when my phone rang. It was Jill, Mr Johnson's secretary ringing to say that he was back and could I come in to see him after I had finished work the following day? I needed to go to the bank with the cheque Eve had paid me on Saturday, so I told Tony the foreman on site that I had to leave early the following day.

I managed to work through the day feeling crappy and was glad 4 pm had come around. I was soon in the van heading back to Lloyd's place. I just hoped he was back. As I drove up the drive, I saw the BMW car parked in front of the house, my heart sank, it was his sister, but what was she doing here?

Lara had seen me coming up the drive, waiting at the door. Oh no, had something happened, or was she going to have another go at me? I parked the van a few yards away from her car as I jumped out, walking towards the house where she was waiting for me.

"I would have thought you would have gone by now, you trollop," said Lara sounding bitter and twisted. I ignored her comment.

"Is Lloyd ok?"

I asked, sounding her out for information.

"What business is it of yours, anyway? You need to pack your bags and go; he's not going to be around for a while, and not only that, he will be seeing more of Lucy now," said Lara sounding pleased with the information she had given.

Chapter Twenty

I pushed past her as tears started to fall, running upstairs to pack the few clothes I had here while living with Lloyd. Within a few minutes, I was back down with my bag; I had wiped the tears away, not wanting her to see that it was getting to me. I felt like punching her, but she would have the police onto me for assault, unlike the guy I punched the other night. I threw my bags on the front seat of my van, jumping in, and started the engine. I revved the engine selecting reverse skidding the van back and then hit the first gear skidding off, and the stones flew up with speed as I went passed Lara. She watched me leave and shouted that I was a slut and a dirty whore.

I was feeling crappy as it was, but now I had sunk into the abyss with Lara's bitter and twisted tongue, which was not giving me any information on Lloyd. I had been texting him all day but had no reply while I was at work. Was he ok, or was this a way of getting rid of me by sending his sister to do the dirty?

I had to pull over to the side of the road. I sobbed my heart out; I was on a downward spiral, why was I feeling like this?. I was having a meltdown in the middle of nowhere; my heart broke in many many pieces. I pulled the nearest piece of clothing out of my bag to wipe the snot and tears. My head was aching more with having a cold and sobbing so much; I tried to pull myself together before setting off back to my flat where Russ would be asking questions.

It was nearly 6 pm when I pulled up outside my flat; there weren't any lights on in the flat. Russ must be out; I was pleased in one way that he won't be asking me questions seeing that I had my bags with me. I dragged my bags into my bedroom and sorted them out before Russ came home. I went straight to bed without having a shower, which normally I always had after work, but I felt so crappy and down. I had been in bed an hour when I heard Russ coming in and filling the kettle in the kitchen.

There was a knock on my bedroom door as Russ entered.

"Hey, what's the matter with my sex goddess?" asked Russ sounding concerned.

"I've got a cold and stinking headache," I grumbled, sniffing. Russ came over, giving me a peck on my cheek.

"Oh baby, would you like coffee and some pain killers?" asked Russ hugging me.

"Yes, please, if you don't mind."

"I'd do anything for you, my goddess," said Russ getting up to make the coffee.

Half an hour later, Russ brought a tray loaded with a mug of coffee and a couple of boiled eggs with toast cut into soldiers.

"I've made you something to eat," said Russ putting the tray on the side with the pain killers.

"Thanks, you're too good." I started to raise myself off the pillow to sit up, sniffing. Russ sat on the other side of the bed while I ate and took the pain killers.

When I had finished, Russ grabbed the tray taking it back into the kitchen. He was gone a while before coming back with fresh mugs of coffee.

"Caz, would you like me to stay the night with you?" asked Russ with concern in his voice.

"Only if you want to catch a cold off me," I sniffed. Russ jumped in the bed alongside me, stroking my hair. "Russ, why do you bother with me? I'm not worth it; I'm just a slut." I murmured.

"Caz, you're not a slut in my eyes,"

said Russ kissing my head.

"You're just saying that,"

I whispered, drifting off to sleep.

I woke up a couple of times in the night with Russ fast asleep by my side. My head had stopped aching, but I was still feeling down. Russ was leaving for work at the same time as me. Since it was January, the mornings were still dark; he had got up to make breakfast bringing it through with a couple more pain killers. We both left at the same time for work; I told him that I would be back around 6 pm. But Russ didn't question why I was coming back to the flat.

The day went quickly, even though I was not feeling well. I left at 3 pm to go to the bank first before going to the solicitors. I managed to find a car park that didn't restrict trade vans with a high restriction as you entered the car park. I pushed in enough coins for the maximum time, so I didn't have to think about the time and to get a ticket for being overdue. I paid the cheque into my account, which boosted my account; I now needed to transfer a substantial amount over into my savings account, leaving enough to pay my rent and general bills.

It was nearly 4.30 pm by the time I reached the solicitor's office, which was down one of the side streets off the main city centre. I sat down in the reception area after speaking with the receptionist and waited, flicking through a couple of newspapers on the table in the seating area.

Why is it that the solicitors always keep you waiting? I thought with frustration having been here nearly half an hour. I could hear someone coming downstairs; I just hoped it was for me. Jill walked through the door, giving her apologies for being late and now ready to take me up to Mr Johnson's office. It was now after 5 pm luckily; I had found a car park with pay and display, not worrying about the time.

"Hello, Miss Jones. I'm sorry it's taken all this time, but we're here now," said Mr Johnson offering me a seat to sit down.

"Hmm, yes, it's been a while," I said with a smile. Mr Johnson opened the file in front of him, picking up a piece of paper. I have some good news and bad news, firstly the bad news, your uncle was worth a substantial amount of money, but unfortunately, there will be inheritance tax to pay on his estate being over a six-figure sum.

"I can't pay that," I said, sounding disappointed.

"Well, the good news is, your uncle had provided for you as you a partner in the company with you being the main shareholder, and he has been paying your taxes in Italy with an account set aside with monies if you needed it on his death."

"So, what you're saying is that my uncle set up the company with me being the main shareholder having a separate account with enough monies to pay death duties on my uncle's death?" I said, trying to process this information.

"Basically, in a nutshell, yes, you have now inherited a substantially profitable business, set up by your uncle since you were eighteen years of age."

"And what happens now?" I asked, still processing this.

"Well, you will have to go over to Marina di Camerota and see the company's solicitor sign some papers; I will send all the details to you in the post which you need to take with you for the company's solicitor." He said.

"So, after I sign the papers, when do I inherit it?" I asked, a little subdued.

"Well, I should say within the week, depending on how quickly they rush it through at their end."

It was after 6 pm when I left the solicitor's office still not believing that my uncle had thought of me all those years without seeing me. A tear fell from my eye as I walked to the van, thinking of him; he had been thinking of me since the death of my parents. Would he have come over to find me when Davide had mentioned that he was going to take a back seat to go travelling? I will now never know the answer to that question.

The traffic was heavy while driving back to the flat so that I couldn't be back until 6.45 pm. Russ had just made himself scrambled eggs on toast and a coffee when I came in.

"Oh, I didn't think you were coming back, or I would have waited," said Russ.

"It's ok I'll sort myself out, you get that down you before it gets cold."

"Here, you can have this. I'll make some more," said Russ handing me the plate and utensils. I kissed him on the cheek, thanking him as I took the plate and utensils, and walked into the living room, plopping myself on the sofa. Ten minutes later, Russ was by my side while I had just finished eating my meal.

Russ cleared the dishes and made a fresh pot of coffee, bringing it through into the living room, we both lay on the sofa the way I used to with Lloyd. I could feel the heat radiating of Russ's body, feeling secure, warm, and comfortable moulding in between his legs with his arm around me. We laid there watching TV most of the evening in silence with Russ making a coffee before going to bed at 10 pm.

I still had a cold but felt better than I did the evening before, which didn't help with seeing Lara giving me verbal abuse.

"Russ, I'm going to bed," I said, stirring to get up,

"I'll come with you if you want me with you." His voice was laced with concern.

"Please, I need your arms around me." I got up to go to the bathroom first. We were snuggled in bed with Russ's arms enveloped around me, "Russ, you are too good for me." I said, feeling the warmth from his body.

"Caz, I want to be with you and have wanted you for a while," said Russ hugging me tightly.

"Russ, we are just fuck buddies at the moment," I said, not wanting to have a relationship with anyone at this time.

"I can wait," said Russ kissing my shoulder.

"I do love you but in a different way," I said, not wanting to lose him.

\

"I've loved you since the day I moved in," said Russ giving me a tight hug.

"Mm," I said, drifting off to sleep.

I received the letter from the solicitors in the next couple of days with all the details needed to see my uncle's company solicitor. Still, the only problem I had was my contract working for the council continued till the end of March, so the council spent their budget for the tax year. I rang Davide with the information I had been told and told him that I wouldn't be over until after March. Davide was over the moon, desperate to see me, and so was Antonio. I missed them too, so thoughtful and protective. Davide said he would explain to the company's solicitor about the delay for me in coming over and would be in touch as soon as I was over.

Over the weeks running up to the end of March, I stayed in the flat. There had not been any contact from Lloyd since that weekend when he had said he would be away and will not be returning. Russ was so romantic with me all this time, but I was still not sure. We spent the weekends in bed mainly with me, demanding him to fuck me hard so I could feel the pain. Russ didn't understand why I needed hard sex; I couldn't explain I just needed it. I think it was down to losing my parents at a young age together with being in love with someone for the first time, but not knowing how he felt about me, feeling severe pain was a coping mechanism.

We were on time finishing the last house with the council a couple of days before the end of March. I was pleased now being released to go to Italy to finalize things with my uncle's estate and also needed a much-needed break from work. The only thing I would miss was Russ, but I would soon be back once things were sorted. Russ wasn't very happy I was going away; he wished he could have come with me but had to work to finish his job for the next stage but had to be approved by the council first. I spent the weekend sucking the life out his length, leaving love bites all over his body to remember me before taking a flight to Italy on Monday morning.

I didn't stay in a hotel before the flight due to the flight at 1 pm and had a leisurely drive to the airport parking, before checking in. It was nearly 6 pm by the time I cleared customs and spotted Davide in his tight black trousers and a white shirt. A huge smile came onto his face as soon he saw me approaching him. He scooped me up, kissing me all over with one passionate at the end. He was so lush I could eat him, which I was hoping to later tonight. Davide took hold of my luggage, walking to a 4x4 parked in front of the airport.

"Hmm, gone up in the world, have we?" I teased.

"No, it's only the company vehicle," said Davide wishing it was his. Davide put the luggage in the back as I climbed into the front.

"So where to, boss?" asked Davide teasing with a grin.

"Back to your place, I'm hungry, hungry for your love," I said, kissing him on the cheek.

"So am I," said Davide as he started the engine, selecting first gear, and pulled off.

"Will Antonio be coming around tonight?"
I asked.

"No, he is away until Friday, but he does know you will be here so he'll be over as soon as he gets back?

"I'll miss him," I said, a little disappointed.

"Yes, I wish we could have both met you at the airport," said Davide. Having a clear run back to his place, we were in the apartment just after 7 pm. Davide took my luggage into his bedroom while I went to make the coffee. Davide came up behind me as I prepared the mugs for the coffee, his arms wrapped around my waist, kissing my neck.

"I've missed you so much."

I started to melt in his arms.

"Davide, make love to me," I whispered. Davide scooped me up, taking me into the bedroom as we both slipped out of our clothes, falling into bed. He made me explode multiple times in heated and intense moments of passion.

It was nearly 10 pm by the time we surfaced, needing a much-needed coffee that I had not made when we first came in. Davide asked if I would like to go to the restaurant for a meal and a bottle of wine. We spent a couple of hours sitting and dining at Davide's father s restaurant with Davide explaining things about the business. I was intrigued, wanting to know as much as possible. Living in Italy was a different experience altogether, was this what I needed, a complete change of scenery?

The following morning Davide had arranged to see the company's solicitor in the afternoon. The morning was spent in lovemaking, with Davide sending me into orbit and back. Davide took me to the solicitor's, which was on the other side of the town.

"I'll wait for you in the car," said Davide, parking up opposite the office.

"No, please come with me just in case I don't understand what they are saying," I said, pleading slightly.

"Caz, it's none of my business, and they do speak English so you won't have a problem understanding them," said Davide.

"Please, Davide, I need you with me," I said, pleading.

"Well, if you insist boss," He smirked at me. We were only in the office for half an hour, having to sign various papers to do with the inheritance tax and the full control of the company. The solicitor said they would confirm by phone and in writing to Mr Johnson in the UK and myself at my home address when the inheritance tax had been transferred and receipted with everything completed with me in solo control of the business.

I was now pleased things had been sorted out but was sad deep down, knowing my uncle had provided for me even though he couldn't take me on when my parents died. For the rest of the week, Davide gave me an in-depth tour of the company going up to the east coast where the vineyard and wine factory was. Apart from Davide giving me an in-depth tour of the company, he was loving and protective towards me, with pleasure and loving making during the early evening through to early hours every day until Antonio came over on Friday evening.

We all dressed for dinner going to Davide's father's restaurant, after which we went up to the night club. Friday was a busy night, and we pushed our way through as Davide and Antonio were greeted by many clubbers. This was something I had to get used to if I was going to live here. I joined in, not wanting to miss out. After our greetings, Davide went behind the bar to get the drinks seeing that the bar was busy, or we would have to wait a while.

The music was good as I started dancing to the rhythm, sipping my wine in between my moves. Antonio came from the back, pressing his body next to mine, his arms around my waist. I could see Davide talking to a dark-haired girl. I noticed the girl batting her eyelashes at him signalling, the come-on move.

I bet she can't satisfy him as I can, I thought. She started to put her arms around his waist, but he didn't stop her despite Antonio having his arms around mine. I was jealous, but why, it never bothered me before, was this normal over here. I had nearly finished my drink as I turned around to kiss Antonio, snogging him hard and started to neck him despite the heat in the night club, causing him to sweat. He tasted good I could have fucked him in the middle of the dance floor there and then, but yeah, we would have been thrown out despite me now owning this club.

I could feel another pair of hands around my waist from the back as I licked Antonio. It was Davide rubbing up behind me. I was now sandwiched between both of them with the heat of their bodies and the sweat it was turning me on.

"Guys, I need to go home," I said, kissing them both and grinning. I needed sex badly and fast. We were soon in the lift going up to Davide's apartment with Antonio behind me, squeezing and pulling my nipples from behind and Davide drinking my wetness as I had stripped off ready to be taken. The pleasure was so intense with multiple explosions of bliss. We soon reached the top as the lift, and the door opened; just as well, no one else lived up here, only being one apartment. I demanded them to keep fucking me as long as they could until they had enough.

The following morning, I woke with a slight headache feeling the weight of Davide and Antonio asleep on my body. The room stank like a brothel, and I needed a good shower stripping off the sweat and sex Davide and Antonio had given me a few hours ago. Their long, taut, slender bodies lay against mine. They would be any woman's dream of sexual bliss, both with longish dark curly hair and dark features they were sex on legs. I was so lucky having two at one time, was I slipping into my uncle's shoes having this much closeness?

Antonio was called back to work; being a male model was demanding to have to go on a call, which could be anywhere all over the world. I said my goodbyes hoping to see him soon giving him so many kisses before he left. I asked Davide if we could go to the villa despite being next to Enrico Caputo's place. I needed to spend some time in the pool and to get some sun on my naked body. We did some grocery shopping before heading for the villa. Although the villa had not been in use, it was spotlessly clean as though we were on holiday having the villa cleaned before the next guests arrived.

"Davide, I'm going in the pool," I called out, walking in, leaving Davide to sort out the groceries. I stripped off my clothes and dived into the pool, coming up, catching my breath with the pool being cold over the winter months. I soon started pacing myself working out hard until Davide joined me having grabbed a couple of towels from the bathroom. I swam up to Davide taking his length by surprise.

"Davide, I need you inside me," I said, pushing my body next to his. Davide pushed me to the side of the pool, pulling me onto his length, shimming me down so quickly, making me go 'Oh.'

I massaged his face with my lips until I reached his mouth, shoving my tongue down into his mouth as our tongues danced with each other. As soon as we were out of the pool drying ourselves Davide's phone rang. He spoke in Italian as the conversation continued in a raised voice.

As soon as we were out of the pool, drying ourselves, Davide's phone rang. He spoke in Italian as the conversation continued in a raised voice.

'I must learn this language.' I made a mental note, feeling left out on conversations that Davide and Antonio had when meeting people. Davide ended the call looking annoyed.

"Is there something wrong?" I asked him.

"I have to go into work; they cocked an order up to one of our best clients, and I need to sort it," said Davide, slightly annoyed. "Are you coming with me?" He asked.

"No, I'll stay here. I need to wash my hair, not only that I'll only be in the way." I said, kissing Davide on the cheek.

"Caz, it's your business; you have a right to be there," said Davide kissing me gently on the lips.

"I know, but I need to learn your language first. I just feel like a fish out of water at the moment," I said, hoping he would understand.

"Yeah, ok, I understand, but I will have to teach you my language," said Davide hugging me before he departed.

I went upstairs to wash my hair in the shower to have a quick rinse from the pool. I dried my hair, curling it with my tongs, making my hair full of curls. I thought I would cook a meal for Davide tonight and dress up for him looking sexy and lush. I must have been upstairs for some time deciding what to wear and finally chose the outfit, leaving it hung on the side of the wardrobe. I was still in my robe as I went downstairs to start preparing the meal when I heard the front door open and close. Davide must have sorted the problem out I thought turning around to ask him if everything was alright, but was taken aback by seeing six men in the hallway staring at me.

I recognized two of the men instantly, Enrico and the other the guy I had punched and kicked in the groin with a scar on his cheek.

"How have you got in with the gates being closed?" I asked, sounding blunt.

"Davide was a little careless for leaving the gate open," said Enrico waving his cigar in the air.

"What do you want?" I asked, tightening my robe a little tighter.

"I have come to talk about some unfinished business your uncle left with me," said Enrico walking toward me.

"Oh, and what is that?" I asked curiously

"Firstly, aren't you going to offer us some refreshment?" asked Enrico walking into the living room with his men following him closely as if I was going to knife him.

"I suppose so," I said, walking into the kitchen to set up the coffee machine. I could feel the guy with the scar watching my moves and my body. Enrico sat down with two others, standing like bodyguards next to him. Scarface came into the kitchen, standing behind me, making me feel uncomfortable by his presence. I avoided eye contact with him as I prepared the tray, ready to take the coffee through into the living room.

"Ti scopero durament," said Scarface in a whisper as though he didn't want anyone knowing what he had said to me. I ignored his comment, not knowing what he had said to me. I took the coffee into the living room, placing it on the coffee table as I sat down. One of the guys sitting on the sofa picked up the coffee pot and poured the coffee.

"So Signora Jones, the cruiser that is moored down by the quay is mine," said Enrico taking a puff on his cigar.

"No, I don't think so, you prove to me that it is yours," I said, raising my voice.

"Mario get the papers out for Signora Jones to sign," asked Enrico clicking his fingers as Mario jumped on command.

"I am not signing anything, and I am not going to be bullied into it," I said, getting up from the sofa. Scarface was stood closely behind me, waiting for me to move.

"You don't understand, I always get what I want," said Enrico sipping his coffee.

"Well tuff, I'm not doing it, and not only that, why are you so keen on having the cruiser?" I said, annoyed.

"That was between your uncle and me," said Enrico starting to raise his voice in annoyance.

I felt as though this conversation wasn't going anywhere, and I was being bullied, just like back in the care home, needing to fight my battles. I needed to get out quickly and fast. I started to move towards the kitchen as Scarface blocked my move. I saw an opening if I was quick enough to make it to the door, I spun around and leaped over the sofa heading to the door, but as I opened the door there stood another guy ready to take me on. I lashed out with a kick to the chest; he fell back, losing his balance. Jumping over him, I ran down the driveway to the gate entrance but was stopped by two more of Enrico's guys.

Fuck, I had to fight, I was cornered his guys were running down the driveway after me. All my training in self- defense kicked in with the guy's thinking I was going to be easy to catch as they lunged at me. Blocking them with my arm, I raised a punch to the gut, with one guy falling to the ground.

One down one to go. The next guy had a little more experience, but I managed to down him as he tried to hold onto my robe, but I kicked him off, running to a vehicle nearby. I just hoped the keys were in the vehicle. Yes, I jumped in and turned the key, revving the engine spinning the tyres in haste to get away.

I was kicking up the dust being so dry and could see I was being chased. I wasn't used to driving on the left-hand side of the road, and I wasn't sure where I was going.

I couldn't remember the turning to the main road as most of the road was a dirt track, so I just floored it and hoped for the best. I must have travelled a couple of miles down the track until the track ended.

Fuck, where to now? I panicked. I slid the vehicle to the right, seeing that the ground was more even to drive on, heading off-road across the landscape into god knows where. I could see the sea in front of me until I had to skid to a halt as I nearly lost it, seeing a drop at the last minute. Crap, that was close. I jumped out, running down the slope my bare feet killing me stepping on sharp stones as I ran sliding part of the way down.

By the time I got to the bottom of the slope, making my way across to the beach, my chasers were on the slope with two of the guys following me. Sweat was pouring off me I was breathing heavy, I needed to hide somewhere amongst the rocks to get my breath back. I saw a crevice in the rocks to squeeze in and hide for a while, hoping they don't find me. I could hear shouting but not understanding the language I was stumped. I readjusted my robe coming to lose with the adrenaline rush kicking in to escape. I waited a while until I could hear the vehicles engines fade in the distance and was sure no one would be about before squeezing myself out of the crevice. I needed to get back to the town somehow, but I was lost.

I started walking along the beach, losing my sense of direction; I didn't know if I was going back to the villa or the town. I must have walked a mile when I saw a building on the clifftop but not recognized it. It must be further down the coast. I had to cross over some rocks to get to the other side; my feet were bleeding and hurting me. I desperately needed to soak my feet and clean them up. I eventually scrambled over the rocks to the other side, seeing a straight stretch of beach in the distance. I continued walking as I approached the bottom of the villa on the clifftop. Then I realized where I was. I had come around the other side of Enrico's villa. I should have turned left instead of right on the dirt track. I made a quick run across the small stretch of private beach and just hoped no one was watching.

I thought I had made it, but my heart sank, seeing half a dozen men surrounding me, I was fucked with nowhere to go. The men closed in on me with the Scarface standing back slightly while the men grabbed hold of me aware of me lashing out. I was outnumbered as they all jumped me pinning down on the sand, bending my arms behind my back and holding my legs down in case I lashed out. My robe was starting to loosen as my cleavage started to show. I was frogged marched up to Enrico's villa. We entered into the large hallway. The villa was similar to my uncle's in the layout as we went through into the living room where Enrico sat looking out of the open bi-folding door to the terrace. I was pushed onto a chair as they released their grip on me. I quickly pulled my robe around me to secure it tightly.

"Signora Jones, you have a lot of spirit; I like that in a woman." said Enrico taking a puff on his cigar. "So back to business, are you going to sign, or do you need a little bit of persuading?" asked Enrico curling his top lip and raising a brow.

"You'll have to kill me first." I spat.

"Be careful what you say it could be arranged," said Enrico looking at the guy with the scar.

"Take her and persuade her to change her mind," said Enrico waving his hand to the guy with the scar. I was grabbed from the chair by two men holding me like a carpet taking me upstairs to one of the bedrooms, dumping me on the bed before leaving the room.

The room was light and airy, with the windows open and a door leading onto the balcony. I heard the door close and a key turn in the lock to find that the guy with the scar was the only person in the room. It was one on one this time it was day time, and I had a feeling this was going to hurt knowing I had kicked the shit out of him a few months ago. I was going down fighting all the way. I slipped off the bed as he walked further into the room. I was thinking about the layout of the villa being similar to the balcony at the front. I couldn't remember if the pool was below the balcony. I moved slowly towards the balcony as he started coming forward. I made a quick dash to the balcony but was rugby tackled to the floor, hitting my head on the floor. The pain shot through my head, stopping me in my tracks. Fuck I had had it. He dragged me onto the bed, looking at me, not saying anything. My eyes became heavy with the pain in my head as I lay there waiting for him to beat me to a pulp.

He pulled open my robe, exposing my naked body as he straddled over me, knowing I wouldn't fight back with hitting my head on the floor. His face was close to mine as he touched my head where I fell, I quince slightly as he touched me. I could smell his garlic breath hovering over me as he ran his fingers over my lips. I couldn't move.

His hand took hold of my throat, rubbing his thumb up and down my throat, pressing slightly for my reaction.

"Do whatever you're going to do. I have no more fight in me." I whispered whether he understood what I was saying. His hand cupped my cheeks as his mouth took mine pushing his tongue down my throat for a few seconds, his mouth started working down my neck biting me; all of my body down to my wetness. I groaned as he bit my breasts, and they were so sensitive. He pulled his trousers down and spread my legs apart, thrusting his over large length inside me, pumping me so hard I felt the pain. I moaned as he pushed harder and harder inside me, making me moan more until he released himself inside. He lied on his mouth over mine with his tongue inside, giving me his surplus saliva from his mouth while his thumb rubbed up and down my throat. He pulled his trousers up and tucked in his shirt as he hovered over me. 'What else is he going to do to try and hurt me?' I thought. He looked at my naked body, my legs apart knowing I was vulnerable and helpless. He watched my face as he started to pummel his fist hard inside. The pain felt as though I had been set of fire; he kept screwing his fist inside me. He was cutting me inside with the rings on his fingers, cutting through my sensitive flesh as I started bleeding from inside. I was groaning in pain, but I couldn't fight back. The last thing I knew, I was seeing his face grinning at me with the pain he was giving me and loving every minute of it until I passed out.

I didn't know how long I was out, but when I came around, I could feel the warmth of a body cradling me stroking my face and hair gently. I looked up to see it was the man with the scar. Why was he doing this to me? I reached up to touch the scar on his cheek, staring into his dark eyes, he was handsome behind the scar, but where did he fit in with Enrico's family.

"You sign papers for my father, and I will look after you," said Scarface in broken English.

"Is that all he wants?"

I whispered, my eyes feeling heavy.

"Yes, that is all," said Scarface.

"I will sign," I whispered. His fingers traced my lips as he gently pressed his mouth onto mine. Why was he doing this to me? I eventually signed the paperwork as Scarface brought the papers to me.

I could hear water running in the bathroom as Scarface came over and scooped me off the bed, slipping my robe off my broken body. Was he going to drown me now that I had signed the paperwork? He gently put me down into the water, my body hurting and aching from the abuse I had taken as he started to bathe my body of what he had endured on me. The blood from below was dried down my legs as though I had started my period, my feet, and bites stinging from the temperature of the water as I lay back groaning with pain. I must have passed out only to be woken to find myself in bed. It was dark outside with a full moon casting a shadow through the windows of the bedroom, giving a little light. Davide would be wondering where I was; I needed to go. I pulled the covers back on the bed in an attempt to get up; my feet were bandaged up sore and aching together with the rest of my body.

I couldn't find my robe, so I substituted a sheet from the bed to wrap around my body and gingerly stepped out of the bedroom. As I slowly walked along the corridor, I could hear raised voices not understanding the language; I didn't know if this was normal or was something wrong. Enrico saw me coming slowly downstairs.

"Nico, go see to your woman," shouted Enrico waving his arms out at me. The guy with the scar must be called Nico as he quickly came over and scooped me up.

"I need to go, Davide will be wondering where I am," I said.

"Davide knows where you are and that you are stopping here for a while with us," said Nico taking me back upstairs.

"I have to go back to England, and where is my robe?" I said, feeling helpless.

"You stay with me for a while until your body is healed, I will bring you some food and drink, and you stay in bed I will look after you." murmured Nico in broken English. I had no option; I was stuck here.

Chapter Twenty-One

I woke up the next morning still feeling sore and aching all over. I felt warm; I rolled over to find Nico in the bed with me, watching me while I slept. He touched my face and kissed me on my lips gently.

"Did you sleep well?" asked Nico; his voice was full of concern.

"Mm, yes, I suppose so," I mumbled, thinking why this didn't make sense, Nico being so concerned and affectionate towards me after he had abused me. Nico slept with me every night until I was well enough to go. He just kissed me and touched my cheek every time he came in to see me but never tried anything on.

I left after a couple of weeks with Nico taking me back to my villa. My bites were starting to fade; I wasn't sure about my insides; I still hadn't had my monthly and was due within a few days. I needed to phone Davide to take me to the airport once I had sorted my flight and packed but had to wait until my phone had recharged. Davide had been so worried and was relieved to hear my voice over the phone.

"Caz, I have been so worried about you, but they told me you were staying with them for a while and that you needed the cruiser and that one of Enrico's men was going to take it," said Davide relieved I was now speaking with him.

"I'll tell you about it when you come over to pick me up, but I need to get back home and can't get a flight until tomorrow evening," I said, sounding relieved and free.

Davide had soon arrived to see me but was shocked to see the markings on my body. He hugged and kissed me, wanting to know what had happened to me when he had left that day. I told him everything; Davide was taken aback with the ordeal I had been through. He hugged me holding on for a few moments.

"You have been through so much; for a moment, I thought they had killed you," said Davide hugging me tightly.

"What do mean killed me?" I squeaked in horror by his comment.

"It has been renowned that if you cause them grief and refuse, they kill you," said Davide, not sure if he should have told me.

"Well, they got what they wanted in the end," I said, walking off into the kitchen to make coffee. "I thought Enrico only had four sons," I said.

"Yes, as far as I know, he has,"
said Davide sounding puzzled.

"So who is Nico, and why does he call Enrico father?" I said, looking perplexed.

"Hmm, I don't know," said Davide raising his brows.

I finished packing and checked that I had packed everything before leaving the villa. Davide was so good not making any advances towards me knowing the ordeal I had been through but was so mad about the bites I had endured on my body. He held me closely kissing and stroking my hair and face as we lay in bed for the last time before I left to go back home the following day.

It was late Saturday night before I got home to the flat; I unlocked the door walking into the flat with my bags; it had been a tiring journey. I could hear music coming from Russ's bedroom, and then I heard giggles, was that a woman he had with him? I switched the living room light on to find women's clothing scattered over the sofa with a pair of heels shoved under the coffee table. The one thing I had asked him not to do he had broken the rule, and he wanted a relationship with me. I couldn't trust him anymore. I went through into my bedroom, dragging the rest of my luggage that needed putting away while I put a washing cycle on for my dirty clothes and checked the post to find the letter I was waiting for. I was officially the full owner of my uncle's business.

This was going to give Russ a wakeup call knowing I was now back on the scene. I switched the living room lights off and banged my bedroom door shut, ensuring that he heard me in the flat. I settled down in bed tired; it was after midnight.

Sunday morning, I was feeling crappy, having started my monthlies. I didn't know if my normal protection would be ok since my ordeal with Nico. It was nearly 7 am as I got up for some painkillers and to make myself a coffee. The woman's clothes and heels had disappeared as I walked through to the kitchen. He must have known I was back with the noise I was making last night. I took my coffee back to my bedroom, thinking I should purchase some pads instead of using my normal protection. I hadn't thought about Lloyd since I had been over in Italy. I hadn't seen him for a few months. Did I love him, or was it a phase I was going through being with him? His sister had cut me with a knife, which was that tongue of hers. Yes, if I looked back, I was having sex with just about anyone who touched me. But that was me needing closeness.

I could hear Russ in the kitchen, making coffee. I turned over and stared at the clock showing it was 9 am. I thought I should better get up and do a little bit of grocery shopping. I also needed to take Lloyd's keys back now I had moved out and completed the job Lloyd had asked me to do assuming he was at home. There was a knock on my bedroom door; then the door opened, and Russ brought me a coffee. I turned over as he put the mug on the side and sat on the bed.

"Hello stranger," said Russ a little sheepish.

"Mm Hi," I said, not jumping for joy to see him.

"I've missed you," said Russ a little coy.

"Well, it didn't look like that last night," I said, sounding sharp.

"I am sorry I've let you down if we were a couple, it would have never happened," said Russ trying to justify his actions.

"I did tell you about bringing women back to the flat before; you are just taking the piss, Russ. I can't trust you anymore." I said, picking up my coffee for a sip. Russ was looking at the exposed parts of my body, which I had covered as he had come in.

"Caz, what's those bite marks doing on your body?" asked Russ, trying to justify his actions by noting that I had been with a guy.

"Russ, I don't want to talk about it, please just go. I don't feel well." I said, placing my mug down and turning my back to him. Russ didn't say a word before picking my empty mug and left my bedroom.

I heard Russ leaving the flat after a couple of minutes, yes I was jealous of him for having a woman in bed with him knowing his sex drive and what we used to do. Although I was like that with all the guys, being protective only wanting it one way. I asked myself then;

'What do I want out of my life, to be a slut, but what would happen when I got older or do I try and settle down with a guy I can trust?' I needed to see if Lloyd was at home and speak to him about my feelings towards him and to see if he was done with me.

I was up and dressed, as I needed my monthly protection urgently. I had padded myself out with toilet paper and nipped to the nearest shop for some pads. I came back to clean myself up and changed into my joggers with a hoody top covering my body as much as possible to hide the bites on my body. I took a couple more pain killers before leaving to see Lloyd; I just hoped he was going to be in after all this time.

I pulled into the driveway pressing the fob key to open the gates. As I drove up there parked in front of the house was a 4x4, it looked familiar, no it can't be, was it, Alex's vehicle? But I couldn't quite remember the registration of his vehicle. I was a little apprehensive when I walked through the door. I could hear voices coming from the study.

Oh, fuck it sounded like Alex's voice, what the fuck was I going to say with Lloyd being there? I tapped on the door as I stuck my head around the door. It was Alex as he stopped talking when he looked up to see who was knocking on the door.

"Hello, my sexy builder," said Alex being jovial. I could have been swept up the carpet as I cringed by his comment in front of Lloyd. Lloyd looked up, having no expression on his face. This wasn't looking good, but I knew the answer.

"Hi, I've brought the keys back now I've finished the shower," I said, keeping it business-like.

"Oh, you've had some work done, have you, Lloyd? This hot chick is our Caz, and she is damn good in the sack," said Alex being flippant. Lloyd could see I was uncomfortable with the remarks.

Lloyd stood up from his desk, "Alex, if you could just give us a few minutes? Go and make some coffees, will you, please?" asked Lloyd looking at him with a false smile. Alex went off, slapping my butt on the way out.

As soon as the door shut, I started. "Lloyd, I'm sorry, I was beside myself not knowing where I was going with my life, and I needed closeness which you gave me, and I fell in love with you, but you didn't return my calls," I said, raising my voice down to a whisper.

"I'm sorry, Caz, but I still love my late wife, and no one will replace her. Lara told me about your sexual exploits with Alex and Jess with the bondage. It wouldn't have gone anywhere Caz, so it's best we leave it and get on with our lives. I'll pay you for the good job you've done in the shower room." said Lloyd sounding negative. Lloyd wrote a cheque out for an amount of money, not asking how much and pushed it in my hand. He kissed my cheek, whispering in my ear, "you should do good business as an exclusive escort giving extra's to the rich." I couldn't believe what he had said; he was like a stranger to me. My eyes started to moisten; he was as bad as his sister.

Alex came through with a tray of coffees; I pushed passed him, throwing Lloyd's keys on the floor running for the front door. I needed to get out of the house without showing that I was so distorted. I jumped in the van making the tyres kick up the stones in the driveway to get a quick getaway; I couldn't believe he could be so callous. I had to pull over to the side of the road as tears in my eyes were pouring out. I was getting weak, was it because there had been so much happening in my life or was it because I was scared that if I got older, would men still want me?

After 10 minutes at the side of the road, weeping, I pulled myself together and set off for the supermarket for groceries, only getting the basics. Russ was still out when I got back. I was pleased; I didn't want to face him with what had just happened to me after hearing Lloyd's venom. I put the groceries away and made myself a coffee. While I was waiting for the kettle to boil, I pulled out the cheque Lloyd had written out. I couldn't believe the amount he had given me; it was too big. Why had he paid me this amount? I was going to phone him, but he would probably ignore my calls or give me more verbal abuse over the phone.

I needed some pain killers again and was starting to feel tired. I was also nursing a headache due to sobbing so much, so I took my coffee through into my bedroom to lie down. It was dark when I woke up, turning over to find it was 4 am. I was still dressed in my joggers and was feeling a little chilly. So, I nipped to the bathroom before undressing to get into my bed and soon fell back to sleep.

I didn't hear Russ going to work that morning either he had not been in that night or was avoiding me. It was nearly 10 am by the time I got up. I could have started the next job with Alex and Jess, but with seeing Alex with Lloyd yesterday, I didn't bother. I decided I just needed a complete change in life; to go and live in Italy filling my uncle's boots and run the business while I lived in the villa near the coast.

I went into the city to deposit the cheque Lloyd had given me.

"Fuck it, come on, Caz toughen up," I said to myself, driving into the same car park as before when I went to see the solicitors. I asked the bank for the full balance on my accounts; I was pleased with the figures on the accounts. I knew a bit of shopping therapy was needed to take me back to Italy, so I drew a wad of cash from the bank and set off for clothes shopping in the city.

After over four hours of shopping and spending just over four figures on clothes, I was heading back to the van with my purchases. I felt good; it was good therapy. I felt a lot better driving back to my flat. I was going to have a good sort out with my wardrobe and general things I didn't use anymore. I forgot the time of day and heard Russ coming in from work. My bedroom door was slightly ajar, and I could see Russ in the kitchen. I continued sorting my stuff until I heard a tap on my door.

"Would you like a coffee?"

asked Russ, smiling at me.

"Yeah, thanks," I said, getting up off the floor.

"Hmm, having a sort out?"

asked Russ making conversation.

"Yeah, Russ, I need to speak to you about the flat," I said, giving him a false smile.

"Oh, do you want me to leave?" asked Russ sounding a little concerned.

"No, just make the coffee, and I'll explain." Russ turned to the kitchen and quickly made the coffee bringing it back into my bedroom. He handed me a mug of coffee while we both sat on my bed.

"Russ, I am giving notice on this flat, so if you want, I could ask the landlord to see if he would allow you to take over the contract of the tenancy," I said, sipping my coffee.

"Caz, where are you going?" asked Russ sounding surprised and disappointed.

"I'm hoping to make a new life in Italy," I said, not going into details.

"So, what has brought this on?" asked Russ curiously.

"I need a change of lifestyle, and I have friends over there," I said, still not giving much away.

"Caz, I'll miss you," said Russ hugging me.

"Oh, you'll soon get over me like you normally do; any way you'll be able to have all the women you want staying with you when I've gone," I said sarcastically.

"When are you planning on leaving?" asked Russ needing more information on my plans.

"Well, I need to sort out a few things here first, but I was hoping within the next couple of weeks."

I had finally done it; I was sitting on the plane heading to Italy with my entire luggage. I had to pay extra for being overweight. I had organized a hire vehicle so I could drive myself not being dependable on Davide chauffeuring me about, but I had to collect the key for the villa from his apartment. The hire car would be temporary until I could obtain a company vehicle. I thought I would surprise Davide and just turn up on his doorstep and give him the news that I was staying to oversee the business and was going to live in the villa. As I stepped off the plane, the heat hit me with the temperature being in the mid-twenties. Luckily, I was only wearing black leggings with a short-sleeved top and sandals, leaving the UK in surprising warm temperatures of twenty degrees for the time of year.

After clearing customs, I found the car hire desk to pick up my keys for the car. I signed the appropriate documents before being given the keys to the vehicle. The car was waiting outside the airport; they provided me with the make and model of the vehicle. I managed to fit in my entire luggage into the car; with having to use the back and front seat of the car. It was only to get me to the villa as a temporary measure until I got my company vehicle.

I set off being a little apprehensive in driving on the opposite side of the road and remembering the route to the villa. I was quite confident driving towards the town, knowing Davide's apartment was alongside the river. After a steady drive from the airport, I pulled alongside

Davide's car parked in the slot allocated for his apartment. Good, he was in.

I knocked on Davide's apartment door, hearing voices from within. The door opened as I stared at a young girl in her late teens.

'Si' said the girl.

'Chi e Gina' shouted Davide from the kitchen. I pushed my way in, seeing the young girl so pretty and full of life. I had caught Davide with a girl in his apartment, and my feelings were shattered by him having someone younger than me. Davide padded through seeing me inside his apartment, which now belonged to the company, and the company was mine, and I was the boss.

"Caz," he shouted out in surprise, raising his arms to envelope me. He seemed fazed by the young girl being in the apartment. "Why didn't you phone me to let me know you were coming?" said Davide kissing my cheek.

The young girl shouted out 'A piu tardi' as she left, leaving the two of us together.

I had to rein in my horns; I was in another country; they do things differently, and I would have to get used to that. Davide seemed pleased I was there; as he gave me a passionate kiss on my lips and a hug.

"So what are you doing here?" asked Davide.

"I've moved over here, and I would like you to show me the business and how it's run. I will be living in a villa near the coast." s

"Good I am pleased you are staying. I will teach you the language and to understand our process of the business," said Davide sounding pleased I was here.

"Good. Could I have the key to the villa? I need to sort my clothes out, and I need some groceries but give a couple of days to settle in, and I will phone you when I am ready." I said, needing to get going before it got dark.

I was loaded to the gunnels, now having purchased my groceries as I fit them in every nook and cranky in the car. The drive out of the town was straight forward, but as soon as I turned off onto the dirt track, I was a little lost with a couple more tracks leading elsewhere, but then I felt the car starting to make a noise with the steering wobbling. Fuck, this was all I needed; out in the middle of nowhere with my battery on my phone at zero.

I stopped the car and got out to walk around the car to see if I could see a visual problem, fuck I had a puncture and the spare was in the boot, which was fully loaded. I dragged my luggage from the boot of the car, having nicely prized it in at the airport. Luckily the heat wasn't as intense like it was when I stepped off the plane, but it would soon be getting dark.

I managed to find the wheel brace and jack with the spare tyre checking to see if it was ok to use before attacking the punctured tyre on the front of the vehicle. I started to try undoing one of the wheel nuts on the front wheel, but it wouldn't budge,

"Fuck, these are tight," I muttered, so I tried jumping on the wheel brace but firstly doing a balancing act before jumping. I heard the nut crack, giving me enough leverage to screw it further. I started doing the remaining nuts, but the last didn't want to budge. I thought I would give it one last go, and if that didn't work, I would have to start walking.

I wished I had started walking when while having one last jump on the brace, I lost my balance slipping off the brace, causing the brace to fly up hitting back of my leg. I fell on my back in pain; the dirt track had stones I had fallen on, sliding my hands on the ground. Fuck, Fuck, Fuck I had made it worse, in the middle of nowhere having a flat phone battery, a car with a flat and now just about crippled myself in the process. I lay on the ground waiting for the pain to subside when I heard a vehicle in the distance. I just hoped the vehicle was coming this way.

I could see the dust rising in the air as the vehicle approached nearer. I managed to drag myself up off the ground to sit in the seat of the car with blood trickling down my leg and my hands sore from skidding them on the ground and covered in dust. A black 4x4 pulled up; it had tinted windows, making it difficult to see how many people were inside. The passenger door opened as a man in black trousers and a black snug fit shirt got out, at first I couldn't see him properly with the sun in my eyes.

"Caz, what are you doing here?" said a voice. I thought I recognized the voice and the Italian accent. As he came nearer I recognized him as Nico, I had called him Scarface because of the scar on his cheek. He was the man who had abused my body.

"You are hurt, let me help you," said Nico bending down to check my leg. "You go to the villa?" asked Nico bluntly.

"Yes, but I'm not sure which track I need to be on to the villa." Nico stood waving at the 4x4 as the driver's door opened, and another guy got out walking over. Nico spoke to the guy as I sat there, helpless, not understanding what they were saying.

"You come with me. I will take you," said Nico holding his hand out for me to get up from the car seat.

"I need my groceries," I said as I grappled my bag pushed in a recess in the car.

"I will get them, come on I will help you." He said, scooping me up in his strong arms, carrying me to the passenger side of the 4x4. He smelt nice; he was strong as I could feel his taut body, while I wrapped my arms around his neck. It had been the first time since my ordeal with him that I had my arms around a man again. It had been nearly two months with no closeness; I was repairing my body inside with this man carrying me now, although he had caused that hurt inside me.

Nico drove me to the villa leaving the other guy changing the wheel on the car, bringing it up to the villa with my luggage. As we pulled up to the door, I opened the car door to get out as I was about to step out of the vehicle. Nico shouted at me before scooping me up, not wanting me to walk to the door. After unlocking the door, he pushed the door with his foot and took me over to the sofa, telling me to stay there. He went to get the first aid kit from the vehicle. He soon came back carrying a green box and placed it on the sofa next to me.

"Caz, you need to take off your leggings," said Nico in his Italian accent. I did as he said, wriggling out of them. Just as well, I was wearing some underwear. The wheel brace had gouged a hole at the back of my leg. Nico started to bathe around the hole as I quince and started pulling faces of pain, wanting to slap him. I persevered with the pain until he had applied a dressing to the wound and bandaged my leg. He continued to bathe my hands covered in dust from the fall and sore with a couple of grazes on each hand.

I need to sort the groceries out." I said, trying to get up after he had finished.

"No, I will do it," said Nico, walking off towards the door. I could hear a vehicle pull up; it must be my car with my luggage. Within a few minutes, I heard a vehicle pull away as Nico came back in with my groceries taking them into the kitchen. He was taking over the situation but was so dominant, telling me to sit. I lifted my feet onto the sofa to lie down for a few minutes, but the tiredness had overwhelmed me, and I was out for the count.

I woke up the following morning as the sun was shining into the bedroom. I rolled over to find Nico in the bed with me naked, and so was I; he had put me to bed. Had he taken advantage of me, but then I realized he hadn't touched me. He had been watching me leaning on the pillow as his fingers touched my cheek and lips.

"Nico, why are you helping me like this when you hurt me so much?" I asked, looking into his dark eyes, running my finger over the scar on his face. He was quite handsome, hiding behind his scar.

"You have spirit and are not afraid, which means a lot to me in a woman," said Nico kissing me gently on my lips.

"I need to sort my stuff out," I said, trying to snap out of the moment.

"I will help you, but first, I make coffee," said Nico slipping out of bed. His naked muscular body showing more scars; some looked as though they had been deep. What had happened to him to get those? He had a nice firm butt as he padded off, slipping his trousers on the way down to the kitchen.

Nico soon came back with two mugs of coffee and sat on the bed with me. I sipped my coffee, gosh I needed this.

"Nico, don't you have to go to work?" I asked, curious about his occupation.

"No, my family can deal with any problems; they don't need me," said Nico firmly. I didn't push the question of the family business, but I would find out at some stage.

I needed a shower, and I was naked in bed with Nico by my side, I felt a little shy despite Nico having already seen my naked body.

"Nico, could you please bring up my luggage while I have a shower?" I asked, making an excuse for him to leave while I nipped into the shower.

"First, we must take off your dressing, and I will dress it when you come back," said Nico, assertive.

"It's ok I can take it off myself, thanks." I smiled, not being helpless.

"No, I will do it," said Nico firmly. I tried to cover my modesty with a sheet from the bed as I readjusted myself for Nico to take off the dressing on my leg. Nico didn't comment, knowing I was feeling a little uncomfortable.

My leg was still sweeping slightly while I showered and washed my hair at the same time. Nico had brought my entire luggage up to the bedroom as I limped through. I could hear Nico coming upstairs as I sat on the bed with a smaller towel wrapped around my leg.

"It has started to leak again," I said, raising my leg onto the bed. Nico had made fresh coffee; he handed me a mug while he took a look at my leg.

"I think you need to go to the hospital for stitches, I will take you," said Nico still looking at my bleeding leg.

I was at the hospital, waiting to be seen. Nico was by my side, holding my hand. Why was he so protective of me after giving me so much pain? We were there just over an hour as Nico took charge of me not speaking the language. I needed to send the hire car back now. I had all my possessions at the villa. Nico arranged for us to be picked up at the rental point, relieving me of an unwanted expense. The only problem was I was now left with no transport at the villa as I was on my own, but I wasn't ready to drive just yet. I was dropped off at the villa with Nico, saying he would be back to see me later.

It took me most of the day sorting my clothes, hanging up and ironing the creases from those that needed it. There was enough space for all my clothes and accessories. The weather was in the mid-twenties outside the villa; unfortunately, I didn't have air conditioning, and sweat was starting to trickle down me. I must look into getting some installed with solar panels to run them saving money in the long run. Now that I was going to be living here, I was going to assess the villa to cut down costs where I could, and once I got my head around the business and learned the language, I would do the same. At least I could save on building costs and repairs.

I was sat out on the terrace with a mug of coffee, watching the sun going down when Nico arrived. Nico came over, kissing me on my lips softly, resting his hand on my shoulder.

"Would you like to come with me to eat with my family?" asked Nico, smiling at me.

"Oh, I don't want to put your wife out," I said, thinking about his wife with Nico sleeping only by my side last night.

"I don't have a wife; we will be at my father's house," said Nico addressing my thoughts on the situation. I had got that wrong. I wondered why he wasn't married with most of Enrico's sons apart from the youngest were married, but no one knew about Nico being a son when I had asked Davide a while back.

"Okay. I will thank you, but I need to have a shower and a change of clothes." I said, smiling back into his dark eyes, wanting to know more about the scars on his body.

It was dark when we arrived at Enrico's place. On opening the door, the smell from the kitchen lingering through hit my nostrils.

"Mm, something smells good," I said, sniffing the air walking through into the living room where Enrico was sat in his chair.

"Ah Caz, I am glad you have come to join us, under different circumstances and that we can do business with you like your uncle," said Enrico getting up hugging and kissing both of my cheeks. I smiled, not knowing the kind of business he was thinking of and just agreed to be polite.

Enrico did more of the talking asking me what I did over in the UK for work. He was surprised and laughed when I told him that I did building work, which annoyed me a little being a bit of chauvinist, which I supposed I would expect here, as a woman's status was to marry, have kids and cook being under the thumb by the husband. This wasn't going to happen to me; I needed my independence and my say on things, which I always had when I started in the building trade and not knowing any difference. The evening went well despite Enrico doing all the talking with glasses of wine loosening the tongue, making it more relaxed.

It was nearly midnight when Nico took me back to the villa, stopping the night but did not touch me, only a kiss on my lips as we slipped side by side. It reminded me of sleeping with Lloyd having no bodily contact until he was ready. Why was Nico doing this to me? Was he protecting me from something, or was it something else? This continued for over a couple of months with Nico disappearing in the morning after bringing me a coffee as Russ used to.

I phoned Davide asking if he could sort a vehicle for me to drive and to learn the Italian language so I could get more involved in the business. Things seemed to have changed since I was now the sole owner of the company, with Davide being a little distant and not being over me like a rash, whether it was because I was now the boss or was it something else. He knew Nico was staying with me at the villa, but did not comment on the situation, or was it to do with the girl in his apartment I had seen, catching him unaware turning up on his doorstep without notice.

Davide had arranged for me to have lessons in speaking Italian locally in the town on a daily basis for two hours a day, starting with the very basics as if I was on holiday. Still, it was a start. I hadn't had any form of sex or pleasure since Nico had abused me that day over signing over my uncle's cruiser to his father. But Nico was showing a different side being so kind and thoughtful, not touching me and only planting a kiss at night before he slipped into bed with me, naked.

I was restless lying in bed next to Nico. I was ready for some closeness, but I wasn't too sure if he would please me gently with not having sex for a while. I rolled over to face him, seeing that he was lying flat on his back; I didn't know if he was asleep, I needed to touch him. His chest was exposed as he lied, I looked at the scars on his chest. What he had done to get those, I thought as I touched them with my fingers. He grabbed my hand tightly all of a sudden making me squeak with the shock of his sudden movement.

"Sorry, I thought you were asleep," I said nervously.

"No, I don't need much sleep," said Nico bluntly.

"Oh, fuck." I thought this could go either way. So, I leaned over to kiss him on his lips gently to see if he responded.

"Caz, I want you to be my woman," said Nico grabbing me and pushing me back into my pillow.

"Nico, make love to me gently. I haven't been since you..." I stammered. He kissed me gently and started to use his mouth down my body kissing me gently, my arousal starting to make me wet below. He was like a new person so gentle and tender, taking my breasts, sucking my nipples to make me come. I wriggled with pure arousal as he went down to drink me.

"Nico, I need you inside me gently," I whispered with the pleasure he was giving me. He slowly started to enter me, pushing slowly, having a large package. I moaned as he entered, staying inside me, kissing me passionately. This man who had abused me now was so gentle; I could feel his love radiating through me.

"Nico, push harder," I whispered, moaning with the pleasure he was giving me. He started to push harder; I could feel his full package as I climaxed. He started pushing back and forth, making me feel his hardness to the max coming with him as he released his hot salty liquid inside me.

We lay there for a few seconds; Nico rolled off me, taking me into his arms, kissing me passionately.

"Caz I have been waiting for this moment, I didn't want to press you, knowing what I had done to you. I am so sorry we have to do things we don't really want to do, but I will never hurt you again, and I want you as my woman," said Nico being so affectionate. I didn't question why he had to do it, but I now knew he was serious about me and would look after me.

Epilogue

Over the next couple of months, I explored Nico's body, kissing and sucking the parts I had endured on him when trying to escape that night he came for me in my bed. I found out that he was Enrico's eldest son to his first wife, who died being shot in a feud by another family doing a little business that went wrong, but he didn't go into detail, and I didn't push it. I asked him about my uncle's death if he knew if his death was an accident or if it was a setup. Nico did not hesitate to say that it was an accident, and he had taken drugs that night being at a party and had decided to drive himself home instead of staying the night having rooms to use. I believed him knowing the truth with my uncle living life to the full.

As time went by, Nico became more playful; he laughed more, was more caring, although we used to wrestle with each other sometimes. As our closeness became more intense, I forgot about my injection for contraception and succumbed to pregnancy with Nico. He was over the moon having a child of his own now he had found his right woman, and I also was happy for finding my perfect man that was protective, gentle, loveable and wouldn't stray.

And they say beauty is in the eye of the beholder; I smiled, seeing his scars over his body. God, I loved this man so much, and he loved me. Now we had a baby on the way to make a perfect family.

About the Author:

Sue Vout, currently living a peaceful secluded life in a **village near Gainsborough, Lincolnshire, England started writing as a student but is now a full-time writer. Her love for nature and animals turned her sensitive and nudged her to share her thoughts through her stories. Finding joy in short walks, music, art and nature, Sue has always loved the idea of spreading joy and beauty of the world through her writing. Her philosophy of life is reaching the stars as you still can, as waiting for the right moment is stupid. Every moment is the right moment if you see it closely. In her world, women are strong, brave and are capable of living life as they want, true love still exists, and chivalry is not dead.**

Made in the USA
Coppell, TX
02 June 2021